# Praise f

"*Love, Unscripted* has it all—the funniest meet-cute ever, unique characters, and a charming beach town setting. If you love sweet romance with a lot of heart, this one has 'Hallmark movie' written all over it. Highly recommended!"

—Colleen Coble, *Publishers Weekly* and
*USA TODAY* bestselling author

"Hunter (*Bookshop by the Sea*) opens this heartwarming romance with Queens, N.Y., western writer Sadie Goodwin learning that her publisher wants her to switch genres to romance . . . Hunter's charismatic and complex characters effortlessly propel the story. Readers won't want to put this down."

—*Publishers Weekly* for *A Novel Proposal*

"A heartwarming tale written by an undisputed queen of the genre, *A Novel Proposal* is a love letter to readers, to writers and, above all, to romance. As Sadie and Sam were forced out of their comfort zones, I sank deeper and deeper into my reading happy place. This cozy, clever, captivating love story is the perfect beach read and an absolute must for fans of happily ever afters. Denise Hunter charmed my socks right off with this one!"

—Bethany Turner, author of *Plot Twist* and *The Do-Over*

"A tragic accident gives a divorced couple a second chance at love in the warmhearted third installment of Hunter's Riverbend Romance series (after *Mulberry Hollow*) . . . Readers looking for an uplifting Christian romance will appreciate how Laurel and Gavin's faith helps dispel their deep-rooted fears so they can find a way to love again. Inspirational fans will find this hard to resist."

—*Publishers Weekly* for *Harvest Moon*

"Denise Hunter has a way of bringing depth and an aching beauty into her stories, and *Harvest Moon* is no different. *Harvest Moon* is a beautiful tale of second chances, self-sacrifice, and renewed romance that addresses hard topics such as child death and dissolved marriages. In a beautiful turn of events, Hunter brings unexpected healing out of a devastating situation, subtly reminding the reader that God can create beauty out of the most painful of circumstances and love from the most broken stories."

—Pepper Basham, author of *The Heart of the Mountains* and *Authentically, Izzy*

"A poignant romance that's perfect for fans of emotional love stories that capture your heart from the very first page. With her signature style, Denise Hunter whisks readers into a world where broken hearts are mended, lives are changed, and love really does conquer all!"

—Courtney Walsh, *New York Times* bestselling author, for *Mulberry Hollow*

"Hunter delivers a touching story of how family dynamics and personal priorities shift when love takes precedence. Hunter's fans will love this."

—*Publishers Weekly* for *Riverbend Gap*

"Denise Hunter has never failed to pen a novel that whispers messages of hope and brings a smile to my face. *Bookshop by the Sea* is no different! With a warmhearted community, a small beachside town, a second-chance romance worth rooting for, and cozy bookshop vibes, this is a story you'll want to snuggle into like a warm blanket."

—Melissa Ferguson, author of *Meet Me in the Margins*

"Sophie and Aiden had me hooked from page one, and I was holding my breath until the very end. Denise nails second-chance romance in *Bookshop by the Sea*. I adored this story! Five giant stars!"

—Jenny Hale, *USA TODAY* bestselling author

"*Autumn Skies* is the perfect roundup to the Bluebell Inn series. The tension and attraction between Grace and Wyatt is done so well, and the mystery kept me wondering what was going to happen next. Prepare to be swept away to the beautiful Blue Ridge Mountains in a flurry of turning pages."

—Nancy Naigle, *USA TODAY* bestselling author of *Christmas Angels*

"*Carolina Breeze* is filled with surprises, enchantment, and a wonderful depth of romance. Denise Hunter gets better with every novel she writes, and that trend has hit a high point with this wonderful story."

—Hannah Alexander, author of *The Wedding Kiss*

"A breeze of brilliance! Denise Hunter's *Carolina Breeze* will blow you away with a masterful merge of mystery, chemistry, and memories restored in this lakeside love story of faith, family, and fortune."

—Julie Lessman, award-winning author

"*Summer by the Tides* is a perfect blend of romance and women's fiction."

—Sherryl Woods, #1 *New York Times* bestselling author

"Denise Hunter once again proves she's the queen of romantic drama. *Summer by the Tides* is both a perfect beach romance and a dramatic story of second chances. If you like Robyn Carr, you'll love Denise Hunter."

—Colleen Coble, *USA TODAY* bestselling author of *One Little Lie*

"I have never read a romance by Denise Hunter that didn't sweep me away into a happily ever after. Treat yourself!"

—Robin Lee Hatcher, bestselling author of *Cross My Heart*, for *On Magnolia Lane*

"*Sweetbriar Cottage* is a story to fall in love with. True-to-life characters, high stakes, and powerful chemistry blend to tell an emotional story of reconciliation."

—Brenda Novak, *New York Times* bestselling author

"*Sweetbriar Cottage* is a wonderful story, full of emotional tension and evocative prose. You'll feel involved in these characters' lives and carried along by their story as tension ratchets up to a climactic and satisfying conclusion. Terrific read. I thoroughly enjoyed it."

—Francine Rivers, *New York Times* bestselling author

"*Falling Like Snowflakes* is charming and fun with a twist of mystery and intrigue. A story that's sure to endure as a classic reader favorite."

—Rachel Hauck, *New York Times* bestselling author of *The Fifth Avenue Story Society*

"*Barefoot Summer* is a satisfying tale of hope, healing, and a love that's meant to be."

—Lisa Wingate, national bestselling author of *Before We Were Yours*

DENISE HUNTER

# love,
## *unscripted*

THOMAS NELSON
*Since 1798*

*Love, Unscripted*

Published in Nashville, Tennessee, by Thomas Nelson. Thomas Nelson is a registered trademark of HarperCollins Christian Publishing, Inc.

Thomas Nelson titles may be purchased in bulk for educational, business, fundraising, or sales promotional use. For information, please email SpecialMarkets@ ThomasNelson.com.

Publisher's Note: This novel is a work of fiction. Names, characters, places, and incidents are either products of the author's imagination or used fictitiously. All characters are fictional, and any similarity to people living or dead is purely coincidental.

Any internet addresses (websites, blogs, etc.) in this book are offered as a resource. They are not intended in any way to be or imply an endorsement by Thomas Nelson, nor does Thomas Nelson vouch for the content of these sites for the life of this book.

**Library of Congress Cataloging-in-Publication Data**

Names: Hunter, Denise, 1968- author.
Title: Love, unscripted / Denise Hunter.
Description: Nashville, Tennessee: Thomas Nelson, 2024. | Summary: "This escapist, summery beach read about a woman who scripted her perfect boyfriend but hates the actor playing him in the on-screen adaptation is perfect for fans of romance, women's fiction, and Hallmark movies"--Provided by publisher.
Identifiers: LCCN 2023044140 (print) | LCCN 2023044141 (ebook) | ISBN 9780840716651 (paperback) | ISBN 9780840716668 (epub) | ISBN 9780840716675
Subjects: LCGFT: Romance fiction. | Novels.
Classification: LCC PS3608.U5925 L68 2024 (print) | LCC PS3608.U5925(ebook) | DDC 813/.6--dc23/eng/20231010
LC record available at https://lccn.loc.gov/2023044140
LC ebook record available at https://lccn.loc.gov/2023044141

*Printed in the United States of America*

24 25 26 27 28 LBC 5 4 3 2 1

# Chapter 1

In a world where surprises were not always the good kind, Chloe Anderson knew she'd better savor the moment. A glimpse of her debut novel in the bookshop window reinforced the thought. Her book baby. Even a year out from publication, the sight of it ushered in feelings of joy and appreciation.

The bell tinkled a welcoming hello as she entered the store. Only concern for her best friend dulled the warm glow of gratitude. She headed straight for the counter where Meghan fielded a phone call. Her long blonde locks, usually worn in waves around her slender shoulders, were pulled back into a low ponytail and her face was bare of even lipstick. In short, her friend's troubles were written all over her face.

The store was quiet just as she'd hoped, except for Meghan's end of the conversation. "I'm sorry, Miss Evelyn. If you bring the book back, we'll exchange the copy for—" Meghan spotted Chloe and waggled her fingers even as she rolled her eyes. "I'm sorry— No, I didn't realize it was for your book club— That's not much time, but you're a fast reader so I'm sure you'll— Yes, I understand. I'll hold the copy behind the counter, so if I'm not here— Again, I'm sorry for the trouble— All right. Good-bye, Miss Evelyn. Tell your mama I said hello."

"What now?" Chloe asked as soon as Meghan ended the call. Miss Evelyn was known for returning every book she bought—even if she'd finished it.

"She actually has a valid complaint this time. The book's missing the entire first chapter."

"What? That can happen? Thank God I didn't know that." She'd worried herself sick over every detail of her novel's release—all for naught, it turned out.

Meghan whipped out her cell phone and began tapping the screen.

"How are you doing?" Chloe asked. "Is there anything you need? Chocolate? Liquor? Cyanide—for him, not you."

"You really don't have to check on me every day," Meghan said without glancing up. "I'm perfectly fine."

"I know. But I also realize how hard this is and I want to be here for you." After losing his job three years ago, Meghan's husband, Kyle, lounged around the house drinking while Meghan struggled to run the Beachfront Bookshop and pay the bills. After two years of Kyle refusing professional help, she filed for separation. She gave him another year to get his act together, but that's not what happened. The divorce was finalized last week.

"I appreciate your concern but I'm really okay. I just need to get through this and on to better days."

"Tell me you aren't on that app again," Chloe said.

Meghan's eyes were still glued to the screen. "I'm not on that app again."

"Liar, liar, pants on fire."

Meghan had been holding up pretty well until six months ago when, while still hoping to reconcile with Kyle, she discovered he'd invited his high school girlfriend to move in. That's when Meghan remembered the app on her phone that remotely controlled the thermostat in their old house.

"It's going to be quite toasty at Kyle's house today," Meghan said. "I'm thinking eighty-five degrees . . ."

She couldn't blame Meghan for feeling bitter, but Chloe hoped she'd get it out of her system soon. "What happened to the 'better days' part? You have your beautiful bookstore—and me. What else could you possibly need?"

Meghan gave the screen a final tap and slipped the phone into her pocket, producing a big cheesy smile. "And just like that, I feel so much better. Speaking of you, did you see my beach-read display in the front window? Your book is front and center and still selling like hotcakes."

"Aw, you're too good to me." Not only was Meghan her biggest fan, but she'd been the one who encouraged Chloe to write the book to begin with. "I should've added your name to the cover."

"Your note in the acknowledgments was perfectly adequate. I show it to practically everyone who enters the store."

"As well you should."

Meghan came around the counter. "When the movie comes out, we should do another signing."

Because—yes, indeedy—Chloe's book was being adapted into a movie. Not a TV or Netflix movie but an actual movie-theater movie. The big screen. Overcome for the millionth time by her uncanny luck, she offered her arm to Meghan, who accommodated by pinching her.

"At some point it's going to sink in."

"Well, not today. And I owe it all to you." She squeezed her friend.

"Nonsense. You did it—you wrote the love story every woman wants to read."

"I wrote the *hero* every woman dreams exists."

"True, true. Ledger Ford is ridiculously swoonworthy. In fact, if you should happen across the real-life version, please send him my direction."

Chloe's heart softened. She wanted nothing more than to see her friend's face light up with a smile again—a real one. "You got it."

"Come admire my handiwork."

Chloe followed Meghan to the window display. Three years ago they'd been bemoaning the lack of real-life heroes. Chloe's boyfriend of nearly a year had cheated on her, leaving her heartbroken. Evan was just the last in a string of romantic disappointments.

Meghan insisted Chloe should pen that novel she'd always wanted to write. And inspiration struck—Chloe could custom-build the hero to her own specifications. If the perfect man didn't exist, she would simply write him into existence!

And that's just what she did.

The epic love story featured a young widow who returned to her seaside hometown and reunited with the childhood sweetheart who'd broken her heart years before. With the help of an agent she'd sold it to Rosewood Press.

Ledger Ford had resonated with romance readers on a scale Chloe hadn't dared to dream of. And then several months after her big launch, her publisher had optioned the story to a major film producer. Was it any wonder Chloe was still pinching herself?

"Any more casting news?" Meghan asked.

Daisy Hughes had been casted as Cate—a perfect pick as far as Chloe was concerned. "I haven't heard anything lately. I'm so nervous about who they'll choose to play Ledger. He's the key to making this movie adaptation work."

"I'm still hoping for Chris Evans."

"I put a word in for him, but we'll see. I hope whoever they settle on has a good reputation, you know?"

"Sure, but the actor and the character aren't the same thing."

"I know. I just don't want any nasty scandals besmirching Ledger's good name."

"Well, you're consulting producer, so you do have some leverage. But I know how important—how personal—this is to you."

Because, yes, Ledger was the hero of Chloe's heart. The man she hoped actually existed in real life, somewhere. One who would love her. One who would be loyal to her. One who would stick around.

She was willing, eager even, to return the favors. "They've been pretty good about keeping me in the loop and hearing my thoughts, but it's not like I have final say on anything."

They stopped at the window display. "Where did you get all this sand?"

"The beach, of course. I'm surprised your brother didn't mention it."

"What does Sean have to do with it?"

"I asked to borrow his truck and then he ended up helping me. Some environmentalist chased us away, but not before we'd absconded with enough sand for the display. It was actually pretty fun."

Chloe frowned at the small smile lifting Meghan's lips. At the secret glimmer in her eyes. Chloe loved her brother, she did. But her friend was in such a vulnerable place, and Sean had a certain charm that tended to leave a trail of heartbroken women in his wake. She feared he'd never settle down.

"What do you think? Are the pails too much?"

"No, it's great. You're so creative." Chloe's eyes sharpened on the cover of a historical and she reached for the novel. "This looks good. I love the muted colors."

"It's set in Chicago in the 1920s. The protagonist is a chocoholic who opens a gourmet chocolate shop."

"Relatable." Chloe tucked it under her arm, and they turned for the register. "I should get home and change for work." She and Sean ran Docksiders Bar and Grille with their mom, who owned the place.

When Meghan was ringing her up, a call buzzed in on Chloe's phone. It was the executive producer of Chloe's movie. Her veins instantly flooded with adrenaline. "It's Simone Jackson."

"Movie news! Answer it."

Heart pulsing in her throat, Chloe swiped the screen and greeted the woman.

"Hello, Chloe," Simone replied. "How are you, dear?"

"Great. I'm doing well. How's everything for you?"

Meghan jabbed at her palm, mouthing, *Speakerphone.*

Chloe acquiesced and Simone's smoky voice filled the bookshop. "I have some excellent news for you, and I couldn't wait to call you."

Meghan silently clapped her hands.

"Well, I can't wait to hear it. You sound so excited."

"You will be too. You know we've been working on casting the past couple months. What would you say if I told you that Ledger will be played by none other than . . . *Liam Hamilton!*"

Chloe's gaze met Meghan's widened eyes. Liam Hamilton was *huge.* But he was also the biggest Hollywood player the town had ever seen. He'd risen to fame several years ago with a role in Chloe's favorite rom-com, playing the man who'd cheated on his fiancée with her maid of honor. A part he'd played quite convincingly!

In real life he was just as unfaithful and irreverent. He was a womanizer. If he wasn't the devil, he was certainly the anti-Ledger!

Simone chuckled. "I can see I've shocked you speechless."

Chloe paced off some of the energy zipping through her like an electric current. She had to speak up. For Ledger, for all his fans, for the good of the movie. Simone had taken some of her feedback on the script. Minor stuff, maybe. But Chloe was the author of the book! She'd *created* Ledger Ford. Surely she should have a say in who played the character some fans (and *Publishers Weekly*) had called the best book boyfriend of all time.

Chloe stopped in front of Meghan. *Say something!* she mouthed.

"Chloe?" Simone said.

"Um, yes, I'm here. And I am quite surprised. It's just . . ." The words bubbled up inside and boiled over. "I honestly can't think of a man *less* qualified to play Ledger Ford. Ledger is *heroic* in every sense of the word. He's larger than life. He exhibits all the qualities that every woman yearns for in a partner. And Liam Hamilton is—"

"Um, Chloe . . ."

"He's just not any of those things, and even though I've only seen him in one movie, his reputation—"

"Liam is—"

"—certainly precedes him, and surely actors carry those qualities onto the set. I just don't think he's—"

"—right here."

"—appropriate for the part. I'm sorry, what did you say?"

"Liam. He's, ah, right here with me, dear. Right now. Listening."

"Hello, Chloe," a deep voice called, sounding somewhat strained.

Chloe's gaze darted to Meghan, whose brown eyes were so wide in her delicate face it would've been comical. Except that it wasn't.

"So Liam has just signed the contract, in fact!" Simone's voice rang with false enthusiasm. Something rustled on the other end of the line, then she continued in a hushed voice. "I stepped away from the table. Well, that was very awkward."

"Did he—?" Chloe cleared the squeak from her voice. "Did he hear everything I just said?"

"I was a little late getting you off speakerphone."

Chole groaned as she sank her head onto the countertop. "Oh no. I'm so sorry." Then she remembered the other thing Simone had said. "Wait. He signed the contract?"

"It's a done deal."

Ugh. She covered her face. Like it or not (not!), *Liam Hamilton* would be playing Ledger. Oh, why hadn't they asked her first? They'd talked about casting and not once had Liam's name come up. Not once!

"I thought you'd be pleased. We found out Chris Evans wasn't available, and Liam is well-known and his work is stellar. The studio is so excited he's taken the role. They're aware of his publicity problem and will be keeping a close watch. We've definitely got some work to do there. But trust me, they'll handle it, and he'll end up drawing a big audience, and that's exactly what we want. I know what I'm doing, Chloe. You have nothing to worry about."

She ignored the terrible sinking sensation in her stomach. Whatever. It was done. This was the woman who was making her movie happen. Time for Chloe to pull up her big-girl pants. She injected some enthusiasm into her voice. "I'm sure you're right. You're the filmmaking expert—I'm just a writer."

"An amazing writer. But you have to trust me on this. Liam will be perfect opposite Daisy. They'll have loads of chemistry, you'll see. The studio wants Ledger's character to shine as much as you do. They realize his importance to the film's success, and we'll do everything possible to make sure your writing magic translates to the big screen."

"Of course. I'm sure you will."

"Everything's on schedule for filming to begin in June." It would take about three months and would take place right here in Stillwater Bay, where her book had been set.

"I can't believe it's just a few months away."

"It'll be amazing, you'll see." A rustle sounded through the phone. "Oh dear. I should get back with Liam—I think you ruffled his feathers a bit."

Chloe winced. "Again . . . I'm so sorry about that."

"Actors and their delicate egos. Not to worry, I'll smooth it over."

A moment later Chloe disconnected the call, her body wilting like a dehydrated begonia under the summer sun. "Well, that's it. My film is ruined."

"Oh, honey. Let's not be hasty. Maybe he won't be so bad. He was very convincing in *Jilted*."

Chloe nailed Meghan with a dry look. "As a philanderer."

"Well, yes, that's true . . ."

"Have you read the most recent scandal about him cheating on Brittney Bloom with Katie Simpson? It's always something with him."

"Those things aren't always true, you know."

"Ha! Maybe there's gossip here and there, but there's practically a monthly column featuring Liam and his escapades." She covered her face. "They literally could not have chosen a worse actor for the part. What was Simone thinking?"

"Well, you didn't exactly get off on the best foot with him."

"Thanks for the recap."

Meghan gave a pained smile and patted her arm awkwardly. "It's gonna be okay. You like the actor they casted to play young Ledger."

"That's true." A fair portion of the story was told in flashback with the teenaged versions of Ledger and Cate. "He's perfect for the role. And the actress playing young Cate is dead-on. But also, I just alienated the actor playing grown-up Ledger!"

"Once Liam gets here you'll win him over. And who knows? Maybe Simone's right. Maybe he'll surprise you and pull it off after all."

This was a disaster of epic proportions. All her hopes and dreams of seeing Ledger brought to life on the big screen had been dashed in one disastrous phone call.

*Liam Hamilton.* Ugh!

"At least he's gorgeous," Meghan offered sheepishly.

Chloe let out a long-suffering sigh.

# Chapter 2

As far as escapes went, Stillwater Bay would do just fine. Liam Hamilton pulled his Braves ball cap low over his sunglasses as he entered the fray along Main Street. To one side of the street, a boardwalk welcomed walkers with a stunning view of the windswept beach. To the other side restaurants flaunted patio seating, and racks of clothing spilled from canopied storefronts. Shoppers sorted through sales racks on this sun-drenched Sunday afternoon.

He wasn't here to shop though, God forbid. He was here to scout out the setting for the movie he was about to film. And yeah, maybe escape Hollywood and his latest scandal.

His phone buzzed with an incoming call. Spencer. Speaking of the latest scandal, his manager and best friend had been trying to reach him all day. Liam declined the call, pocketed his phone, and let his gaze sweep the summer scene.

The town had a nice laid-back vibe. Very different from the California coast. Fewer name brands and tall, skinny actress wannabes. More casual attire, natural faces, and southern pleasantries. He could dig it.

He continued along the boardwalk a few minutes, then crossed the street and strolled the busy sidewalk. His phone vibrated again. He checked the screen. Then, steeling himself, he left the crowd and stepped into the shadows between a boutique and bakery.

"Hi, Mom. How's it going?"

"Oh, much the same. I was just reading through the newspaper."

Likely perusing his dad's real estate ads. "I'm on the East Coast at the moment. North Carolina. It's beautiful out here."

"I can hear the ocean. Oh, the life you lead. And here I thought you'd be a musician."

Barely afternoon and her words were already slurred a bit. "Maybe I'll play one in a movie."

His mother laughed too boisterously. "You're doing so well. If we could just get those awful tabloids to stop gossiping about you."

"You promised to stop reading them."

"I did no such thing."

He thought of the latest scandal and the two-year-old photo accompanying it and rolled his eyes. "I didn't cheat on anyone, you know."

"Of course you didn't. Speaking of cheaters, have you heard from your father?" Her hopeful tone made him want to shake her—and throat-punch his dad in equal measure.

"Not really. He's busy with his work, I guess." Dad was a successful Realtor in Riverside, California, where Liam had grown up. Now his divorced parents lived across town from each other.

"Is he still seeing that redhead?"

"As far as I know."

Mom sighed.

It had been many years since he'd left his wife—for a blonde twenty years his junior. There'd been a flavor of the month ever since. And yet his mom still held out hope.

She needed to move on. Maybe then she'd stop drinking and find someone else to love. She was an attractive fifty, and she deserved better than anything his father could offer—every woman did.

"Well, I'll let you go. Relax and enjoy your break."

He said good-bye and pocketed his phone, breathing a sigh of relief that she hadn't asked for money. That seemed to be happening more often lately. He always gave it to her. Even if she hadn't exactly been Mom of the Year, he'd always had what he needed. She'd put up with his prolonged defiant phase and endured his punk stage wherein he started a band and played bad heavy metal in their attached garage. She hadn't complained when he announced three days after high school graduation that he was moving to Hollywood to become a star. (What he'd actually become was a waiter and a barista and at one point a dancing pig on the sidewalk in front of Barnyard Joe's BBQ.)

His gaze caught on a woman a few stores away, browsing the sidewalk sale. Her shoulder-length brown hair swung forward as she glanced at a price tag. When she hung the garment, the shiny curtain fell back, revealing familiar wide blue eyes set under arched brows. Her mouth was too wide, her face too angular, and yet the combined effect worked somehow.

It worked quite well.

His recent research revealed that Chloe Anderson was the author of only one book, though it had been a smashing success. In her interviews she spoke eloquently about the writing process and her life in North Carolina. She was close to her family (parents and a brother) and, unlike Liam, had a squeaky-clean reputation. Even her book was squeaky clean—yes, he'd read it after he got the part—and somehow realistic and layered and compelling too.

Much to his irritation, after weeks of reading up on her, he couldn't find a thing about her to dislike.

The same, however, could not be said of Chloe when it came to her opinion of him. Her response to Simone's big news had been pretty insulting, even if it was delivered with a charming southern accent.

* * *

Chloe was flipping through a rack of gaudy Hawaiian shirts when her phone buzzed. After a quick check of the screen, she greeted her brother.

"How do sriracha deviled eggs sound?" Sean said without preamble.

"Mmm. I'm definitely gonna need a sample."

"They're cooling in the fridge as we speak."

"Working on a Sunday?"

"Creating dishes isn't work."

Her brother-chef had gotten all their mom's cooking genes. They were planning to add a new appetizer to the summer menu. She tucked the phone between her shoulder and ear and held up a shirt. Too long for her short torso. "I'll try one when I come in tomorrow."

"Maybe you could arrive an hour early and help with prep? We're short-staffed."

As she moved to the next rack, her eyes caught on a man standing in the narrow alley between the shops. Was that . . . ? She blinked at the guy.

It was definitely Liam Hamilton.

He wore his public disguise (ball cap and sunglasses), because yes, she'd seen all the candid photos and read every salacious article about him in the past three months. She'd know that perfect square jaw anywhere.

Was he staring at her? Hard to tell with the sunglasses, but he was definitely looking in her direction. She glanced behind her. He could be staring at anyone really, not necessarily the woman who'd cut him down to size over the phone.

"Chloe?" Sean asked. "You there?"

Liam began walking her way!

"Gotta go!" she squeaked.

She ducked out of view, seeking a place to hide. The clothing rounder. She dove inside, hangers clattering. One of them hit the ground at her feet. It wasn't until she was safely, if somewhat precariously, squatting on the pavement that it hit her—Liam would have no reason to recognize her. No reason at all!

Oh well. Might as well wait until he passed. What was he doing here so early anyway? The actors weren't scheduled to arrive for the prep work until next week. Then the movie started filming the week after. At that point she'd be seeing him almost daily.

The garment shielding her face seemed to have feathers attached. Very tickly feathers. Since her hands were on the ground, keeping her balanced, she blew the feathers away. One of them returned with a vengeance, a heat-seeking missile heading straight for her nostril.

She sneezed. Then sneezed again.

A pair of Birkenstock flip-flops, visible through the clothing, appeared on the ground at her side. "Hello, Chloe."

*Crap.* She closed her eyes, pretending for one delusional moment she could disappear. But another sneeze was building up. Darn those feathers! She pressed her lips together. Held her breath.

"Need some help in there?"

"Aaa-choo!"

"Bless you."

She peeked out from the clothes, following the line of his muscular legs past his low-slung trunks and fitted white tee to the man she'd thought she wouldn't have to face for at least a week, if not two.

"Uh, hi. Hi there. You're Liam. I was just . . ." She groped frantically along the ground and grasped a stray hanger for dear life. "I, uh, dropped something . . . just picking it up." Gathering herself, she oh so casually slipped from the clothing rack and came to her full five-foot-three-inch height. He was taller than she realized—must be those statuesque actresses he always had on his arm.

"Got it!" She held up the rescued item. "Accidently dropped my new—"

"String bikini?"

Her gaze flew to the article of clothing. Yep. A highlighter-yellow thong—practically a ribbon really—dangled from the hanger. There was no top.

"Will you be wearing that on set then?"

She wouldn't be wearing it anywhere! "On second thought"—she shoved the bathing suit back onto the rack—"not really my color."

She hoisted her purse onto her shoulder, lifted her chin, and tried to look cool and breezy. It was hard to tell what he was thinking behind those sunglasses, but his posture and smug little grin screamed arrogance. "I thought— What are you doing in town already?"

"I like to show up early. Get the lay of the land."

She didn't know what that meant. But they'd gotten off on the wrong foot—twice now. And she'd decided weeks ago that if she had any hope of rescuing her film, it began and ended with him. Maybe he could bring Ledger to life if he just knew him the way she did. And the only way to make that happen was to get on the same page—so to speak.

Time to swallow her pride. "Listen, I'm actually glad I ran into you."

A skeptical crease appeared over the rim of his glasses.

Right. Ruffled feathers. "I wanted to apologize for my hasty reaction when Simone called a few months ago." Her contrite (and distorted) face peered back at her in the reflection of his sunglasses. When he didn't respond she added, "So I'm sorry if I, uh, hurt your feelings or anything."

He tilted his head, ushering in an uncomfortable silence that filled the space between them. It seemed to swell like a wave under the sea, growing and growing and . . .

"It's just that I saw you in *Jilted* and of course I've come across articles about you in the, uh, tabloids and, well, I know they're not called gossip rags for nothing, but I mean, you know, where there's smoke there's fire." Her nervous laugh seemed to hang in the air between them, then plummet with a thunk at their feet.

"So it's my lifestyle you disapprove of."

His monotone delivery didn't exactly reveal his feelings. "Well, uh . . . *disapprove* is kind of a loaded word. I don't really, um . . ." *Change the subject!* She cleared her throat. "Well, listen, what I wanted to explain is that the character you're playing is the most crucial role in the whole story. So congratulations on that!" More nervous laughter. Hers, apparently. "See, Ledger *is* the whole story. He's the reason the book developed such a large following, and I think it might help you, uh, get into his skin if you read the actual book—I don't suppose you've read it?"

"Are you unhappy with the script then too?"

He was not making this easy! Her cheeks flared with heat. "The script is wonderfully written, but screenplays are just dialogue and dry directives. A novel allows you inside the heads of the characters. You get to know their thoughts and feelings, and only then do their actions make full sense, you know?" And even if he wouldn't say so now, he hadn't read the darn book. He'd admitted as much in *Vanity Fair*.

"Sounds like you're trying to tell me how to do my job."

She resisted the urge to stamp her foot. "You're deliberately being obtuse. This is not about your acting skills—"

"You're the one who mentioned *Jilted*."

"My concern is about this particular *character*, and since I created him, I know him better than anyone else. And since you're playing him in the film, perhaps you could read the book and learn everything there is to know about him, all the reasons a million readers have fallen in love with him."

He shifted his weight but his expression remained an enigma. *Oh, take off those stupid sunglasses!*

"And you?" he asked.

"And me, what?"

"Have you fallen in love with Ledger too?"

She opened her mouth. Closed it again. *Getting a little personal, aren't you, Mr. Big Shot?* And somehow this seemed like a trick question. "He—he was lovingly created in my mind and poured out onto the page with my blood, sweat, and tears. I realize he may be just another fictional character to you, but to many women he's the best book boyfriend ever written, and it's important that you—"

"Book boyfriend?"

She huffed. "It's a literary term used to describe—"

"I can infer the meaning, thanks. And I appreciate that the film has a ready-made audience in your fans. I'll try not to disappoint them. Now, I should let you get back to your, ah . . ."—he glanced at the bikini bottom—"shopping excursion. See you on set."

# Chapter 3

"Ugh! He was just so smug with his little half grin and haughty looks and those stupid sunglasses. I'm telling you, he's not taking this role seriously enough." Chloe brought the knife down with more force than necessary.

"Hey, easy on my innocent tomatoes." Sean tugged the brim of his ball cap lower, calling attention to his deep-set blue eyes. A black apron worn over his black tee and pants completed his uniform.

"Liam Hamilton is the antithesis of my entire list." Because, yes, after her heart-stomping breakup with Evan, she'd made a list of the top five qualities she desired in a potential mate. She wanted a man who was loyal, steadfast, protective, self-sacrificing, and sentimental. All the things Evan—not to mention her father—had never been. And when writing the book she'd made Ledger the embodiment of all those traits. Because even if such a man didn't exist in real life, he could certainly exist on the page.

"Well, it's not like you have to marry him."

She glared at him.

He tossed a white hand towel over his shoulder where it would sit the rest of the night. "Sorry. I know how much this movie means to you. But he is an actor—a pretty sought-after one too. Maybe he can pull it off."

"I don't even think a guy like him could understand a man like Ledger."

"Maybe you could make him understand."

"How am I supposed to do that? I'm just a consulting producer. He won't take my direction."

"You could start by making peace with the guy."

"I tried! He's impossible. He—he hardly said a dozen words, but they were all the wrong ones."

"He really pushed your buttons."

"You don't have to sound so pleased about that. There's just so much on the line with this movie, and he holds all the cards. Plus, it's hard to respect a notorious womanizer."

"Would now be a good time to remind you that you've called me the very same?"

She snorted. Okay, Sean wasn't really a womanizer. But he did go through women like a fish through water. Men. Did any of them want to settle down into married bliss with one woman? Time to think about something else. "Speaking of your love life . . . how's it going with Haley?"

"Haden." Sean made quick work of the green onions. "It's going fine, I guess."

Haden delivered their fresh produce from a local organic farm. "It's about that time, isn't it? It's been five, six weeks now. What's wrong with her?"

Sean scowled. "Nothing's wrong with her. She's great."

"But . . ."

He scraped the onions into the bowl. "But nothing. She's smart and attractive and we have a lot of fun together."

She nudged his shoulder. "Does she bruise your apples? Root for the Mets? Dislike your Mexican street corn? What is it?"

Sean winced. "Stop it."

But she knew her brother all too well. Whatever Haden's "fatal flaw," he'd discovered it even if he wouldn't share. "I told you not to date someone we do business with. Where will we get our fresh produce now?"

"I *know*. I've already been beating myself up—you don't have to pile it on. The last delivery service was awful."

"Looks like someone's headed back to the farmer's market."

"Don't remind me."

She thought of Meghan's mention of her sand run with Sean a few months ago and that secret grin that had formed on her friend's face. Fortunately, Sean hadn't come up in conversation since. Anyway, Meghan knew all too well about Sean's pathetic dating history. Besides, her BFF probably wasn't ready for another relationship. She was still making Kyle's home, by turns, into a sauna or a frozen tundra.

"So are we adding sriracha eggs to the menu?" she asked. "It's going to the printers next week." The deviled eggs, as predicted, were delicious—spicy and tangy-sweet with just a hint of garlic. Her brother was a culinary genius.

"Let's do it. I'll have Mom write up the description."

"She's so good at it."

Years ago Mom had bought a two-story shanty at the end of a dock shortly after she discovered her husband had a secret family in Connecticut—and *not* a job as a traveling salesman as they'd believed. The Hartford family had come first, so just like that Mom's marriage was null and void. And apparently their father's parenting obligations were too, as he seemed to drop off the face of the earth shortly after he'd been caught in his epic lie.

A civil lawsuit, however, had been very kind to their mom— hence her dream restaurant. She now filled in at the restaurant as needed and seemed content to let Chloe and Sean run Docksiders. It worked well since Sean had the kitchen covered, and Chloe excelled in front-of-house matters like staffing, customer care, and general management issues. If it wasn't her dream job . . . well, it was a decent living and she loved working with her family.

Sean began slicing and dicing a green pepper. "So what are

you gonna do about Liam Hamilton now that you've burned that bridge?"

"Hey, you weren't there. I was being really nice."

"After you cut him down to a nub over the phone? A guy's got his pride, you know."

"I didn't know I was on speaker! I didn't even know he was there." Then she muttered, "Darn that Simone."

"But if I know you, you haven't given up yet."

"He's in town a week early—that must be a sign. I have to get through to him somehow."

"How are you gonna track him down? I get the feeling you two didn't swap numbers."

She sent her brother a withering look. "I'll get his info from Simone and explain I'd like to make peace with him. I'm sure she'll be in favor—harmony on the set and all that."

"But then what? You can't exactly force-feed him your novel."

She thought of Liam's smug little grin and brought the knife down with extra force. "I don't know. But I'd better think of something, and fast."

# Chapter 4

The repetitive buzzing of incoming texts woke Liam from a deep sleep. He opened his eyes to filmy sunlight flooding the room of his beach rental. It was a newer house, sporting wood floors, cozy area rugs, and a fireplace he wouldn't be using this time of year. A nice change from his contemporary home in Santa Monica.

He stretched. The bedding was pretty awesome too. He'd slept through the night for a change. And now the rhythmic sound of waves filtering through the open windows called his name. He'd have a nice long jog on the beach, lift weights, then scope out the area where some of the filming would take place. A little precarious since that was actually Chloe's property.

He thought of the pretty brunette holding up that little piece of nothing and grinned. Those eyes of hers had transfixed him at first glance. He'd flustered her—and enjoyed doing it. She hadn't known quite what to make of him at first, and he enjoyed that too. Watching her cheeks flush pink and her elfin chin notch upward had been the highlight of his week. And he could listen to her talk for hours with that sweet southern accent. He almost hoped he ran into her at the filming location just so he could get under her skin again.

His phone buzzed once more, this time a call. He grabbed the phone. Spencer. He wasn't exactly eager to think of his LA life right now with the beach awaiting him, but he'd ignored his manager yesterday—and he'd apparently missed a few texts from him this morning.

He swiped the screen. "Spencer, buddy, how's it going?"

"I can't decide if you flew to North Carolina or fell off the face of the earth."

"What time is it there?"

"Early. From what I remember, we were going to talk about your little problem before you flew across the country. The studio is concerned."

"You know I like to arrive before prep work begins."

"Not a week early. You ditched me."

"I was ditching LA, not you."

"Well, let's talk now since you bothered to answer the phone."

His reputation was the last thing he wanted to talk about, but he couldn't deny the gossip had gotten out of hand. What started as honest coverage of his casual dating style had morphed into something uglier. The tabloids had begun painting him as a heartless playboy. They'd recently announced he was cheating on Brittney Bloom with Katie Simpson, and Brittney seemed all too willing to play the victim even though they'd only gone out once. So now he was an unfaithful cad.

"This is bad for your career, Liam. The old adage 'All publicity is good publicity' isn't really true. You're gonna start losing parts."

"I don't know what you want me to do. I can't tell the press what to print, and I can't stop them from using old photos that make me look like a cheating tool."

"No, but we can try to control the narrative." Spencer's psychology degree sometimes came in handy despite his radical career shift. "Did you get my texts this morning?"

"Uh, yeah." Liam quickly tapped a couple of buttons and scanned the texts.

"So who's the girl?"

"What girl?"

"The pretty brunette with the skimpy bathing suit . . . Ring a bell?"

Liam touched the live link Spencer had sent, and the *Tattletale* website opened. There, front and center, was a photo of Chloe and him outside that shop yesterday. She was holding up the bikini and the headline read, "Has Liam Ditched Katie for Southern Squeeze?"

"You've got to be kidding me," he muttered.

Now Chloe was being pulled into the sticky web of his gossip-laden life. It was unlikely the paparazzi was here already, which meant some pedestrian must've recognized him and snapped and posted the photo. The tabloids picked it up. He scanned the article. Thankfully the gossip site hadn't identified Chloe. But it was only a matter a time.

"Hello? Care to elaborate?"

"She's just— It's Chloe Anderson. Author of *Beneath the Summer Skies*."

There was a beat of silence. "The one who insulted you over the phone?" Spencer's amusement came through loud and clear. He'd laughed uproariously when hearing about that phone call. It wasn't every day a woman shot Liam down so bluntly. Sometimes having a friend for a manager sucked rotten eggs.

"Yeah, laugh it up. Happy to entertain you."

"Why was she getting your opinion on a piece of lingerie?"

"She wasn't. I ran into her downtown, that's all. We exchanged words."

"You're smiling at her."

"*Smirking.*"

"Whatever. I didn't expect this, but since it just kind of fell into our laps, I have to ask: Is she single?"

"What? How would I know?" But he did know because he'd re-searched her in great detail. She never went into specifics about her love life, but given that her book was a romance, it followed that journalists would ask about her relationship status.

"Yep, she's single," Spencer said. "Says right here in *Southern*

*Living.* 'There's no one special at the moment, but of course I want a happily ever after just like everyone else.' The article's only six weeks old."

Liam had read that one already. "What's your point?"

A full ten seconds of silence passed.

"*Spence.*"

"Wait, I'm reading."

Liam sat up in bed and ran a hand through his hair. A seagull called outside the window, drawing his attention to the horizon where the clear blue sky met the sapphire sea. The morning sun gleamed off its surface like glittering diamonds.

He threw back the covers and got out of bed. Only a few people were on the beach. Two sea shellers, a walker, and a jogger with a golden retriever in tow. He wanted to get out there before the heat soared well into the nineties.

"Listen, I'm gonna go for a jog. I'll just call you later."

"No, no. I think I've seen enough . . . ," Spencer said, though it was pretty clear to Liam he was still reading. "Never would've thought of her given that you got off on the wrong foot and all, but—"

"I didn't do anything!"

"—she might be just what we're looking for."

"What are you talking about?"

"I've been on the phone with the studio—that's what I wanted to talk to you about before you left town. Patty from PR thinks it would be helpful if you were in a steady relationship for a while. This author, Chloe, is attractive, well spoken, wholesome . . . close-knit family, quiet life . . . Very different from your usual."

He didn't like the direction of this conversation. "My usual *what?*"

"Your taste in women isn't exactly a mystery, buddy. You only date beautiful actresses."

"I'm not dating Chloe, if that's where you're going with this."

"Afraid she'd turn you down?"

No doubt she'd do just that. But he also disliked the idea of the tabloids gossiping about her. There was something kind of adorably innocent about her. Something he wanted to protect. It'd be a shame to rob her of a quality he'd found to be quite rare. He gave his head a shake.

"Listen, it doesn't have to be real. It just has to *look* real. Actors do PR relationships all the time. Do I have to start naming names?"

"Maybe I'd consider something like this, but not with her. Someone in the business. Someone used to being hounded by the paps and smeared in the tabloids. We can talk about it when I get home."

"I don't think you understand the damage being done to your career with each negative story. The studio wants to get on top of this. If you're worried about getting Chloe on board, use the film as leverage. She won't want your negative reputation tanking her movie."

*Ouch.* But fair point. His female fans wouldn't continue supporting him if they thought he was a womanizer. They'd stop going to his movies and he'd soon find himself a has-been.

He wanted the film to be a success too. Not only for his career but to prove to Chloe that he could, indeed, play her paragon of a hero and quite well, thank you very much.

"Plus a relationship between the two of you would be great publicity for the movie."

Another idea flittered into his brain. "What about Daisy? Wouldn't it make more sense to involve my costar?"

"Daisy's engaged, remember? You need to stay far, far away from her off set. You get that, right?"

"Hey, I'm not a home-wrecker."

"I know you'd never do that. But you have to avoid the appearance of anything romantic once the cameras are off. You know better than anyone how an innocent picture can be misconstrued."

"I got it. Jeez. This isn't my fault."

Spencer sighed. "I know it's not, buddy. But would it kill you to have a long-term relationship once in a while? This casual dating thing has to be getting old."

"We can't all settle down to married bliss at the age of eighteen."

"I was twenty-four. And Gwenn and I couldn't be happier. You don't know what you're missing."

He really didn't. He hadn't exactly had the best example in his parents. "I'm not opposed to the idea of marriage; I just haven't met the right person." At least that's what he told himself. It was true, wasn't it? He was almost sure.

"For now let's just work on salvaging your reputation. Do you think Chloe will be agreeable? This would also help avert the whole Liam-Daisy love affair that's bound to be splashed across the gossip sites if you're not seeing someone else during the filming. If Chloe's reluctant, maybe I can talk to the studio about letting her coach you a bit. Simone made it clear she's very particular about the portrayal of your character."

"You think they'd go for that?"

"I can ask. It would give you more leverage with Chloe, and Patty really liked the idea of a PR relationship. You've already got the ball rolling with Chloe."

He couldn't imagine the author getting on board with this. She wouldn't give two figs about salvaging his reputation. But maybe she'd do it for the movie's sake.

"I can't make any promises, but I'll see what I can do."

"You can do it. Just turn on the charm. It's never failed you before."

When they got off the phone, Liam recalled his contentious conversation with Chloe in front of the shop. Spencer was grossly overestimating Liam's appeal.

# Chapter 5

Chloe had meant to get an earlier start on the day, but she'd stayed up late paying restaurant bills, then lain in bed overthinking. It was a specialty of hers.

She rode the mower across the property she never could've afforded on her own, even with her blockbuster novel. The grassy parcel sloped down toward a pier that extended across the salt marsh to the gently flowing Dutchman's Creek. She enjoyed quiet mornings reading on the pier and paddling her kayak down the lazy creek, all the way to the mouth of the Cape Fear River.

The briny breeze scented the air and shimmied the leaves on the live oaks, their branches sprawling across her yard like a canopy.

"Thanks, Dad." Sarcasm laced her tone.

Because, yes, Mom had insisted on sharing her lawsuit winnings with Sean and her. *After all, you were his victims too. Why shouldn't you be compensated?*

The humidity beaded on Chloe's arms, and sweat trickled down her neck because it was already hades-like at eleven o'clock.

This Liam thing was intruding on her peace of mind. But her midnight ruminations had at least resulted in a solid plan. At ten this morning she'd gotten his number from Simone and called him, her heart jackhammering in her chest because who liked eating crow?

Her apology yesterday hadn't gone over especially well, and okay, maybe it hadn't been the best apology ever delivered. It was time to dig deep.

Alas, he hadn't answered his phone, so she'd simply left a voice mail asking him to return her call. She would've been relieved, but he didn't strike her as the type who returned calls. She couldn't get that image of his smirking face out of her mind. And those obnoxious sunglasses perched on his nose. He probably thought he was hot stuff with all those gorgeous actresses falling at his feet.

She finished mowing the row and turned at her property line. As she completed the maneuver, a movement nearby startled her. A man.

*Liam Hamilton.*

She eased her foot off the gas and the mower stalled, sputtering to a stop. He approached wearing shorts and a tee and the aforementioned sunglasses, despite the widespread shade.

"Hello, Chloe." He'd left his ball cap at home apparently, exposing his famous hairstyle—short cropped at the sides and longer on top with a perfect dark swoop that was apparently unaffected by humidity.

Chloe pushed back the tendrils that had escaped her ponytail. "You could've just called."

He stopped a few feet away and pulled off his sunglasses. "Pardon?"

At least that's what she thought he said. She was momentarily mesmerized by eyes that were utterly gray. Not greenish or blue-gray but perfectly colorless gray. Which sounded rather boring but in reality was quite striking against his bronzed skin.

Which reminded her that she was makeup-less, frizzy, and, oh yeah, dripping with sweat.

He glanced down at her shirt, no doubt reading the slogan: *Hand over the chocolate and no one gets hurt.* Meeting her eyes again, he tilted his head, the corner of his lips pulling up.

Right. She should probably say something. "How'd you know where I live?"

"We'll be filming here, remember?"

"Right." She should probably lose the attitude, but the man seemed to bring out the worst in her. She couldn't deny he was a treat for the eyes though. "I—uh—I guess you got my voice mail."

"What voice mail?"

"You didn't get it?"

"Obviously not. Another half-hearted apology?"

"Nooo . . . I just said I wanted to talk to you. Why are you here then?"

He stuffed his hands in his pockets as his gaze swept over the yard. "Scoping out the area. So this is where some of the scenes will happen. Nice property. A good choice—and kind of charming that it's the author's backyard."

"Thank you." She was glad he seemed serious about the movie, coming out early and all. But this movie wasn't about the setting.

"It faces west," he said. "So you really do get the sunset. I wondered about that one scene since you're on the East Coast."

"The creek bends and curves every which direction."

"I see that." He glanced at her, his expression unreadable. "I guess you saw the gossip site. I'd apologize, but unfortunately, I have no control over it."

A warning flare fired deep in her belly. "What gossip site?"

He lifted a brow. "You didn't see it?"

"You'd better tell me what's going on."

"Do you have your phone? I left mine in the car."

She handed hers over and he tapped the screen.

"What happened?"

"Someone saw us together yesterday and snapped a photo. It ended up on a tabloid site." He turned the phone around and showed her the picture.

There they were, up close and personal. And of course the

shutterbug had caught her holding up that ridiculous thong. The scene appeared much more intimate than it had actually been. Her cheeks warmed.

"I'm afraid the story's already spread to other sites."

She skimmed the headline and frowned. "'Southern Squeeze'? Wow, I've been reduced to a ripe lemon."

"It's what they do. At least they didn't identify you."

"No, they just suggested I horned in on your relationship with Katie Simpson. Oh my gosh, has she seen this? I'm so embarrassed."

"You didn't horn in on anything. I'm not even dating Katie—or Brittney."

She snatched her phone. "Well, that's not how this makes it seem!"

He gave a smug smile. "Welcome to my world."

She spared him a glance before scanning the brief article. She was no dummy. It wouldn't take any time at all for the tabloids to identify her if they wanted to. It was a small town. All they had to do was ask around. And she was hardly famous, but she'd certainly done the publicity circuit on her release. She might even be recognized from that. She didn't want people thinking she was Liam Hamilton's new plaything! It might even affect how her movie was perceived. "I don't want my movie tainted with fake gossip."

"I don't want that either." He cleared his throat. "My manager and the studio suggested we try to control the narrative."

"Well, how do we do that?"

"I'm glad you asked." He tilted his head, those gray eyes zeroed in on her like a laser. "I have a proposal for you."

She narrowed her eyes.

"Not that kind of proposal. A business proposal. You might be aware my reputation has taken something of a hit recently."

Gross understatement.

"Right. Well, I'm sure you realize the negative publicity isn't particularly good for your movie. Obviously my female fans would prefer to root for an actor they admire."

"Obviously."

"We're on the same side here. We both want the film to be a resounding success. And I think we agree that the negative publicity about me or *us* won't help matters."

*Us?* Seriously, how was this even happening? She crossed her arms, a flimsy barrier against whatever was coming next. "Go on."

"My manager, Spencer, and the studio's PR person, Patty, think the appearance of a relationship between us would help matters."

Tired of him towering over her, she dismounted the mower. "So instead of them just gossiping about me being your plaything, I'd actually pretend to *be* your plaything. Ha! No thanks."

"That's not at all what we're suggesting."

"That's what it sounds like."

"We're talking about an actual dating relationship."

"Do you even know what that is?"

His jaw knotted as those gray lasers cut right into her.

Probably shouldn't have said that out loud. She hadn't meant to get personal, but the man got under her skin. She opened her mouth to apologize, but he spoke first.

"The studio thinks it's brilliant. Think about this from your fans' point of view: their favorite author is in an exclusive relationship with the man playing the hero she penned. As far as publicity goes, what could be better?"

She closed her mouth as his words hit their target. That did sound rather perfect. She was no publicist, but even she could see this playing well in the media.

Still. She swept her gaze over Liam. It also might turn into a disaster. She took a few steps toward the shoreline, seeking the peace the rippling creek offered even as she envisioned this ruse going off the tracks.

"You're not seeing anyone, right?"

Nice of him to assume so. She sent a scowl over her shoulder.

"Spencer read your interviews." He stepped up beside her. "What are you so worried about then?"

"How do you know I'm worried?"

"It's written all over your face."

She threw her arms up. "Exactly. I'm no good at pretending, Liam. How do you expect me to convince the public I like you?"

He flinched. "Don't feel like you have to sugarcoat it."

"I didn't mean it the way it sounded. But we do seem to rub each other the wrong way."

"We got off on the wrong foot, that's all."

"Well, I'm not an actor! Maybe you can pull this off, but I'm not so sure I can."

His brow bounced. "Will it be that difficult pretending you like me?"

What she really feared was that the tabloids, not to mention his fans, would find her completely unworthy of his attention. Would the public believe a man with his reputation might finally be won over by . . . *her*? She glanced down at her ratty T-shirt and grass-stained tennis shoes. Even on a good day, barring humidity and hormonal breakouts, she was maybe an eight. The women he dated were off the charts with their poreless complexions and legs up to their armpits.

But she wasn't admitting that. "I'd probably wind up as fodder for your next scandal—the one in which you throw me over for the next gorgeous starlet."

"That's not gonna happen because we'll control the narrative. We'll give them a real relationship. Lots of photo ops and candid shots of us. If they post a two-year-old photo of me and someone else, we'll come back with a lovey-dovey shot of us. They'll eat it up. You'll see."

Chloe hadn't even stopped to consider all the time they'd have to spend together. "That sounds like a lot of pretending. Anyway, it's completely unrealistic. We live on opposite coasts and we just met two days ago."

"They don't know that. I'm acting in the adaptation of the book you authored. We could've been in contact for weeks or months. It could've started with that phone call with Simone."

"Oh, it started, all right."

"Only a handful of people know how it really went down. Or maybe we keep that piece of the puzzle and add to it. You called me later to beg my forgiveness and—"

"Or you called me to beg me for the role."

His lips twitched. "Fine, have it your way. I called you. Sparks flew right away and we kept in contact regularly. I flew out here early to spend time with you before the filming started."

"And all those women you've been seen with over the past few months?"

"No women. I've been lying low at the recommendation of my manager and the studio."

Hmm. His plan actually seemed plausible. If a hot Hollywood actor dating her could actually be plausible. But what if this went the wrong way, and she came off like just another of his castoffs? Being abandoned in real life was bad enough. What would it feel like to be publicly humiliated? Not good, she was pretty darn sure.

"It would be good for your platform," he added. "I'm sure an author can never have enough followers."

He couldn't know that her publishing team had been encouraging her to grow her dismal social media following. They'd been begging for a proposal, but she wanted to write a historical novel next, and they were nervous about the change. A relationship with Liam would surely gain her followers by the thousands and make Rosewood happy in the process. Then all she'd need is inspiration. She needed the kind of idea that set her on fire the way *Summer Skies* had. The story had meant everything to her, and getting it onto paper had been pure magic.

"Well?"

She considered his proposal. Tempting. But there was that possible humiliation. "I don't know. It's probably not worth it."

"Not worth the success of your film?"

"The success of my film is largely up to *you*—I think I've made that clear."

"Fine, then. Be my fake girlfriend and I'll do whatever you want."

Chloe blinked. "Whatever I want?"

"Whatever you want."

Her mind spun at the carte blanche offer. Wasn't this just what she'd been wishing for? The opportunity to make Liam understand exactly who Ledger was?

She pinned him with a skeptical look. "You'll read the book?"

"Done. I'll even take your direction on the role."

She snorted. "I don't see the studio going along with that, not to mention the director."

"Au contraire. The studio and director have already agreed. I just heard from Spencer—he ran it by them."

She gaped. "Seriously?"

"Hey, you created the guy and they have a lot of respect for you."

She could hardly believe the studio would give her this much leverage. Or that Liam really wanted *her* to be his fake girlfriend. She scanned his features, searching for sincerity and finding it. (Among other things because, jeez, that face.) But of course he could just be faking the sincerity. He was an actor after all.

"We all want the same thing here, Chloe. We're on the same team."

She weighed his words. Somehow they'd found themselves on the same page. Her stomach fluttered at the thought of what she was about to agree to. There were risks but there were also rewards. Rewards that just might equate to the success of her movie—not to mention a social media following that would excite her publishing team.

Still, she wasn't sure exactly what she was signing up for. "I have no idea how this sort of thing works."

"I'll guide you through it step-by-step. We can talk about it in detail and make a plan you're comfortable with."

She checked her watch. "It's getting late. I have to get ready for work."

"Breakfast tomorrow?"

"Sure, where at?"

"Come over to my place. We shouldn't discuss this in public. I'll send you my address."

"All right."

He gave her a long, searching look. "All right, you'll do it?"

Chloe took a deep breath. Found strength in the confidence on Liam's face. "All right, I'll do it."

# Chapter 6

To say Chloe had a lot on her mind was an understatement. And the work of a bustling restaurant offered a welcome reprieve from her worries.

She skirted the full tables on the deck, smiling at regulars as she went. A sea breeze ruffled the canopy overhead, and water lapped against the pilings in a sound so constant she heard it in her sleep. Nearby in the marina, white masts poked skyward and metal hardware pinged against a flagpole.

She went back inside. It was busy, as it was most summer nights. The restaurant was a far cry from the shack their mother had purchased. The walls had been reinforced and the roof re-shingled. Décor was simple and casual, with lots of corrugated metal, wooden planks, and boat parts utilized whenever possible. White twinkle lights and country music gave the place a party vibe. But people really came for Sean's food. He could turn a burger into a culinary sensation.

They were short a server tonight. She caught up with Lindy, who'd been with them seven years. "Can you get drinks from the bar for table nine, please? Sara's in the weeds with a party of twelve."

"Sure thing, Boss."

Chloe headed toward the window to retrieve a dish. The salmon looked great to her, but then the first had seemed fine too. Second time was the charm.

"Eighty-six the surf and turf for the rest of dinner service," Sean called from the grill.

"Got it!" Chloe said.

She took the plated salmon to the customer and passed the word to the other servers. Since everything was running smoothly in the front and beginning to wind down, she returned to the kitchen. "Need help back here?"

"It's under control," Sean said, then called, "Four fish tacos all day!"

"Got it, Chef!" Their sous chef, Raymond, got to work.

Chloe grabbed her water bottle and took a sip. It was after eight and they closed at nine tonight. The evening would slow down from here since it was a weeknight and there was no live music.

The back door opened, ushering in a briny breeze and their mom, arms stacked with white pie boxes. She was a brunette and petite like Chloe with a slender frame, but her teased-up crown gave her an extra two inches.

"Somebody need cheesecakes?" Mom said over the kitchen noise.

"Hey, Mom," Sean called from the grill.

Chloe went to relieve her mom of the load. "You're just in time. I thought the lady at table six was gonna cry when I told her we were out."

"Can't have that now."

Chloe opened a box and grabbed a spatula. "Oooh, chocolate raspberry—my favorite. Kaitlyn, can you take this to six, please?"

"I'm on it." She swooped the plate away.

Chloe plated several slices while her mom hovered nearby. Her stillness—and silence—made Chloe cut her a look. Mom stared at her, head tilted, eyes curious.

"Do I have food on my face?"

She leaned a hip next to Chloe. "Do you have something to tell me, daughter dearest?"

"No . . ."

"Something special that a mother should know about her favorite daughter . . . ?"

Sean approached, wiping his hand on his apron before giving Mom a sideways hug. "Thanks for bringing the cheesecakes, Mom."

"Does he know?" Mom asked.

Sean's gaze toggled between them. "Know what?"

Great. It had to be the tabloid story. What else could it be? Chloe's stomach sank. She wasn't ready for questions.

"It seems Chloe here has been keeping secrets from us. Mary Lou showed me a very interesting picture today—from one of those tabloid sites."

"You were on a gossip site?"

"With none other than Liam Hamilton."

"I can explain."

Mom laughed heartily. "Oh, the picture said it all, sweetheart. I'm only mad I wasn't the first one you told." She gave Chloe a little whack on the back of the head. "You know I've always loved him. He's such a cutie pie. Way too young for *me*, I know, but as you're aware, my youth was wasted on your father."

"I don't understand," Sean said.

"Your sister's dating Liam Hamilton—on the sly it seems. But not anymore! The news is out now."

Chloe opened her mouth but the words tangled in her throat.

"Mary Lou said people are Twittering about it and everything." Mom wrapped her arm around Chloe. "Liam's been a little naughty lately, but he and Katie Simpson or Brittney Bloom? No way. He took one look at my baby girl and lost his heart, didn't he, sweetie?"

"Well, I—"

"The expression on his face in that photo . . ." Mom pressed a hand to her heart. "You've got him wrapped around your little finger,

I could see it just plain as day. And why not? My baby's as beautiful as all those starlets and twice as nice."

Sean's eyes narrowed on Chloe.

What should she say? She hadn't discussed strategy with Liam and she was afraid to—

"I need a salmon on the fly!" a server called through the window. "This one's dead."

"I got it, Chef!"

Mom gave Chloe's shoulders a squeeze. "Well, you guys are busy. Do you need an extra set of hands?"

"We've got it covered," Chloe said. "Enjoy your night off."

"If you're sure. See y'all later." Her gaze homed in on Chloe. "Call me. We'll set up a coffee date—I want all the details."

"Uh, sure, Mom."

She left as quickly as she'd arrived.

Chloe returned to the cheesecake, trying to ignore her brother who lingered nearby, waiting, arms crossed. She hadn't expected the news to get out so fast. It was only online, after all, and Stillwater Bay seemed a million miles from Hollywood.

"What did you do?" Sean asked finally.

"I didn't do anything!"

"Just yesterday you were moaning and groaning about him, and today everyone thinks you're together?"

He did nothing but hover and stare. And stare. And stare.

"Someone took a picture of us when we ran into each other Sunday, that's all. It got posted on some tabloid site and it was . . . misconstrued."

He tilted his head. "And you didn't set Mom straight because . . . ?"

That explanation was a little trickier. "Don't you have some fish to fry?"

"You're hiding something."

"Am not."

"Are too. You're blinking like crazy and avoiding eye contact."

She forced her eyes wide open and met his gaze. She and Liam hadn't talked about who they would or wouldn't tell. No doubt, the fewer who knew the truth, the better. Her eye started twitching.

"You look deranged."

She couldn't keep this a secret from Sean. She'd never get away with it.

"Fine." She lowered her voice in a hiss. "Liam and I made a deal today. I'm gonna be his fake girlfriend, and he'll take my direction on the role of Ledger."

"Why would he want you to be his fake girlfriend?"

"Hey!"

He waved away her indignation. "You know what I mean."

Okay. Fair question. No sense hiding the rest at this point. "He's trying to salvage his image, which would be good for him, and what's good for him is good for the movie. And you can't tell anyone about this. Not a soul. This can't get out or it'll spoil our plan. He agreed to read the book and everything."

"Wow, the whole book? And all you have to do is become fodder for every gossip site in America?"

"This will work in both our favors. You know I need more followers anyway if I'm gonna switch to historicals. And a relationship with him will get me zillions of them."

"So honorable."

Chloe glared. "Not to mention I'll have a say in Liam's role—the studio said so."

Sean gave his head a shake. "Why's that so important to you anyway? I know it was the 'book of your heart' and all. But you didn't even expect a movie deal out of this. Why does it matter so much? The book's already a raging success."

"I just want them to get it right. I want them to do Ledger justice." He was her Mr. Right—maybe the only one she'd ever get.

Sean's gaze zeroed in on her face and after a long moment his eyes softened. "He'd better not hurt you."

Her heart melted a little. "Come on. How could he hurt me when I don't give a flying fig about him? As long as he gets the role right, we're golden."

"I hope you know what you're doing."

She so didn't know what she was doing. She gave her widest smile. "Piece of cake."

While he headed back to the grill, she boxed a cheesecake slice for later and put the rest away. Then she detoured to her office, which was really just a paneled closet with a desk. She dug her phone from her purse, her heart faltering at Meghan's text, sent an hour ago.

*Um, did you know you're on a celebrity site with Liam Hamilton? Also, hope you passed on the thong. Not your color.*

Crap. The news was spreading fast. And how was she supposed to keep her deal with Liam a secret from her best friend? Was there any scenario in which she'd get away with that?

She sent Liam a text. *I know we were planning to meet in the morning, but that article has leaked and people are asking me about it. Help!*

She was shoving her phone back into her purse when it rang. Liam's number appeared on the screen. She answered.

"Hey," he replied. "Yeah, it's gone viral."

She'd never noticed the low, sexy timbre of his voice before. "I'm kind of freaking out here. My mom, brother, and best friend already know about the article."

"Relax, it'll be fine. Why don't I come over after you get off work?"

"That won't be till almost ten. Sorry, I probably should've just waited till morning at this point."

"No worries, I'm still on Pacific time. Unless you're too tired."

She snorted. "I don't know if I'll be able to sleep at all."

"Nothing's changed. People were going to find out—they're *supposed* to find out. That was the plan."

"I know, I just . . ." She hadn't expected things to escalate so quickly.

"It's all new to you—I get it. We'll walk through it together. Everything's gonna be fine."

Right. Everything would be fine. "I'll see you around ten."

"See you then."

# Chapter 7

Chloe had a cat.

Liam didn't see the feline as Chloe ushered him inside the two-story Cape Cod. He didn't hear the cat or smell the cat. But his eyes had started itching the second he entered the house.

He followed Chloe into the living room. She wore a pair of leggings and a loose olive T-shirt that read, *I closed my book to be here.* She'd twisted her brown hair, still damp from a shower, into a messy bun.

"Sorry if I was freaking out on the phone earlier. This is just moving faster than I expected. I was just on Twitter." She winced.

"Rule number one: don't go digging around social media." He rubbed his itchy eyes.

"But don't we need to know what people are saying?"

"That's what my manager and Patty are for. They'll stay on top of all that. If we need to know anything, they'll pass it along."

"Have a seat. Can I get you something to drink?"

"No, I'm good."

"Well, I'd like something. Be right back."

He sat on one end of a black leather sofa and took in Chloe's home. The floor plan was open, with the dining room and kitchen just off the living room. The wood-plank floors appeared to be original and were stained a rich brown. The low ceilings, whitewashed brick, and snug area rugs gave the place a homey feel while the sleek black countertops and stainless-steel appliances lent a more modern vibe.

A minute later she returned with her glass and curled up in the recliner across from him. He didn't know much about her, and that would have to change if they were going to pull off this fake relationship. "Where exactly do you work? I assumed the author gig was working out pretty well."

"I've only written one book so far. My family owns a restaurant—Docksiders, down on one of the piers by the marina."

"I've seen it. Great location."

"That's the idea. My brother runs the back and I run the front. Weeknights are pretty mellow, but we have live music on summer weekends and it gets rather lively."

"Do you enjoy the work?"

She shrugged. "Sure."

"And your mom and dad? Are they involved in the business too?"

Her left eye ticked. "My mom's the one who started the restaurant. My father's not really in the picture anymore."

"Sorry to hear that."

She lifted a shoulder. "His choice."

Liam had a feeling there was a lot more to the story but didn't want to press.

"I have a stepdad—I actually call him *Dad*. He's the pastor at Surfside Community Church. He adopted Sean and me soon after he married our mother."

"That's great." Good information to have about someone he was supposed to be dating.

Chloe cleared her throat. "So maybe we should talk about how this is supposed to go. I should tell you right up front, my brother already knows about our . . . arrangement."

That wasn't ideal. "It's imperative we keep this under wraps."

"I understand that, but yesterday I told my brother about our run-in downtown and—" Her cheeks bloomed with color. "Well. Let's just say he didn't buy the tabloid's version of things."

Liam filled in the blanks and bit back a grin. "You said derogatory things about me."

"They weren't very flattering." She gave him a sheepish look. "I did say you have nice hair."

"You're too kind. So basically your brother wants to beat me up."

"Don't worry. He needs his hands in the kitchen."

"That's good. I need my face in the movie. What about the others? You said your mom and best friend saw the article."

"Ah yes, my mom. She was all aflutter, believing every juicy word because, yes, of course a hot celebrity would be over the moon for her perfectly average restaurant-managing daughter."

Average? Not in this lifetime. "For the record I'm disputing that statement, but for the sake of clarity . . . you let your mom believe we're an item?"

"I didn't know what else to do." She closed her eyes, then palmed her face. "I'm a terrible daughter."

"I'm sure that's not true. And your best friend?"

"She's a great daughter. Kidding. I haven't texted her back—except about the thong. Never mind. I don't know if I can lie to her. As you pointed out, I'm not very good at it."

One of the things he liked about her actually. "You should use your own discretion, but obviously the more people who know, the greater the chance this gets leaked."

"And Simone, the director, and the cast? Will they know?"

"The studio knows of course. And we'll have to run all the social media by Patty before posting. But there's no need to inform the cast and crew. Some of them might suspect a PR relationship." He shrugged. "Daisy'll probably be relieved to hear the rumors about you. The tabloids are less likely to pair me up with her if I'm already in a committed relationship."

"Is that what this is?" She blushed again. "I mean, is that what we're pretending to be?"

"I think so, yes. Newly committed maybe, since we only just met in person."

"But we clicked so well long distance and one thing led to another?"

Liam nodded. "Exactly."

She set her drink on the table. Shifted in her chair. "I'm not sure how I feel about making everyone believe a version of the story that isn't true. Doesn't it bother you?"

"I'm pretty tired of those rags exploiting me. I won't mind exploiting them for a change. Most of what they print about me is no more real than our relationship will be."

She appeared to weigh that. Did she believe everything she'd read about him? If his fans did, that didn't bode well for his image or his future in film.

He had to allay her concerns. He leaned forward, elbows on his knees. "Listen, we're not hurting anyone, right? Who cares if the public believes we're a couple? We have to remember the greater good."

"The movie."

"Right. The movie."

A cat hopped up on the couch beside him, making him jump. Not because of its sudden appearance but because of, well . . . its general appearance. It had a weird smashed-in face, and its yellow coat gave off a recently electrocuted vibe. It arched its back and waved a scrawny tail.

Poor thing. He gave the cat a stroke. "Hey, buddy. Who's this guy?"

"That's Buttercup. She's a rescue kitty."

*You don't say.* Buttercup seemed friendly enough at least. She rubbed her side against his hand, climbed up on his lap, plopped down, and curled into a ball.

"She normally doesn't take to strangers. Or anyone, really. I guess your Casanova appeal extends to felines."

"Seems friendly enough to me." Liam's nose was suddenly stopped up and his eyes began itching like mad. A sneeze ripped through him.

"Are you allergic?"

"Just a bit." Another sneeze exploded from him. Tears pooled and trickled from his eyes.

Unbothered, Buttercup lowered her head and closed her eyes.

"I'm so sorry."

The cat screeched as Chloe removed her from Liam's lap.

He wiped his eyes. Then remembered he'd touched the cat with that hand. Another sneeze.

"Oh dear." Chloe handed him a tissue. "Maybe you should wash your hands. I'll put Buttercup in my room. We'll find Mousey, won't we, sweetheart? Where did Mousey go, huh?"

Liam washed his hands in the kitchen sink as he scanned the kitchen out of curiosity. Just who was Chloe Anderson, his new girlfriend? She owned a fancy Breville espresso machine that looked like it might somehow also offer one-hour massages. But her toaster could've come from Walmart. Photos of (presumably) family and friends adorned the fridge, held in place by seashell magnets. A box of gourmet chocolates sat on top of the fridge, and a sign above the stove read, *If you don't like my cooking, lower your standards.*

"You doing okay?" She entered the kitchen. "Need to leave? We can do this tomorrow if you'd rather."

"I'm feeling better. Let's just go over any questions you have so you can get comfortable with all this. I don't want you up late worrying for nothing."

They settled in the living room. He could almost breathe through his nose again.

"So what happens next?" she asked.

"Well, basically we make sure we're seen together in public. Photographers will do the rest."

"The paparazzi?"

"Or bystanders or the regular press. I didn't anticipate them being here until the movie started filming at least, but now that word's out that I'm here and there's a possible love squeeze in the mix . . ."

She hurled a pillow at him.

It hit him in the stomach. "Oof," he said even though it didn't hurt. "Just kidding, short stuff."

"Wow, we haven't been together twenty-four hours, and you're already hating on my height."

"No hate here."

"Yes, I can tell you love short women by all the tall actresses you date."

"I don't date them because they're tall; I date them because they're actresses."

She tilted her head. "Explain."

"They know the drill—the paparazzi, the rumors, the business. It's a lot to take sometimes."

"Fair point. I guess I'm about to find out for myself."

She was. And he should probably prepare her. "I'll be honest—their so-called reports can be less than flattering. It's not much fun to read negative things about yourself that may or may not be true."

"Thanks for the warning. I'm sure that won't be very pleasant. And I'll be honest with you too—part of my reason for agreeing to this is that I need to grow my social media following. I'm planning a slight genre shift, and my publisher wants me to have a bigger platform."

"Understood. I think we can make that happen." This kind of thing was hardly new to him. Other celebs usually liked going out with him for the attention. Oftentimes he was just a commodity. It didn't feel great, but he was using them too. Sometimes he needed a date for an event, and he enjoyed the female companionship. At least Chloe was honest about what she would get out of it.

"Is this your first time doing this?"

"What, a PR relationship? Yes."

"Will the media ask me questions?"

"Sure, but you can just say, 'No comment,' and leave it at that."

"You make it sound so simple."

"Hopefully it will be."

"But shouldn't we know things about each other that a normal couple would know? And what about your family? Won't they want to know what's really going on?"

"There's just my mom and she'll be fine. She won't pry." Half the time she had her head down a bottle and the other half she was too obsessed with getting his dad back to worry about Liam's love life. "But yes, knowing some basics about each other wouldn't hurt."

She covered a yawn.

"But all that can wait till tomorrow."

"Do we have plans tomorrow?"

He stood. "We do. I'll pick you up at noon."

She cut him a wary look on the way to the door. "You're a little bossy."

"I'm used to getting my way."

"Is that so?"

He turned at the door. "Wear comfortable clothes and expect to be photographed."

She groaned.

He bit back another grin. "Let the games begin."

# Chapter 8

Dread slowed Chloe's steps as she took the stairs to Meghan's porch. Then she tapped on the door. Despite a late night, she'd awakened early this morning, uneasy about her deal with Liam and all the implications it might have on her life.

Meghan opened the door. Even in a ratty robe with zero makeup and an exaggerated scowl, her friend was beautiful. "It's about time. You're dating Liam Hamilton and forgot to mention it to your best friend?"

"Can I come in?"

"Only if you promise to tell me everything. I thought we hated him. What is happening?"

What had Chloe been thinking? She'd never be able to keep the truth from Meghan. "Let me in and I'll tell you everything."

Chloe entered the home, complete with old wood floors and cushy seating. Its seaside palette featuring subtle shades of blue, green, and beige invited guests to sit and rest awhile.

"I'll get you some orange juice and then I want to know what's going on."

Chloe collapsed on the sand-colored sofa, sinking into its welcoming embrace. She stared across the living room at the focal point of the room—an entire wall of built-in bookshelves, fully stocked with everything from genre fiction to classics. Never mind that Meghan had a store full of books down the street. Yes, in some ways, her friend led a charmed life. In others . . .

She glanced around the home that screamed *Single woman lives here!* Gone were the wedding photos and Kyle's ugly green recliner. No stray socks or empty beer bottles littered the room. Instead the place was embellished with feminine touches: candles, a planter, a candid photo of Meghan and her sisters.

Her friend returned with two glasses of freshly squeezed orange juice. "Drink up. You need your vitamin C."

Because yes, Meghan was a health nut. Chloe did as she was told.

"First things first; did you buy the thong?"

Chloe snorted. "It was a bathing suit, and do I own anything in highlighter yellow?" She went on to tell Meghan about her run-in with Liam on the sidewalk downtown. Her friend nearly spewed orange juice when she got to the part where he caught her hiding in the clothing rack.

"What did he say?" she asked.

"He said"—she lowered her voice—"'Hello, Chloe.'" She made sure to use that arrogant tone.

Meghan only laughed harder. "I love it!"

"Hey, you're supposed to be on my side. It was embarrassing." But it was so good to hear Meghan laughing again, Chloe couldn't even take offense.

"I can't help it. You paint such a vivid picture. What happened next?"

"Not much of anything really. We kind of had words about the role of Ledger. He got my back up."

Meghan's eyes sparkled. "You don't seem upset about that now. Have you heard from him since the story broke?"

"I texted him last night and he came over after work."

Meghan's jaw dropped. "Liam Hamilton came to your house last night?"

"You can stop using his last name. Especially since he's my boyfriend now."

Meghan's eyes widened. "It's *true?*"

Chloe savored the moment for an extra beat before expounding. "Yep, we're official."

"Chloe . . . for real. You're not getting mixed up with that guy."

At the note of worry in Meghan's tone, Chloe came clean. "Relax. We're officially in a *fake* relationship. Liam's concerned about his image, what with the recent negative publicity, and I want to coach him in his role as Ledger. So we made a deal: I pretend to be his girlfriend and in return he'll take my direction on the role. The studio is on board and everything."

Meghan took a slow sip of juice, then set the glass on the table. "I see."

"He approached me about it yesterday. Apparently a committed relationship with me, in all my chaste wholesomeness, will make him look like a steady kind of guy."

Meghan just stared at her.

"*What?* Why are you looking at me like that?"

"I can't believe you're in a fake relationship with Liam Hamilton."

She could hardly believe it herself. But hearing the words aloud made it seem even more real. "Tell me I'm not crazy. That I haven't just made the biggest mistake of my life."

"You're not crazy. You haven't made the biggest mistake of your life."

Chloe gave her the side eye. "But really."

"Really . . . Have you thought it through? This seems so sudden."

"I know, but I can't pass up this opportunity. He seems really open to my direction now. He seems . . . different than I assumed he was at first. I just don't know how I'm going to show him who Ledger is."

"He could start by reading the book."

"Definitely my first goal. But I want to go deeper than that. He has to be in Ledger's skin to play this part."

"Maybe you should start with your list—the top five qualities."

"That feels so personal. I haven't shared that publicly."

"I know, but don't you think it's necessary to understand Ledger at that level?"

Maybe she could just focus on the qualities and not necessarily why she chose them. "You're right about one thing. Unpacking those characteristics is important. I can't assume even after he reads the story that he will have deduced them all."

"Some readers don't see beyond the surface."

A long, thoughtful moment passed as Meghan's gaze sharpened on Chloe.

"What?"

"I'm just worried about you, that's all. This could bring a lot of attention your way. If he's in the spotlight, you'll be right there with him, and who knows what they'll say about you."

"The publicity could be good for the book and the movie. And I forgot this part: Remember how Rosewood wanted me to up my social media game because of the genre switch?"

"I guess this is one way to do it. But are you sure this is what you want?"

Chloe reflected. "It's only temporary. How bad could it be?"

"Well . . ."

"Don't answer that. Liam and I will just be a quiet, steady couple. No drama, no antics, just a nice simple romance."

"There's nothing quiet or simple about Liam's life, sweetheart."

Meghan's words gave her pause, but she dredged up a cheeky grin. "Well, there is now."

# Chapter 9

Chloe waited until Liam pulled into her drive—in a shiny red Camaro—before she stepped down from her porch.

He exited the coupe as she approached. "I was gonna go to your door like a proper gentleman."

"No need. I don't see any cameras." She gave his fancy rental a once-over. "I guess you weren't planning on blending in around here."

He flashed that Hollywood smile as he opened her door. "No point in making money if I can't enjoy it." He circled the car in navy shorts and a navy tee that did nice things for his biceps. He wore a matching ball cap but no sunglasses—basically half his disguise.

She'd apparently dressed appropriately in white shorts and a red wraparound shirt. She'd done her makeup and curled her hair, putting the top back in a barrette because, the wind. In short, she was at her casual best. The plan, after all, was to be photographed, and she could do without disparaging remarks about her appearance.

Liam lowered himself into his seat, then swept his gaze over her, lingering an extra beat on her legs. "You look very nice."

Before the compliment went straight to her head, she checked herself. He'd no doubt splintered many a heart with that silver tongue and those dashing good looks. Hers would not be one of them. "Eyes off the legs, big shot."

"We're dating, aren't we?" He tossed her a playful grin. "And those are some very nice legs."

Warmth flushed up her neck. "*Pretending* to date."

"Details."

She snorted as he put the car in Reverse and backed from the drive. "Seriously, you realize this car will only draw attention."

"That's a good thing, right? Besides, I couldn't resist. She corners like she's on rails."

Boys and their toys. Oh well, might as well enjoy the luxury. Her seven-year-old Camry wasn't nearly this appealing.

Because his muscled leg, complete with California tan, was *right there*, she turned and stared out her window. She'd tossed and turned all night, worrying about this plan and wondering if she'd soon regret it.

But no, it would be worth it when he nailed the part of Ledger. When the movie lived up to the book. When her social media followers climbed into the stratosphere. At least that's what she told herself.

He reached the end of her street and turned away from town.

"So what's on the agenda? Or are you still keeping me in the dark?"

"You don't seem to like surprises much."

He probably hadn't noticed, but they weren't always good.

"Thought I'd take you on a quiet picnic. But if you'd rather do something else, I'm flexible. We could just stroll around town or sit at the coffee shop and gaze across the table at each other."

She was being a poor sport. "A picnic sounds great. Sorry, I'm a little on edge. I get that way when I'm nervous."

"I make you nervous, huh?"

She scowled at him. "About the gossip sites. Jeez, the ego on you."

"I gotta keep you on your toes. If for no other reason than it'll give you a few inches of height."

*"Hey."*

He chuckled. "You are too easy, sweetheart. We might have an agenda, but while we're at it, we can have a good time too."

That sounded dangerous. But maybe he was right. It would be hard to fake it. If she were actually having a good time, the photos would be more authentic. More believable.

A few minutes later he pulled into Waterfront Park and eased the car into one of the many empty spaces. "You know there's a park right in the center of town, right? You'd be recognized there for sure."

"Too obvious. We're a couple falling in love and trying to avoid the limelight. Don't worry, we'll be spotted. Stay right there." He exited the car, came around her side, and opened the door.

"Are you always such a gentleman?"

"My mother would have my head if I didn't open a woman's door."

"Your mother's not here."

"Sure she is." He tapped his temple. "Right here. It was ingrained from an early age. Apparently my dad wasn't good about that stuff, so she coached me pretty hard."

Interesting note about his parents. She was curious to know more about them, but that would mean opening up herself, and he didn't need more than the basics.

At the thought of her family's past, a finger of dread pricked her spine. What if someone dug around and discovered the truth of what her father had done? The thought of that secret being exposed filled her core with cold dread.

But no, that wasn't possible. Only a handful knew her father was a bigamist, and there were no records of her parents' so-called marriage. There was nothing to find. She pushed away the concern.

He popped the trunk and pulled out a bona fide picnic basket.

"Well, aren't you prepared." Chloe grabbed the blanket and

followed him down the park's sloped lawn, surveying the area. Down closer to the water, a couple rested on a bench, enjoying the sea view. A man tossed a Frisbee to his Labrador. And on the boardwalk in front of the waterline, joggers and walkers passed by.

He stopped under one of the live oak trees a good distance from the shore. "You sure we'll be spotted from here?"

He shrugged. "If I'm wrong—and I'm not—we'll take a stroll through town later."

She had to trust that he knew what he was doing. This was his way of life, not hers. She spread out the blanket. "So what's it like, living in a fishbowl?"

"Never a dull moment. But you gotta take the good with the bad. I love what I do and it comes with a lack of privacy. Every job has its problems. What's the downside of writing?"

She considered his question as they settled on the blanket. She'd loved writing that story. It flowed from her imagination like spring water from the ground. After it was published, she enjoyed meeting readers and even doing the publicity circuit.

"Having the wrong actor cast as your male lead?" he guessed, eyes twinkling.

She hadn't expected him to be playful. Charming even. Who was this guy? "There is that."

He chuckled. "I think you might be the one keeping me on my toes, Anderson." He unloaded the food, all of it packed in clear plastic containers.

She removed the lids. A salad with three kinds of greens, grated cheese, hard-boiled eggs, and grape tomatoes. A tub of mixed berries. A loaf of French bread. And chicken that was still warm and smelled as if it had been grilled. Her stomach rumbled as she inhaled the savory scent. "You *cook?*"

"I'm more than just a pretty face, you know."

She rolled her eyes. "I don't remember reading about that in the tabloids."

"My pretty face?" He flashed a smile. "No, I tell them as little as possible. Which might explain why they make up so much. I hope you like chicken. A lot of my friends are vegetarian, but I figured chances were good a southern woman would eat meat."

"Bring it on. I love my proteins." She dished out food onto porcelain plates while he poured them drinks in stemless glasses.

"Your rental must be very well appointed if it came with a picnic basket."

"It is pretty nice, but I DoorDashed the basket."

She laughed. "Of course you did."

"What? Sometimes a guy just needs a picnic basket."

"Most people simply run to Walmart."

"Most people don't have cameras following them around."

"Fair point." She went for the warm chicken first and nodded in approval. Definitely grilled and flavorful with bursts of lemon and thyme. She couldn't believe he'd gone to all this trouble when he could've just grabbed it from the deli. Then again, those pesky cameras. She couldn't imagine living that kind of lifestyle, but he seemed to take it in stride.

She swallowed the chicken. "My brother would approve."

"Tell me about him. You two must be close, working together the way you do."

"We're only a year apart—"

"And that would make you . . . ?"

"Twenty-five. Right, I guess you should know my age. How old are you?"

"Thirty-two," he said. "Sorry, you were telling me about your brother."

"Sean and I are close. He can be a pain in the butt, but he's always there when I need him."

"I always wanted a sibling. There was no one to play with in my neighborhood, and my school friends lived too far away."

"Sounds kind of lonely. I'm grateful I had Sean growing up. But now that you're an adult, I'm sure you've found lots of people to connect with. Your manager, for instance. How'd you meet him?"

"I tried for three years to find an agent or manager. Not an easy task when you're a full-time barista trying to work your way into film. After I got my first role, I called Spencer and he ended up taking me on. It was a good fit in many ways. But as far as connecting with people, it's not easy making friends once you're in the business."

She stabbed another bite of chicken. "How so?"

He seemed to reflect a bit before he answered. "When you reach a certain level of success, people often want something from you other than friendship. Sometimes it's hard to tell who's genuine and who's not."

That was pretty vague, but she could imagine what those things might be. Old friends might come around wanting money. Wannabe actors would want a part in his movie. B-listers might want to share his spotlight. She'd never considered the cost of fame.

But he didn't seem to want to talk about it, so she changed the subject. Even though she was dreading the next topic, it was better to just get it out there. "I talked to my friend Meghan this morning and told her about our arrangement."

His face fell.

"I know, I know. I wasn't going to tell her, but I couldn't keep it from her. She'd never say a word to anyone though, I promise."

"I hope you're right. The media can be brutal. I'm used to it, but you're not. I'd hate for them to drag your name through the mud."

"Meghan's been my best friend since middle school. We've been together through thick and thin. We can trust her."

"Spencer will want an NDA from Sean and Meghan." At her questioning look he said, "A nondisclosure. He wanted one from you too, but I told him it wasn't necessary."

"I'd never betray your confidences."

"I believe that. And I realize you also have a lot on the line with your book and movie."

It was nice that he trusted her even though he hardly knew her. "I don't mind signing it. And I'm sure Sean and Meghan wouldn't either."

His mouth ticked up in a grin as he gazed at her. "Which just goes to show my instincts about you are right. Spencer would appreciate that if you don't think it'll cause any hard feelings between you and Meghan or Sean."

"Not at all. They're not like that."

She finished the chicken and moved on to the salad, which featured a tangy citrus vinaigrette. "Very nice. I might have to get the recipe for this dressing—for Sean, mind you."

"Passed down from my great-grandmother."

"Really?"

"No, I got it online."

She chuckled. He was surprisingly down-to-earth. She supposed that made him a *little* like Ledger. But there was still a huge gap between the two men. Liam didn't have to be Ledger to understand who he was though.

Speaking of . . . "So, I brought you a copy of my book. How long do you think it'll take you to get through it? You could always download the audio if you prefer, but I find that reading print immerses me in the story more thoroughly. Maybe that's just me though."

He finished a bite and took a sip from his glass. "Yeah, about that . . . I have a confession to make."

"You don't know how to read? You're allergic to fiction? My writing gives you hives?"

"Funny. No, my confession is"—he gave her a sheepish look— "I've actually already read your book."

She blinked. "What? You lied to me!"

"No . . . You just assumed I hadn't read it and I didn't correct you."

"Yesterday at my house when you were talking me into this whole thing, I asked if you would read my book and you said . . ."

He gave a dramatic shrug. "I said, 'Done.' And I was."

Sneaky. She scowled at him as their gazes locked.

"I'm still open to your insights on the character. Anything you want to teach me." He lifted a shoulder. "But if this is a deal breaker for you, I understand. I'll let you out of our arrangement if that's what you want. But I hope it's not."

He seemed earnest enough. And she was actually relieved he'd already read it. She'd thought she'd have to badger him about it. After publication it had taken six weeks and a few not-so-subtle threats for Sean to get through the book. A reader he was not.

"So why'd you read the book?"

"Despite what you seem to think, I take my job seriously. You were obviously worried I wasn't up to the role, so after that phone call I wanted to make sure I understood the character. And maybe prove you wrong in the meantime."

"You're competitive."

"You don't get very far in this business if you're not."

She could see that. Both publishing and acting were full of competition. If you didn't embrace it, you probably wouldn't last long. She almost hated to ask the next question, but it couldn't be avoided. "Well, don't keep me in suspense. What did you think of it?"

"The book or the character?"

"Both." She steeled herself for disapproval as she did when she read online reviews. Somehow criticism would feel more personal coming from Liam. Besides, a man might have an entirely different take on Ledger.

"I liked the story. I read it in two days, so that says a lot. It gripped me. The setting was palpable—and dead-on, I can say now that I'm here. You really captured the essence of the place." He tilted his head, his gaze intent on her. "Also, now that I think of it, there's a lot of you in it. I didn't know that when I was reading it though."

She squirmed. Took a sip. "What do you mean?"

"The voice, I guess. It has your quippy voice. A little sarcasm, not biting, just humorous in a low-key way. But there's a vulnerability in the tone of the story that kind of balances out the edge."

His assessment took her aback, made her feel a little exposed. She hadn't realized so much of her had leaked into the story. None of her reviews had put it quite that way. Then again, the readers didn't know her. On the other hand, neither did he.

She'd rather talk about her hero. "And Ledger? What are your thoughts on him?"

"He's quite the hero. A man who came from very little but has an innate sense of right and wrong. He's brave, even in love, which is maybe the hardest thing of all to be brave at."

She blinked at his evaluation. Maybe he understood Ledger better than she thought. "I like that. What else?"

"Do you want me to be honest?"

"Of course," she said even as she braced herself.

"Well . . . and this is a man's perspective, but he's a lot to live up to. When Cate starts pushing him away, I don't know many men who'd continue to pursue her so patiently."

"But she only does it because she's scared. She'd lost him years before and then her husband died. She's deeply scarred and afraid of loss."

"I realize that. I'm not saying she didn't have her reasons. I'm just saying he's impressive in his ability to see her through that fear and press on."

"It's because he loves so deeply. He lost her before and he's not about to lose her again. But he has his flaws too. He's admirable but he's not perfect. For instance, he's loyal to a fault. Even though his brother constantly took advantage of him, he still wouldn't give up on him."

"That's true. Ultimately, I was rooting for Ledger and Cate. Rooting for him to stick by her, so you did your job. The ending was very rewarding."

"You liked the storm scene?"

"It was moving and passionate, dynamic. It'll be a great scene to film. Very visual."

Pleasure bloomed inside at his compliments. At the way he stared at her, his eyes full of admiration. "I'm glad you liked it."

She couldn't believe she was sitting here with Liam Hamilton, discussing her book, and he'd actually enjoyed it. But he might not understand Ledger's background and how that propelled him to become the man he was. Or the depth of love he felt for Cate. Chloe still had some work to do.

She was staring at him. She pulled her gaze away, surprised to realize she'd finished her meal. They both had.

"Well, we've had at least three different people taking photos," he said. "That's a good start. Someone'll post on their socials or a tabloid site."

She glanced around the park, suddenly remembering where they were and what they were supposed to be doing here. "What? Why didn't you tell me?" No one was looking their way at the moment.

"Because we were doing just fine, making conversation, connecting. Better to keep it natural."

"Especially where I'm concerned. Hey, wait a minute, is that the only reason you laughed at my joke?"

He just chuckled and tossed his napkin at her.

# Chapter 10

The call came in just after Liam finished dinner—picnic leftovers. He'd been sitting on his deck, enjoying the evening sunshine, the briny breeze, and the gorgeous beach view when his phone vibrated in his pocket.

Spencer. He accepted the call. "Hey, what's up?"

"I'm staring at a nice photo of you and Miss Wholesome enjoying a picnic for two. *CelebWire* picked it up. Looks like a couple other sites have followed suit. Nice job, buddy."

That was good news. "Send me the link, would you?"

"Doing that now."

"What are people saying?"

"Haven't had a chance to get on socials yet, but the tabloid coverage I've seen so far is positive."

The link came in. Liam put Spencer on speaker and clicked it. The photo appeared at the top of their site. "'Liam Hamilton's New Fling?' I wish they hadn't used the word *fling*. Sounds cheap."

"Give it a minute. That'll change when you add some longevity to the relationship. When they see you're not going out with other women."

Liam read on. "They've identified her. 'Liam's newest conquest is the author of the book-turned-movie that features Liam's latest role. Will the author fall in love with the hero she created, or will Liam break her heart? Stay tuned.'"

"Nice turn of phrase, huh? Patty thinks it's a great start."

Liam scowled. "Chloe won't love being referred to as my conquest."

"As I said, give it time. That's a good picture. You seem relaxed and she appears to be eating up whatever you're saying. She's a looker. I did a little research on her. Those eyes . . ."

"They're striking." And they betrayed her every mood. When she was all fired up, they flashed silver. And when she was listening intently, they were a warm, liquid blue he wouldn't mind falling into for a while.

Liam zoomed in on the photo. It was a frontal view of him grinning at her. Chloe's profile also revealed a smile. Objectively, it appeared to be a private little picnic between a pair of lovebirds. Perfect.

"Keep up the good work," Spencer said. "I emailed you the NDA. Try to get it back to me by the end of day tomorrow."

"About that. Chloe also confided in her best friend."

"Aw, man."

"Hey, I confided in my best friend too."

"Your best friend is your manager."

"It's only two people and she trusts them. She has as much at stake as I do."

"Hardly. Your career could ride on this. With your reputation already in the crapper, if it gets out you tried to fool your fans, it won't be good."

"It won't get out. We're both invested in this."

"Get those NDAs. The studio doesn't like that we didn't get right on this."

"I'm on it."

A few minutes later they signed off, and Liam clicked on the other gossip sites that had reported the story. The captions and content were more salacious than he would've liked, but he'd expected as much. Of course they'd make Chloe out to be his plaything, just as they had most of the actresses he'd gone out with. That was inevitable since he rarely went out with the same woman twice.

Funny, he and Chloe had talked just yesterday about two of Ledger's most prominent qualities. They'd stayed in the park well into the afternoon discussing his sentimentality and fierce loyalty. Liam wasn't particularly sentimental. And as for loyalty, Liam could only relate to the characteristic where his family and friends were concerned. He'd never been in love or even reached a point in a relationship where loyalty was expected.

Moreover, he'd observed his father being unfaithful to his mother. She, however, had been loyal to her husband—to a fault. Even after he'd left her for another woman, she'd begged him to come home. It turned Liam's stomach to remember all the ways she'd tried to win back her philandering ex-husband.

Was it any wonder Liam shied away from commitment?

But he didn't have to *be* Ledger. He just had to understand the character well enough to get into his skin. He could handle that. He'd played many characters who were different from him: a shyster tycoon, a disabled veteran, a grieving widower. He could surely play a sentimental boatbuilder.

He woke up his phone and sent one of the links to Chloe. *And so it begins . . . Stay off the socials!* She was working so he didn't expect to hear back from her right away.

Tomorrow they had plans to meet at the coffee shop, and he found himself looking forward to it. They had a little over a week before filming began. She was holding up her end of the bargain, and he was determined to hold up his as well. He'd nail the part of Ledger if it killed him.

His Milwaukee ball cap and sunglasses did little to fool the barista behind the counter. She stood frozen, wearing a blank stare as he ordered Chloe's and his drinks.

When he finished, the young brunette closed her gaping mouth and attempted speech. "Um . . . sorry, I guess I missed that?"

He repeated the order and she entered it into the computer with hands that trembled. When she was finished she gazed up at him wide-eyed. "That'll be eleven dollars and thirty-five cents. You're Liam Hamilton."

He flashed a smile. "Guilty."

She blushed. "I've seen all your movies. *Valor* was my favorite."

The military romance had been a hit, especially with teens. "Thank you"—he glanced at her name tag—"Veronica. I appreciate that."

"I can't believe you're filming a movie in my hometown. Or standing in front of my register right now. Shoot. I should've comped your coffee. I'm a little starstruck."

He chuckled as he paid via his phone. "You're doing fine. You should come over to the set one day if you can work it out with your schedule."

She handed him the receipt. "Really? I could come watch?"

He took one of the coffee-shop cards and jotted Simone's name and number on the back, then handed it to Veronica. "Give this woman a call and she'll set it up for you. I'll let her know you'll be calling."

"Oh my gosh. You're so nice."

"Bring a friend if you like. But keep the number to yourself, please. We can't have the whole town turning out." He softened the words with a smile. The studio was careful about who came on set since they wanted to control the narrative about the movie.

"I will, I promise. Um, there's a table in the corner that's kinda private." She winced. "Jeez, I forgot to ask—here or to go?"

"We'll be sticking around awhile."

"The table's over there, around the corner. I'll bring you the drinks."

"Thanks, Veronica."

\* \* \*

As Chloe made her way through the coffee shop, she tried to shake the disgust that had been roiling in her gut since late last night. An eighties melody played in the background, and the scent of coffee beans was so strong it nearly gave her the caffeine buzz she sought.

She glanced around the café in case Liam had beat her here. Not likely since she was a few minutes—oh, there he was. He'd taken a table on the smaller side of the shop, facing the wall. Since there were already two steaming mugs on the table, she joined him.

"Good morning." She lowered herself into the seat opposite him.

"Morning."

There were only two other customers in view, and they were far enough away not to overhear their conversation if they spoke quietly. "Thank you for the coffee." She took a sip. Double-chocolate mocha. He'd been paying attention when they'd discussed their preferences yesterday.

His gaze narrowed on her as he leaned back in his chair and crossed his arms over his chest. "You went digging around, didn't you?"

"They've made me out to be your little plaything."

"Of course you're not. I did warn you about this though."

"I'm an independent woman. I run a restaurant—which is not an easy business, my friend—and I wrote a book that soared to the top of the bestseller lists. I don't need a relationship with a man to validate my existence."

"I know that. I'm sorry. I know some of the tabloid sites portrayed you in an unflattering light."

"If they'd shown you in the same light, I don't think *unflattering* would quite cover it. You should read what your fans are saying about me."

"I understand how you feel. But I've dated around a lot, so of course everyone's going to assume that come tomorrow you'll be yesterday's news."

She exhaled a deep breath. Now that she'd vented, she felt a little better. "I know this isn't your fault. You have no control over what they say, and this was bound to happen, I guess. I just didn't expect it to affect me so much. Shoot, you must deal with this all the time yourself." Half of what they'd said about him probably wasn't even true. Guilt pricked. She'd judged him pretty harshly before she'd met him.

Something shifted in his eyes. He leaned forward. "Look, I know this doesn't feel very good. But it'll self-correct, you'll see."

She studied him—the concerned knot of his brow, the flash of fear in his eyes—and softened a bit. "Yeah, how's that?"

"The tone of the conversation will soon shift because you and I will have the one thing I've never had with any other woman."

He'd raised her curiosity with that one. "What's that?"

"*Time.* This will appear to be our third date—a real rarity for me. Then there'll be a fourth and a fifth and before you know it, you'll be the one who finally captured my heart."

His words stole some of the starch from her posture, tweaked her heartstrings just a little. Man, he was good. But what he was saying made sense. Surely he knew what he was talking about; he wasn't new to this whole scandal business. She sure hoped he was right, because being dismissed felt pretty crummy. Some of his fans had even claimed their meeting must've been strictly business—that he couldn't possibly be interested in *her*. That hit a sore spot. Nobody liked falling short.

"Just be patient, okay? This will work out, but we have to give it some time."

Her gaze flickered to Liam's left, where a twentysomething customer peeked around her friend to stare at Liam. "I think you've been made."

"That's okay. Most people just stare or snap a photo. They usually don't approach me." He took a sip of his coffee. "Are we good on this? You'll give it more time?"

She pursed her lips. "It had better turn around for both our sakes."

"It will. You'll see. You ready to get down to business? I've been thinking about Ledger since we talked yesterday. Loyalty is probably a top attribute for anyone seeking a partner. But can't a person take loyalty too far?"

"What do you mean?"

"Well, what if, for instance, Cate didn't return his feelings? Wouldn't Ledger's loyalty to her then be kind of . . . pathetic or even stalkerish?"

"But she did return his feelings, so it's a moot point."

"But how did he know that?"

"Because he's intuitive enough to see through the walls she's built around her heart."

A woman appeared at Liam's side.

"Hi, y'all. I'm so sorry to interrupt, but aren't you Liam Hamilton? I heard you'd be in town for that movie, and I saw you sitting over here and just had to pop over and say hi. I'm Savannah and this is my friend Leah."

Liam rose, wearing a friendly expression, and shook their hands. "Nice to meet you both. This is Chloe—she wrote the book the movie's been adapted from."

The attractive women barely glanced her way. They must've been tourists because Chloe didn't recognize them.

"When does the filming start?" Leah asked.

"A little over a week. Just getting the lay of the land for now."

Savannah touched Liam's arm. "Well, if you have some time to fill, we're staying in a beautiful home over on Culver's Cove. We'd love to take you out on the sailboat. Leah's been sailing since she was just a wee thing."

"That's very kind of you, but I'm kind of booked up." He tossed an intimate smile Chloe's way, but that didn't deter Leah from handing him a card with her number on it.

A few long minutes and two photos later, they left and he sat back down. "Sorry about that. Where were we?"

Before she could answer they were interrupted by a middle-aged couple who'd seen his most recent movie. They were townies, though Chloe didn't know their names until now.

Once they left, Liam sat down again. "Maybe this was a bad idea. People know I'm here for the movie so they're on the lookout. Let's meet someplace more private when we're working on Ledger's role and keep the public appearances for the other end of our bargain."

"That's probably a good idea. We can alternate days: work on Ledger's role one day and your image the next, at least until filming starts."

"Agreed." He emptied his mug. "My place or yours?"

She felt stronger on her own turf. "Mine, if you wouldn't mind. We can sit outside so your cat allergy isn't an issue."

"Sounds good."

They decided they'd ride together in her car, which wouldn't draw attention. But when they neared her house, media vans were parked out front. "Oh boy."

"Keep driving." Liam ducked. "Don't slow down."

"I thought we wanted to be seen together?"

"Not right now. And I don't want them following us. I'd rather they not know where I'm staying just yet."

It was impossible not to gape at the media mingling at the end of her drive as she passed. It was such a strange sight to see in her quiet little neighborhood. "You've got to be kidding me."

"I'm sorry, but it was only a matter of time. They'll lose interest soon enough."

"But I have to go home eventually."

"They can't come into your yard. If they do, call the police. Just say, 'No comment,' and keep moving. You might want to close your blinds though. They have telephoto lenses."

*For heaven's sake.* "Great."

"It'll be fine. It'll be easier if you can park your car in the garage and enter that way."

"It's full of junk."

"You might want to clean it out then."

She checked the rearview mirror. No one had paid much attention to her vehicle. "Okay, we're past. You can sit up now. I don't think they recognized me."

He did as she suggested. "Let's head to my place."

He hadn't been kidding about the house he'd rented. It was on the strip of beach north of town and boasted a large beautiful deck with comfy outdoor furniture.

The inside was tastefully decorated. It was clean but for the sandals lying by the french doors, a newspaper splayed on the sofa, and a few pillows askew. The house held the faint aroma of Liam's cologne.

They spent the morning talking shop on the deck. They discussed two more of Ledger's qualities—protectiveness and selflessness—and talked about the scenes in the story where he demonstrated those traits.

Liam threw together sandwiches for lunch, and afterward she helped him run lines from the scene where Ledger and Cate meet. Chloe was impressed. His voice held just the right awestruck tone.

His expressions betrayed interest in Cate while his gestures gave away the adorable awkwardness she'd written into the scene. With only a few prompts from her, he nailed it. And that was such a relief. She could tolerate the tabloids' insulting interpretation of their relationship if their work produced results like this.

Chloe would've liked to have gone home to change for work, but the gaggle of reporters in her yard deterred her. Later that night as she was preparing for bed, she received a text from Liam. *Was the paparazzi there when you got home?*

She settled against the pillows and responded. *They were gone, thank God. My morning agenda is cleaning out the garage.*

She'd leveled with Sean last night about the photographers. After all, they might show up at Docksiders too. Although she wasn't really the person of interest here. They were trying to catch Liam and her together.

*I'll come over and help out. It's the least I can do.*

*What if they're back? Besides, we're supposed to be working on your public image tomorrow.*

*This could serve as a photo op too. Naturally I'd be visiting my girlfriend's house while I'm in town. And also a new couple would be seeking privacy. It won't seem genuine if we're parading around town every day.*

*That's true. But we could certainly do something more fun than hauling boxes.* 😊

*It needs to be done. You'll feel more comfortable if you don't have to face the media directly. It can be a little intimidating if you're not used to it.*

*Such a strange life you lead.*

*Right? I should let you get to bed. Does nine o'clock work?*

*Sure.*

*I can bring donuts . . .*

*Chocolate, please.* 😊

# Chapter 11

When Chloe checked the front yard the next morning, only two photographers lingered out by the street. She let the drapes fall and set the table with plates and napkins. A few minutes later the rumbling of Liam's Camaro alerted her to his arrival.

She unlocked the front door and watched as he shut off and exited the vehicle. The photographers' voices carried through the screen door as he approached the house.

"Liam, are you dating Chloe?"

"What's in the bag, Liam?"

"How long have you known her?"

"Can we get a picture of you two?"

"Liam, over here!"

Liam ignored them as he strode purposefully down the walk and hopped onto the porch.

Chloe let him in, then closed the door and leaned against it, palm pressed to her heart. "I don't know why *my* heart's beating so fast."

He grinned, clearly not the least bit ruffled. "At least they kept it classy."

"So that's how you do it? You just ignore them and go about your business?"

"There are times I smile their way or give a wave, but only when I'm out in public, not when they're invading my privacy. And be warned, they might try to provoke you by saying something offensive.

But just say, 'No comment,' or nothing at all. Try to keep your facial expression blank."

Uh-oh. "Have you met me?"

His expression warmed. "You'll be fine. Once we start giving them more of what they want in public, they'll stop coming around here. Well, until your property turns into a set at least." He held up the sack. "Where should I put this?"

"On the table's fine."

She followed him to the dining room. He wore a pair of khaki shorts with a white T-shirt that showed off his muscles and tanned skin. The broad shoulders were impressive too. He must work hard at that physique. She'd bet her favorite handbag there was a six-pack under that tee. No wonder he had such ardent fans.

He turned and caught her staring. Arched a brow.

Her cheeks heated as she turned for the kitchen. "Um, would you like some orange juice? Coffee?"

"Water's fine."

She pulled glasses from the cabinets and tried to ignore the way his powerful presence seemed to shrink her house. "The photographers know what kind of car you're driving now."

"They would've figured it out soon enough anyway." He glanced around. "Where's Buttercup?"

She stopped midpour. "Oh, I'm sorry, I forgot about your allergies. Will you be okay in the garage? Buttercup doesn't go out there. She's afraid of the furnace room."

"I'll be fine. There she is," he said upon sighting the cat, then squatted as Buttercup approached.

After sniffing and licking his hand, the cat slid against his leg, purring softly.

Chloe scowled at the animal. "Really? You come out of hiding for *him*? She's been mad at me for being gone all day yesterday."

He scratched Buttercup's neck. "Aw, that was my fault, honey. You shouldn't take it out on Mommy."

"Someone needs to remember who does the feeding around here." Chloe opened a can of chow—the good stuff, mind you—and placed it in the cat's dish.

That got Buttercup's attention.

"And don't you forget it," Chloe said as the cat dug into the food.

Liam washed his hands while Chloe finished their drinks, then they sat at the table.

"Were you recognized at the donut shop?"

"I don't think so. They had a variety of chocolate donuts, so I got them all."

"I haven't met a chocolate donut I didn't like." She selected the chocolate-frosted custard and bit in. "Yum."

"These are good."

"Doreen makes the best donuts in the world. Her work hours are the pits though."

"Do you know everyone in town?"

"Just about. It's a small community till the tourists arrive in the summer."

"Do the townspeople hate that?"

"Oh, we take the good with the bad. Fact is, most businesses—ours included—couldn't survive without them. If we have longer lines and packed beaches, that just goes with the territory. Summer weekends get really crowded around here."

"Speaking of weekends, most of the cast and crew will be arriving Saturday."

Chloe was starting to get nervous about the filming. "That's what Simone said. I don't really know what to expect. I've never been on a set before. What's it like?"

"You'll get the hang of it. You've probably been told we film out of chronological order. It's about location and actor availability. And they try to keep the filming locations fairly close to each other because moving is a huge production. We're talking like ten massive trucks full of equipment. If we have a few scenes set in one location, we film them together whenever possible, even if one's at the beginning of the movie and one's at the end. There are quite a few takes of each scene to make sure they're getting the right coverage for editing. It's time-consuming. Some long days. But you'll be amazed how the crew works together so efficiently. And I will say the table reading went exceptionally well."

"That's what Simone said." Chloe took a bite of her donut.

"Will you be on set every day?"

She finished chewing and swallowed. "As much as I can, given my job hours. Do you know Daisy very well?"

"I've met her a few times, but I can't say I really know her. She has a good reputation for working hard and she's very talented."

"I agree."

He cocked an eyebrow, watching her closely. "So you weren't concerned about *her* role in the movie?"

Chloe's face heated. "It's not that. It's just that Ledger is really the key to making this story work. He's the one the readers swooned over."

"So you said. And you didn't think I could pull it off."

"I've hardly even seen you on-screen at all!"

His eyebrows shot up. "Ouch."

*Oh, for heaven's sake.* "I didn't mean it that way. The only movie I've seen you in is *Jilted* and—"

"You thought I played the role of cheating fiancé a little too well."

She couldn't seem to say the right thing to save her soul. *"Argh."*

He chuckled. "Settle down, I'm just kidding. I'll even take that as a compliment since I've never even had a fiancée, much less cheated on one. You bought the part, right? That's what matters."

He had a point. But truly all her fears had been allayed when they'd read lines yesterday. "I overreacted when Simone called three months ago. I believe I've already apologized for that."

He flashed a grin. "I just like to give you a hard time. You're so easy to rile."

She pursed her mouth in a scowl, but it was more to prevent the smile that teased her lips than anything else.


"Well, well, well . . . What is *this*?" From his corner of the garage, Liam held up a familiar white binder covered in tacky flowers, hearts, satin ribbon, and the words *My Dream Wedding* scrawled in fancy script.

Chloe hurdled over a row of boxes and ripped the hefty binder from his arms. "Never you mind." Face burning, she dumped the scrapbook into a box and carried it to the edge of the garage. The scrapbook was an ill-conceived creation, made back when she thought Mr. Right would sweep her away just in time for her twenty-first birthday—the ideal bridal age, she'd thought.

Liam made a show of brushing the white glitter from his arms. It rained down like a monsoon.

She hurled a balled-up sock at him, missing entirely.

A few minutes later he snagged her attention once again. "Aw . . . lookie here." He held up her seventh-grade photo, complete with braces, acne, and hair that had yet to see a straight iron.

She dashed over and jerked the photo away. "Every child goes through an ugly phase." She glanced down into the box at his feet. It contained her boy band paraphernalia (including her shrine to One Direction), her stash of diaries (filled with romantic melo-drama), the complete set of the Twilight series, and her old band uniform. Why hadn't she realized her garage was a virtual land mine of embarrassing memorabilia?

"You played an instrument?" he asked. "Maybe we could form a band."

"You need a clarinet?" she asked drolly, then grabbed the box. "I'll just take this. You're supposed to be moving them, not pawing through them."

He chuckled. "You're no fun. I'll bet those diaries contain some interesting material."

"Guess who's not gonna find out?" Chloe went back to work.

She paused a few minutes later to wipe the sweat from her forehead. The back door they'd opened offered only a bit of warm breeze. "Sure would be nice if we could open the garage door. This will take a while."

"We're getting there. It's not that bad really. You should see my mom's garage. When she moved, she refused to toss anything, even my old stuff. She has stacks of boxes she'll probably never open again."

"Wouldn't the paparazzi like to get their hands on that? What would I find if I cleaned out her garage?"

"Oh, let's see . . . My starter guitar—a used Glarry made of basswood—several amps, and various pieces of band equipment. A few soccer trophies and jerseys—I played goalie because I was too chubby to play anywhere else."

Her gaze swept over his form. *"You?"*

"I didn't hit a growth spurt until my junior year. Just in time to finally get a girl to go out with me."

Hard to imagine him that way, chubby and unpopular with the girls. "I'll bet they're kicking themselves now. What else?"

"Oh, the usual. Schoolwork, artwork—and I was bad. Like, really bad. That's pretty much it, I guess. Oh, and everything my dad left behind. Scratch that. I think she still keeps that stuff in her bedroom closet."

"Most people toss their ex's stuff when they divorce, don't they? My mom couldn't get rid of my father's things quickly enough."

Liam gave a mirthless laugh. "Well, my mom's still hoping he'll come back, so there's that."

There was a lot of feeling behind those words, behind that scowl. She couldn't imagine her mom still pining away for her father. Even Chloe wanted nothing to do with him. After all, he'd chosen to permanently exit her life. She had no interest in being part of his now. She'd never even had the desire to look him up. "How long's it been since the divorce?"

"Oh, about twenty-five years and a dozen women. He's not coming back, though there's no making my mom understand that."

She felt a pang of sympathy for his mother—and him. "That must be hard to watch."

"Yeah, it's not great."

A moment of silence ensued as they stacked boxes along the perimeter. Apparently he didn't want to talk about his mom. That was all right. They had their work cut out here, and this wasn't a real relationship.

"Hey, what's this?"

She glanced up, cringing at what else he might've found. Her baby teeth? The sophomoric poetry from her middle-school years? Her Justin Bieber doll?

But no, it was just the boat.

Liam whipped off the tarp.

She'd saved up for the used wooden dinghy when she and Evan were dating. She wanted to share her love of the water. The peace she found as she paddled around the quiet tributaries like an explorer of old. Evan hadn't been interested in kayaking, and a rowboat seemed more romantic. Turned out, he hadn't enjoyed that either, so the thing had just sat at the end of her pier for a season. She hadn't bothered putting it back in the water since.

Liam ran his hand over the mahogany gunwale. "Reminds me of the one Ledger and Cate take out on the water in that one scene."

It was exactly the boat she'd pictured as she wrote it. "Well, they say to 'write what you know.'"

"We should get it out on the river. It'll clear up some space in here. We can take her out when we're done and talk more about Ledger. What do you say?"

"Today's supposed to be your day, and you're already waist-deep in my junk."

"I'm sure they got plenty of photos of me entering your house. Besides, I'll be rowing a boat like this for the movie and—full disclosure—I've never done that before. I'd rather not look like a dweeb."

Chloe laughed. "Since Ledger's a boatbuilder, he'd definitely know how to row one."

He stuffed the tarp under the shelving. "Exactly. This is great. I was a little worried about that actually."

Liam seemed so confident—even in the face of her doubts. It hadn't occurred to her he might have uncertainties. It made him seem a bit more human somehow. More relatable.

"What are some things you've had to learn for parts in movies?"

"Well, I had to learn to ride a horse for *Unbridled*. And not just sit the horse—I had to have a really good seat."

Chloe glanced over as he bent to pick up a box, then jerked her gaze away from his backside.

"The character managed a horse ranch, so I had to be a proficient rider. Took a few months, but I think we pulled it off. I still ride occasionally. I was a chef in a movie that you wouldn't have heard of. That's when I actually started getting into cooking. There was a lot to learn in *Valor* about being a Marine and living as an amputee. I learn new things with every role really. Keeps things interesting."

"What do you know about boatbuilding?"

"I've been doing my research, don't you worry. Your boat is a wheelbarrow dinghy, which makes it easy to transport on land." He pointed to the front of the boat. "That's the bow. Port is left, starboard, right. This is the gunwale. The oars are made up of the blade, shaft, and loom."

"Very impressive. Now we just have to teach you to row."

# Chapter 12

It took a bit of doing, but Liam managed to maneuver the rowboat away from the pier into the middle of the river where it flowed gently toward the ocean. However, they were sideways. He used the paddles to point them the right direction, then began powering them downstream.

He sat in the boat's center facing backward, and Chloe sat at the stern, leaning toward him, elbows on her knees. "You're doing great."

Generous, given it had taken him ten minutes to get this far. He chuckled. "Let's just say I'm glad this isn't happening in front of the cast and crew, much less the cameras."

"You're getting the hang of it. You've got good instincts."

He didn't know about that, but all this upper-body work made him grateful for his daily workouts. "Don't you ever use the boat?"

"I thought it would be nice to come out here with my exboyfriend, but he didn't like it much." She stretched out her legs, her feet coming alongside his.

It was a small boat. Cozy. Every time he leaned forward to pull back the oars, it brought them closer together.

He gave his head a shake and focused on his surroundings. Trees lined the river on both sides, concealing the homes farther back on the properties. Piers stretched out into the water. A weeping willow dipped into the edges of the stream.

The salt marshes near the shoreline petered out to water so

clear he could see fish swimming below. A sultry breeze stirred the branches above, and the salty scent of the ocean hung in the air. A seagull cried from somewhere nearby, the sound mingling with the splash of the oar dipping into the water.

He stopped rowing a minute just to relax and enjoy the moment. Drew in a deep breath and let it empty from his lungs. His chest loosened.

Until this moment he hadn't realized how stressed he was. Between his publicity problems, the upcoming film, and (according to his dad) his mom leaving slurred voice mails on his phone, Liam had been a little tense lately.

It had been a long time since he was so far out in nature that he couldn't hear the signs of human existence. No beeping horns or sirens. Just the whispering treetops and the gurgle of water. "It's peaceful. The world seems so far away."

"I kayak out here all the time. It's my best thinking spot."

He hoped the paparazzi wouldn't ruin this for her. Still, it warmed him that she'd share her favorite spot with him. Their gazes tangled for a long moment. The connection stirred something in him. A longing maybe, but for what? He lifted the oars from the water and eased them forward.

"There are streams coming into the river, and you can wind your way back, taking tributaries till you get lost."

"Have you ever gotten lost?"

"Only once and it was getting dark. I learned to pay better attention. And now I've been out here so many times I know my way by heart."

He fell into a steady rhythm. "You have an amazing getaway, not to mention a pretty good workout, right in your backyard."

She flashed a smile. "I'm a lucky girl."

Something behind those eyes intrigued him. Made him want to ask questions. But they were virtual strangers. Two people involved in a simple quid pro quo. She didn't owe him personal information, and he'd gotten into the habit of playing his own cards close to his chest. The first thing you lost when you made it in Hollywood was trust in other people.

But Chloe seemed trustworthy. His mind flashed back to the garage and that tacky wedding book. He'd never had sisters. Was that a common thing young girls did? Somehow he didn't think so. Chloe was a romantic.

He remembered the pile of diaries, complete with keyed locks, and the cute picture of her with freckles, braces, and those familiar wide blue eyes.

"What's that look for?"

He forced an innocent expression. "Nothing."

"You're thinking about that stuff you found in my garage."

"No comment."

"Maybe I should've had *you* sign an NDA."

He laughed. And man, it felt good. When was the last time he'd laughed for real? The indignation on Chloe's face only made him laugh harder. And seeing the white glitter still clinging to his forearms and hands didn't help matters.

"Sorry, sorry," he squeezed out, but the image of that scrapbook flashed in his mind.

Her cheeks flushed. "It's the bridal book, isn't it?"

"You sure had a thing for glitter. Can I see the inside of the book? Just a little peek?"

"I'm burning it when I get home."

A moment later his laughter faded, but a smile lingered as he tried for a turn, taking a wide tributary that led back into the marsh.

Chloe's attention was on the landscape, so he let his gaze feast on her. She appeared so young today with her hair pulled back. Some strands had escaped the ponytail and curled alongside her pinkened cheeks. She embarrassed easily and he wasn't used to that. The women in Hollywood . . . they were more likely to embarrass *him*.

Hard to believe he'd met Chloe only five days ago. He enjoyed her company. She was fun and funny and *real*. In fact, she was fast on her way to becoming one of his favorite people to spend time with. He felt at ease around her somehow, as if he didn't have to impress her or be someone he wasn't.

And unlike so many of his Hollywood friends, she'd been up front about what she wanted from him.

While he was here in Stillwater Bay, he wanted to enjoy her company. Fill some of his hours when he wasn't working. She could swing by his place for brunch while they talked about Ledger and ran lines.

Satisfied, he put his back into his efforts as he propelled them through the shaded sanctuary.

\* \* \*

Chloe should probably bring up the next characteristic on her agenda. It was the perfect place to talk about Ledger's steadfastness. She'd thought this would be a difficult concept for someone like him.

But when Liam was away from the crowds, he actually had the steady thing pretty well perfected. Like now, he paddled quietly upstream, seemingly soaking in the sights and sounds of nature. She liked that he didn't seem compelled to fill every second with chatter. Even when he was teasing her, he wasn't so bad. A little exasperating maybe, but he wasn't a meanie about it.

"Wanna talk about Ledger?" he asked as if reading her mind. "Might as well since we've got all this time."

"Sure, I guess. I thought we'd talk about his steady presence next."

"Steady presence." He said the words as if testing them on his tongue. "What does that mean exactly?"

"He's always there for Cate, through thick and thin. Like when she has that health scare and toward the end when she's pushing him away. He's a solid foundation for her."

"Kind of like loyalty then."

She tried to nail it down. "Kind of like that. But it's more that he stays calm through it all. He's steady in a crisis. He doesn't let his emotions get away from him."

"He's a pretty sensitive guy though. So why's he so steady? His childhood was pretty chaotic. I'd think that would make him anything but calm in a crisis."

"Or maybe the chaos made him crave calm. But in his case it was his military background. Twelve years of preparing for the worst trained him to respond thoughtfully instead of freezing or lashing out or running."

"Makes sense." His brow furrowed. He made two more scoops with the paddles, seeming to let that sink in. "My friend Spencer's like that, though he wasn't in the military. Nothing rattles him. He just buckles down and finds solutions. He's methodical. Why's that characteristic so important to Cate?" He cut her a grin. "And a million other women, apparently."

"For Cate it's more that his steadiness keeps him there. He doesn't run at the first sign of trouble. In fact, there's no amount of trouble that would tear him away from her."

"And she feels so strongly about that because of the loss she's experienced?"

"Right."

"Makes sense," Liam said.

His low voice scraped at the old wound. She caught his unwavering stare and shifted in her seat. It was as if he were seeing right inside her. Right back to her own childhood. Her father's "traveling job" had kept their household in a state of flux. And when they found out about his other family, his departure was immediate—and permanent. Devastating.

This particular trait of Ledger's had been the cornerstone of many reviews and private messages. It seemed Chloe hadn't been the only one unable to find a man who stayed through thick and thin.

Wedding vows weren't taken seriously anymore. For better or worse. For richer or poorer. In sickness and in health. Not that Chloe had kept a man long enough to make it down the aisle. She wanted to, though. The little girl who'd made that tacky dream book was still alive and well—albeit with better fashion sense.

Liam turned into another stream, checking over his shoulder as he rowed, maneuvering the boat smoothly.

"You're getting pretty good with this thing."

"I wouldn't mind a little more practice before the boating scene is filmed. I'm a long way from boatbuilder proficiency."

"You're welcome to use it anytime."

"I think it would be helpful if we could run lines again tomorrow. We can work on the scenes I'll be rehearsing Monday with Daisy."

She was surprised he wanted to run lines again. He'd done so well yesterday. "Sure. Maybe we can do that at your place so we don't have to worry about the paparazzi."

"Sounds good. Hey, Spencer mentioned that we should probably post something on our socials about us."

"Something like . . . ?"

"You know, a relationship status update, maybe a picture or two."

Everyone she knew was about to find out she was dating Liam Hamilton. This was about to get very personal. Was she ready for that?

He studied her face. "Is that okay?"

"Of course. It makes sense. There's just a lot more to all this than I anticipated."

He tilted his head. "Is there someone you don't want to know about us?"

"No, it's not that. It's just that this keeps getting bigger and bigger.

My mom texted me last night and asked when I was bringing my 'Hollywood hunk' over to meet her and my dad."

He chuckled. "She sounds like someone I need to meet. How about if I have you all over for dinner this weekend before prep work gets underway? Next week is going to be insanely busy."

"That's sweet of you, but she'd like to have you over to her place. She loves to cook and of course my brother will be there too."

"The more the merrier."

He truly seemed unbothered. Of course, it wasn't his family he was duping. "Or I could just tell my parents the truth and then we wouldn't have to go through the motions."

"It's up to you, but I hope you won't."

Her parents had a hands-off approach to adult parenting. They were close in other ways, but Chloe didn't really open up to them about the men in her life. Meghan was the one whose shoulder she cried on.

"You're probably right. I guess we should have a meet 'n' greet with the folks anyway, just for appearances' sake."

"Good point." Liam stopped paddling and let the boat drift to a stop.

"What are you doing?"

"Come up here. Let's take our first selfie."

She glanced down at her shirt, which bore the words *This is a clean shirt. I just have a cat.* "I didn't exactly dress for this."

"You look great. But I have to ask, do you have a slogan tee for every day of the week?"

"Meghan gets one for me every Christmas, so I probably have one for every day of the month."

He held out his hand. "Get over here."

Guess they were gonna do this. The boat rocked gently as she slid off the seat. Before she could determine where to sit, he pulled her onto his lap.

Okay then. Her hands clung to each other in her lap. His thigh was like a boulder under her rear end but somehow comfy too, and his arm was a welcoming support around her waist.

He held his phone in front of them.

Chloe turned her attention to the screen and grinned. It felt stilted. Fake. Her pulse raced and her mouth was dry as dust. Also, she didn't exactly look her best after sorting through her garage. "Maybe we should do this later after I've fixed myself up."

He turned, his gaze roving over her face. "You look great. Cute. Natural." He faced the screen and snapped a shot, seeming for all the world like he was having the time of his life.

"I'm pretty sure 'natural' is a euphemism for 'ugly,'" she said through her plastic smile.

He leaned closer until their cheeks almost touched. "You could never be ugly." He took another picture. "Turn this way."

She did—and froze when he did the same. Their faces were inches apart. His warm breath whispered over her mouth. His eyes were *right there*. Had she called them gray? Silly her. Specks of silver and blue gave them a depth she hadn't noticed before.

His lips were nicely shaped, the lower one lush. There was a tiny scar at the corner of his mouth she'd never noticed.

She dragged in the smooth scent of his cologne. Nice. It smelled like man and money, because let's face it, that wasn't drugstore cologne he was wearing.

"Close your eyes," he said softly.

"Huh? What?"

"Just do it."

She did as he asked, bracing herself—for what, she didn't know. Her heart, beating like a bass drum, seemed to have gotten the memo though. All her senses were on high alert. Water dripped off the oars. His fingers tightened at her waist. The boat swayed gently as he leaned forward.

Something warm and gentle settled on her forehead. A kiss, her brain worked out. He stayed for a delicious beat. She might've purred. She definitely felt like it.

Then it was over and the air stirred around them. She opened her eyes to find him making a study of her features. At least she thought he was. But his gaze snapped toward his phone so quickly she might have just imagined it.

"Let's see what we have here." He sounded perfectly calm and collected.

Her heart hammered and her thoughts spun, distracting her as he thumbed back to the first photos and swiped slowly through them. The memory of that kiss was like a brand on her forehead. Had anyone ever given her a forehead kiss? Also his arm was still around her.

"This is the one." He aimed the phone her way. "Don't you think?"

Oh, right. The phone. The pictures. She blinked them into focus. It was the shot of the forehead kiss. Could that be her, lips parted, wearing that dreamy look? The background was blurred and the sunlight glinted off wisps of hair, giving the picture a romantic feel.

And *him*. Liam's eyes were closed too, his lashes fanning his upper cheeks. He was gorgeous. She gave a soft sigh.

"Okay?"

"Sure," she breathed.

"No signal out here," he said, "but I'll okay it with Patty when we get back to the house, then forward it to you if she's good with it."

She didn't need a picture to remember that kiss. She hadn't expected his nearness to affect her this way. But surely her reaction was perfectly normal. Of course she was attracted to Liam Hamilton. Every woman in America was attracted to him. He was hot and sexy and his forehead kisses (she could now attest) were eleventy million out of ten stars.

But attraction and feelings were very different animals. She knew better than to develop feelings for a man whose dating habits resembled those of a lion.

Liam cleared his throat. He'd already put his phone away. He shot her an awkward glance.

Oh. She was still on his lap. She jumped up so quickly, the boat pitched precariously. She grabbed the gunwale, and thankfully the boat settled as she slid silently into her seat.

# Chapter 13

Chloe blocked out the sound of the surf and the way the breeze tugged at Liam's hair. She stared across the beach blanket at him, homing in on his words. On his tone. On the expression on his face. They'd been at this for twenty minutes.

He was delivering the lines from a scene that would film early on. Ledger and Cate would be on her pier. He was bringing up their past for the first time since the two had serendipitously reconnected after seven years apart.

He nudged her bare foot. "Your line."

She'd missed her cue. She dropped her attention to the script in her lap and found her place. "'Really? You're bringing that up now?'"

"'Somebody has to. If it were up to you, we'd just pretend it never happened. But it did, Cate. It did happen.'"

He had the lines memorized, so their gazes connected as he said the lines. Chloe watched the expressions flitter across his face. During a heavy pause, his jaw twitched with frustration. His eyes tightened with restraint. Then he delivered his last line, and Chloe picked up her part.

They read lines until the glare of the sun on the page was about to blind Chloe. She had to hand it to Liam—he was a good sport. He took her criticism well and was quick to adjust to her direction.

She checked her watch. "I think that's good enough for now. Why don't we call it a day?" She had to be at work in two hours and she was already exhausted.

"I was hoping you'd say that."

They set the scripts aside and, as if by silent agreement, lay back on the beach blanket to soak in the afternoon sun.

"It's been a long day." She'd awakened to a phone call from Meghan and over seventy comments from friends and loved ones on her Instagram page. Everyone wanted the scoop on their relationship, but Chloe just played it cool with her responses. How was this all going to go when they "broke up"? They probably should've talked about that, but they had plenty on their plate for now.

"How's the image coming along?" she asked. "I've been a good girl and haven't gone looking for trouble."

"Good for you. You'll be happy to know the tone is shifting now that we're formally out as a couple."

"Good to know. And you've been very good for my following—my numbers have more than doubled already."

"That's great. And Spencer said the general opinions are favorable. I'm happy, you're happy, and the studio's happy."

"Favorable." She tested the word on her tongue. What did that mean exactly?

"It's just like I told you. My fans can see you're something different."

She snorted. "I'll say."

Still basking in the sun, he gave a wry smile. "They've even started blending our names. We're Chliam now, just so you know."

*"Chliam?"*

"Don't look at me. I didn't make it up."

"That's ridiculous."

"It's a good sign. They're seeing us as a couple. We've joined the ranks of Brangelina and TomKat."

"I don't recall either of those working out so well."

"Well, let's just ride the wave. That picture of us I posted already has over two hundred thousand likes."

She gaped at him. He was still sprawled out beside her, calmly soaking in the sun like half the universe hadn't paid homage to their picture. *"What?"*

*"They think you're in love with me,"* he singsonged through a grin.

She elbowed him in the side even as her face warmed. "Shut up. They do not."

"They do. They think you're completely smitten."

"That's absurd. We've known each other a grand total of six days."

"Ah-ah-ah. Let's not forget all those midnight phone calls over the past few months. I wooed you from afar and posted a photo, and now everyone's seen that moony expression on your face."

"It wasn't moony. I was grimacing. Your kiss was, was . . . it was *wet*."

He burst out laughing, eyes still closed. "You are so full of it. That kiss was perfect."

"It was waterlogged. You drooled in my hair." Since he wouldn't stop laughing, she poked him in the side again—and found a ticklish spot.

He jumped, his eyes snapping open. *"Hey.* Watch it."

"I am." She poked him again.

He rolled toward her, a threatening glint in his eyes. "Now you've done it."

"Is your side a little ticklish, Liam? Do you have—aaAHH!"

His hands were all over her, jabbing and poking every ticklish bone in her ribs. She tried to push away his hands. Couldn't evade them. Rolled away.

But he followed. "Not so funny now, is it, sweetheart?"

"I'm laughing, aren't I?"

And oh, how he made her regret those defiant words. She was gonna pee her pants if he didn't stop. She went for a counterassault that had sand flying and caught him just in the right spot, over and over.

He jerked away. "Okay, okay, truce."

They were both sitting up, breathing heavy. The sunlight glinted off his hair. His eyes sparkled with the remnants of his laughter. And his grin was something to behold. Yeah, she could definitely see how a woman would fall in love with Liam.

But it wouldn't be her.

# Chapter 14

Chloe took her parents' porch steps, then placed her hand over her stomach to tame the pterodactyls flapping around in there.

Liam paused beside her, clutching a bouquet of flowers. "Smile, for heaven's sake. You're not on your way to your execution."

"Says you." Faking it in public was one thing. Her family was another.

"It'll be fun." Liam pushed the doorbell.

She tapped her foot as she took in the house, trying to see it through fresh eyes. Hollywood eyes. The modest Cape Cod with its small stoop and weathered red door was a long way from a Beverly Hills mansion.

*Welcome to middle-class America, Liam Hamilton.*

Mom flung open the door and beamed from the well-lit entry. "What are you doing ringing the doorbell, darlin'? Get in here, you two."

Liam ushered her inside with a hand at the small of her back. It was all Chloe felt until he released her into Mom's arms.

When they parted Chloe made the introductions. "Mama, this is Liam Hamilton. Liam, meet my mother. Oh, and this is my dad, Jerry," she added as the man rounded the corner. He was a big teddy bear of a guy with brown hair, a brown beard, and a gentle smile.

Dad shook hands with Liam, then Mom gave him a big ol' southern hug. "Honey, it's so good to meet you. I've heard such wonderful things about you."

"Same here, ma'am." Liam extended the bouquet. "These are for you."

"Well, aren't you sweet! You have to call me Millie, though, or you're gonna make me feel old. Supper's almost ready. Jerry, get 'em something to drink, will you, sugar?"

"Can I help, Mom?"

"Not a chance. You two just go on and make yourselves at home in the living room."

Chloe led Liam into the room to their immediate left, while her mom and dad continued through the dining room to the kitchen. The house was immaculate—all three hundred throw pillows in their places and not a stray sock in sight. The lights were dimmed and candles flickered on the table. *Candles.* She didn't even know Mom owned decorative candles.

The TV was off—an occasion she was pretty sure hadn't happened since Hurricane Isaias—and soft country music played in the background.

Chloe sat on the plush gray sofa and Liam sank beside her, thighs touching. "Nice place. This is where you grew up?"

"Yeah. They've done some remodeling over the years, though, and added a sunroom on the back."

His gaze flittered over the space.

What was he thinking over there? And why did she care so much?

The front door squeaked open, then Sean came around the corner and stopped at the sight of Liam and Chloe on the sofa. "Hey."

"Hey, Brother."

Liam stood and approached, extending a hand. "Hi, Sean. I'm Liam."

Sean's lips pressed together.

Chloe tensed as the moment lengthened. So yeah, Sean had been a little sour on her fake boyfriend since the paparazzi showed up at

Docksiders last night and caused a scene. The restaurant was busy so they hadn't had a chance to talk about it.

But then Sean took Liam's hand and the two exchanged pleasantries. Chloe's shoulders loosened.

"Supper's on, y'all!" Mom called.

They exchanged greetings with Sean, then gathered around the table. Dad said grace and moments later they dug into the food.

They made small talk, mostly Mom and Dad asking about Liam's life and his upbringing because "Chloe's hardly told us a thing about you."

In broad strokes he painted a picture of an ordinary suburb upbringing with his single mom. Chloe had a feeling he'd omitted a lot, glossed over some things. He didn't reveal anything he hadn't already divulged to dozens of reporters. But that was all right. He didn't have to wear his heart on his sleeve.

"I'd love to meet her someday," Mom said. "She must be so proud of you."

"Yes, ma'am. I mean Millie. She'd like that for sure."

Dad cleared his throat. "How did you decide you wanted to be an actor, Liam? That seems like quite the undertaking."

"I was in a couple high school productions and really enjoyed it. The director of theater encouraged me to pursue it in college as a minor." He flashed a smile. "But I decided to skip college altogether and just go for it. Moved to Hollywood right after graduation."

"Seems it's worked out pretty well," Mom said.

Liam chuckled. "Believe me, I paid my dues working minimum-wage jobs."

"Why's it so dark in here?" Sean asked.

Mom patted his shoulder. "It's called ambience, honey. More potatoes, Liam?"

"Yes, please. And this chicken is delicious. I've never had anything quite like it."

Mom blushed prettily. "Why, thank you, honey."

She'd made her spicy fried chicken breasts with her special white gravy. "She used to be the chef at Docksiders," Chloe told Liam. Then, because they were supposed to be a couple, she added, "I've probably mentioned that already."

"I can see why."

"Mind if I turn on the game?" Sean half rose from his seat.

"Why don't we wait until we're finished," Mom said. "The Braves are probably whupping them anyway."

Sean fell back into his chair.

"What's wrong, honey?" Mom asked. "I hope everything's okay with you and Haden. She seems like a nice girl. Such good manners on that one."

Since Sean only mumbled something and picked at his food, Chloe spoke up. "They broke up this week. And now he has to find a new produce vendor."

Sean frowned at her.

*What?* she mouthed.

"Oh, honey. I'm so sorry." Mom covered his hand. "The two of you were really cute together. Are you heartbroken?"

Chloe rolled her eyes. "Only over the fresh produce."

Dad cleared his throat again. "So, uh, filming on the movie starts tomorrow, isn't that right? You both must be pretty excited about that."

"Not the filming per se, but the prep work: rehearsals, costume fittings, et cetera. I'll be pretty busy with that right up to filming, which starts a week from tomorrow."

Chloe beamed. "He's doing great with the role. He's very convincing."

"No doubt," Sean said.

Chloe scowled at her brother.

Mom touched Liam's shoulder. "Well, my goodness! I can't imagine you didn't have more important things to do tonight than hanging out over here."

Liam took Chloe's hand. "Well, I will have to make it an early evening so I can be fresh in the morning. But what could be more important than meeting Chloe's family?"

"Dinner was great, Mom." Sean got up and took his plate to the kitchen. A moment later the sound of a baseball game filtered in from the living room.

Mom turned off the music, leaned her elbows on the table, and set her chin in her hands. "Now tell me about the first time you met Chloe. I want all the details."

Liam turned to Chloe, his lips curling into a wistful smile. His gaze held her hostage while he spoke. "It was on the phone actually. The producer had brought the paperwork over for me to sign, and she wanted to call Chloe and spring the news on her."

"You didn't tell me that," Mom said.

Liam chuckled. "I'll bet she didn't. Simone neglected to mention she had me on speaker, and when she made the announcement, Chloe told her exactly what she thought of the casting."

"Oh no! You didn't!"

Chloe's cheeks heated. "It wasn't that bad."

"She managed to tear me apart personally and professionally before she realized I was listening."

Jerry chuckled. "Oh no."

"Set my therapy back months."

Chloe swatted his arm. "Stop it."

Liam caught her hand and squeezed it. He had such nice hands. Big and strong, tanned flesh with fingers that tapered down to neatly trimmed nails.

"I knew right then and there I had to meet her," Liam said.

A scoffing sound came from the living room. The others probably attributed it to the game, but Chloe knew better. She didn't know what Sean's deal was. This wasn't like him at all.

"That's just so sweet," Mom said. "I knew she wasn't pleased with the casting at first, but apparently you've more than won her over, Liam."

He lifted Chloe's hand and pressed a kiss to the back of it.

The warm sensation both soothed and stirred.

His gaze clung to hers as he lowered her hand. "She won me over too."

"What is your problem?" Chloe hissed as she dropped onto the sofa next to Sean. Liam had somehow talked Mom and Dad into letting him help clean up. Chloe was too eager to confront her brother to insist on helping too. "You've been sulking since you got here, and you've been all but rude to Liam."

"So what? It's not like you're a real couple."

She glanced toward the kitchen. "*Shush.* Since when do you care about that?"

"Since we've had a horde of photographers outside the restaurant, impeding our customers."

"Well, I don't like that either, but there's nothing we can do about it. And it's not Liam's fault. He's a nice guy. You should give him a chance."

Sean aimed his laser gaze at her. "Like you are?"

His words were a flaming arrow aimed straight at his target. It was not a bull's-eye. In fact, it practically missed the board altogether. "What are you implying, Sean?"

"I see the way you blush around him."

"I always blush!"

"And that picture you posted." He rolled his eyes. "The way you stare at him."

"My eyes were closed."

"Not then. Now. Tonight."

"He's looking at me the same way—it's called *acting*."

Sean smirked. "Well, only one of you is a professional."

"What's that supposed to mean?"

"It means he's using you, that's what it means, and I don't like it."

"It's a trade. I'm getting something I want too. My followers are growing by leaps and bounds, and he's going to rock the part of Ledger and make this movie awesome!"

"That's his *job*. Meanwhile, strangers are posting things about you online for the whole world to see."

"What kinds of— Never mind, I don't want to know. Besides, Liam says it's mostly positive."

Sean huffed.

What if Liam wasn't shooting straight with her? What if people were making her out to be an attention seeker? Or worse, just pathetic? But no, Liam said with time his fans would see she was someone he cared about.

At least, until he didn't anymore.

"You practically invited those tabloid leeches into your life—into *our* lives—and I don't like what I'm seeing. Liam's image is coming up roses, and all you're going to get out of this is a broken heart."

She snorted. "That's ridiculous. We've known each other *seven days*."

"I see what I see. Don't come crying to me when this movie ends and he leaves you here in a soggy puddle."

"Don't worry, I won't!"

Liam stopped on the threshold of the room. His gaze toggled between them. "Uh . . . your mom shooed me out of the kitchen."

Had he heard their conversation? Chloe pasted on a smile and tried for a casual tone. "Come sit down. The Braves are winning." Okay, she had no clue what the score was, but the Braves always seemed to be winning this season.

She'd sat close to her brother on the sofa so they could talk quietly, and now Liam sat on her other side, and they were wedged together like an awkward sandwich.

And she knew her brother. He was too stubborn to leave even if tension practically vibrated off the walls.

"So your brother hates me." Liam was first to speak once they were in his car and on the drive back to her place.

The trio had sat in silence ten interminable minutes, until Mom and Dad joined them. Then it was another long forty minutes of pretending to enjoy the game while Sean said little to nothing.

"He doesn't hate you. He doesn't even know you. And he's normally not so surly. It's just that the paparazzi showed up at work last night and made a nuisance of themselves." *And also he thinks I'm in love with you.* She rolled her eyes.

"Why didn't you tell me that?"

"I didn't think it was that big of a deal."

"I don't want them bothering any of you. Maybe it's time we make a statement. Give them enough of a story that they give us some space."

"Will that work?"

"Probably." He gave her a sheepish look. "This is kind of uncharted territory for me."

By which he meant, of course, that actual relationships were new to him. For some reason the thought pinched at her chest. "How do we go about that? I wouldn't even know what to say."

"Don't worry. I'll arrange it and do the talking. For now, let's focus on tomorrow. It's a big day." His eyes smiled at her. "And in just one week we'll begin filming your book-to-movie adaptation."

"I'm so excited—and a little nervous."

"It's gonna be great, you'll see."

Chloe could only hope he was right.

# Chapter 15

With the arrival of the movie crowd, the town was already abuzz with excitement. The studio had rented a production office in town, and Chloe had stopped in to say hello and chat with Simone and some of the others.

But she hardly saw Liam over the next week as he was swamped with meetings, costume fittings, screen tests, and rehearsals.

The movie was all the talk around town, and there was some mention of it in the newspaper each day. The excitement was contagious. Chloe could hardly sleep for anticipating the first day of filming.

Now, after a week of prep, day one was finally about to get underway. Chloe's entire property was a frenzy of activity. Nine huge trucks were parked in her sizable front yard. A team erected a big tent for craft services, otherwise known as *crafty*, to feed the cast and crew. She'd been nicely compensated for the use of her property, but her imagination hadn't quite conjured up the reality of using her home as one of the filming locations.

Her back patio had become the *video village*, which was set up with monitors and chairs from which the powers that be would view the scenes being filmed on the property with an eye to how they would look in their finished format.

All in all forty or fifty people were running around, setting up lights and cameras and making decisions about the scenes to be shot.

"Let's head to hair and makeup, Chloe." Simone took her elbow.

Her black hair, fashioned in tight braids, would withstand today's heat and humidity, which was more than Chloe could say for her own hair. "I want to introduce you to Daisy. She just arrived." The actress hadn't been around when Chloe stopped by the production office.

Hair and makeup was set up in a trailer. Simone led the way across the lawn, up the stairs, and into the trailer. She'd already introduced Chloe to more people than she would ever remember by name. Her head was spinning and she found herself wishing someone she knew would arrive soon. Someone like Liam. She'd missed him this week.

Before the realization could settle, Simone called to the stunning blonde in the makeup chair. "Daisy, I brought someone to meet you."

"Do not dare open your eyes," Sophía, the makeup artist, said. "You will mess up my handiwork."

"Hi, Simone," Daisy said. "I'd say it's great to see you again, but . . ."

Simone laughed. "Wouldn't want to mess up the eyeliner. I brought Chloe Anderson over to meet you."

"The author! How wonderful to meet you in person. I loved the novel—I read it before I even knew there would be a movie. And when I was offered the part of Cate, I jumped at it." Somehow she'd said all that without so much as twitching.

Chloe instantly warmed to the woman. "You're too kind. I was so thrilled when Simone suggested you for the part."

"The same, however, cannot be said of me." Liam had somehow slipped into the trailer. He put his arm around Chloe and kissed her temple.

"I'm never gonna live that down," Chloe said.

The others laughed.

Liam winked at Chloe. "I'll make sure she doesn't."

His teasing nature was growing on her. It had been such a turnoff at first. She'd taken it personally, had misread him because she was in such a panic about the role. Chloe tried not to savor the delicious weight of his arm draped over her shoulder. It wasn't because she'd missed him this past week. He was just familiar and comfortable, that was all. Also hot.

Simone—who was well aware of the PR relationship—eyed the two of them. "I have to say, you two look good together." She nudged Chloe. "I have a feeling you'll keep his ego in check."

Chloe patted his chest. "Oh, it's my first priority." That and, well, patting his chest. So solid.

Daisy laughed. "I like this girl. Just what Liam needs to keep him in line."

"Hey, I'm feeling a little ganged up on over here."

"Poor baby," Daisy teased, eyes still closed.

Simone turned to Chloe, a ready smile on her face. "Ready to say hello to our director? He should be freed up now."

"Let's do it."

Liam gave Chloe a parting hug. She was reluctant to leave his side. He seemed so comfortable in this world of his.

On the way out Simone called back to Daisy, "Don't forget to take that rock off your finger before we film."

Chloe's pulse hadn't stopped racing since she'd awakened at six filled with nervous energy. She was nervous for herself—she was so out of her element. Nervous for the movie itself. She was nervous for Liam too—probably more so than he was.

But at the moment, watching everyone scurry about on the job, she felt like a third wheel. She'd already met everyone on set, and now there was really nothing to do but wait. Might as well get comfy and get ready to watch the action.

She stepped into the video village and sank onto the nearest chair, the wood-framed kind that sat high and sported a canvas seat and back.

Everyone was so nice. Busy, but nice. Back toward the house Liam and Daisy, finished with hair and makeup, were holding the script between them, probably running lines or discussing the first scene they'd shoot. The filming would begin soon.

They were putting final touches on the set. The two white Adirondack chairs they'd planted close to the water seemed like a prime-time reading spot. Why hadn't she thought of that? Greenery had also been added along the shoreline. It looked so nice and lush. When all this was over she'd be making a trip to the nursery.

Rex gave direction to the lighting crew, his deep voice booming across the shaded yard. (Who knew you even needed lighting during the day?) Before meeting Simone, Rex, and the studio execs in January, Chloe had done a little research on the director, who'd been credited with many successful films. He was known in the industry for being intensely dedicated to his work but also for being painfully direct and lacking a sense of humor. He was certainly on the gruff side.

*Note to self: stay out of his way.*

She spotted her next-door neighbors, Vicki and Rod, sitting on their deck, enjoying the show. The location guide had gone door to door long ago, informing her neighbors of the filming and getting their permission. They all seemed excited to have scenes from a movie shooting on their street.

Her gaze drifted again over the action in her backyard. Hard to believe all this was happening because of her book. Her story. These scenes, these characters, all products of her imagination, were coming alive before her eyes. And all these people running about, doing their jobs, were here for one purpose only: to bring her story to life.

Time seemed to stop. The activity in her yard seemed to morph into slow motion as a wave of awe swept over her. Wow, this was actually happening. Her book was being adapted into a movie.

"Do I look tired?" Daisy patted under her eyes. "I'm still jet-lagged. Those three hours get me every time."

Liam scanned the yard and found Chloe standing in front of the video village, taking it all in. He was happy for her. Maybe even a little proud. "You're fine, but if you don't stop touching your face, Sophía's gonna be over here with the powder."

"She's a miracle worker. I had a zit the size of Mount Vesuvius and now it's nowhere to be seen."

Liam's production assistant, Elliot, handed him a water bottle and Liam thanked him before he scurried off.

Liam returned his attention to Chloe, who brushed at something on her flowy white skirt, probably cat hair. Buttercup shed like a German shepherd. Liam couldn't see Chloe's expression as she faced the river, but he'd bet she was biting her lip. She wore her brown hair back in a classy bun today, leaving her long, graceful neck exposed. A strand of hair had come loose from the knot and played in the cradle between her neck and shoulder.

He'd missed being around her this past week. He'd reflected several times on dinner with her family. He'd enjoyed meeting them last weekend, even if her brother hadn't exactly put out the welcome mat. Her mom was an angel, affectionate and accepting. And it was obvious Jerry viewed Chloe and Sean as his own. The couple had treated Liam like a regular person—something he'd come to miss. Their house might be on the small side, but it was cozy and clean. He envied Chloe for having been raised in such a warm environment.

"So . . . you and the author, huh?" Daisy's voice cut through his thoughts. "That's a little different for you, isn't it?"

"Very different."

"She's cute and seems like a nice person. And having read her book, I feel like I know her a little. She has a unique voice."

"She's really special." He was looking forward to more time with her over the next few months. She intrigued him. He couldn't re-member feeling that way about another woman.

"She must be to have captured your heart. Is she excited about the movie?"

"Very much so. Nervous too, I think. She hopes it'll accurately reflect the book."

"I imagine every author wants that. But I think the script does a great job of capturing the essence of her story. Now it's up to us to bring it alive. I'm excited about playing Cate. There are so many nuances to her character and to the relationship between her and Ledger . . ."

Daisy's words faded away as Chloe sank into a chair in the video village—the chair marked very clearly on the back in large white letters: *DIRECTOR*. She crossed her legs, getting comfy.

"Places, everyone!" Rex called. He'd just finished with the light-ing crew, and he and Simone were now headed up the slope of the lawn toward Chloe.

"Break a leg." Daisy headed toward the pier.

"Chloe," Liam called quietly. She didn't hear him and he didn't want to draw attention to her gaffe. "Chloe!"

She turned and her smile slipped, no doubt at his sober expres-sion. He waved her over.

Frowning thoughtfully, she scooted from the chair. Her feet got hung up on the footrest, and she nearly took the chair down. She steadied it, glancing around sheepishly to see if anyone had noticed, then strolled toward him.

Rex and company arrived at the video village just as Chloe reached Liam's side, a rosy blush blooming on her cheeks. "What's wrong?"

"Nothing, it's just . . ." He gestured toward the seats, now filled with bodies. "You were in the wrong chair."

Her eyes widened as they fell on the chair's caption. She

covered her mouth. "Oh my gosh! I was sitting in the director's chair."

"It's okay, nobody noticed. It's not a big deal." But it was a big deal to Chloe, and he didn't want her feeling embarrassed today. Her first day on set should be perfect.

She leveled a gaze at him. "I'm an idiot. Thank you *so much*."

"No worries." He took her by the shoulders. "Hey, try to relax and enjoy this. It's your big day." And with a wink he set off toward the pier.

# Chapter 16

The smell of books welcomed Chloe as Liam ushered her through the back door of the Beachfront Bookshop. He'd set it all up. Upon their exit they'd run into the photographers out front (his manager had tipped them off to the time and place), answer a few questions, and be on their way.

The bookshop had been Liam's idea. *"Would your friend like a little free publicity?"*

Why, yes, she certainly would.

Sadly, they hadn't had a break in their schedule until Thursday. Liam wasn't on today's call sheet, and Chloe didn't have to be at work until four.

Meghan came around the checkout counter, aiming a big grin at Chloe. "They're already gathering on the sidewalk, making a nuisance of themselves—and hopefully getting a nice shot of my display window, which still features your book, by the way." She glanced at Liam. Her smile slipped a little but remained congenial as she extended her hand. "I'm Meghan."

He shook her hand, flashing his handsome Hollywood grin. "Liam. Nice to meet you. I've heard good things about you."

Meghan tilted her head. "Hmm. I've received mixed reviews about you. The jury's still out."

Chloe speared her friend with an appalled look. "Meghan!"

Liam chuckled. "That's okay. That was very, um, honest of you. I can appreciate that."

Chloe huffed. Meghan was only trying to protect her. It was hard to be angry about that. Chloe glanced at Liam. "So, what's the strategy?"

He let his gaze drift around the rows of new books, looking a little like a kid in a candy store. "Well, first we browse these shelves. I haven't been inside a bookstore in ages. Where's the crime section?"

"In the next room, three rows down on the right." Meghan watched him go.

Chloe caught the flicker of female appreciation in her eyes. "Hey, stop checking out my boyfriend."

Meghan turned to her with an arched brow. "Your *pretend* boyfriend, you mean?"

Good point. "Well, he's——he's not a sex object either."

"He kind of is. But enough about him. Tell me about the filming. I've been dying to know, and those cryptic texts you keep sending are exasperating."

"I'm sorry, but this week has been crazy. The filming is going great. Liam's doing an amazing job as Ledger. All those hours prepping and reading lines with him are paying off. The director and studio are pleased, and I can't tell you how relieved I am."

"I'm glad to hear that. I know how anxious you were. What's Daisy Hughes like? She's a diva, isn't she? It would be unfair if she was beautiful, talented, *and* a decent human being. You can tell me; I won't say a word. And also, when do I get to meet her?"

"Sorry to disappoint, but she's actually really nice and down-to-earth. And you can meet her when you decide to take one darned day off work and come on set with me."

"Let me just call my manager and——oh, wait, I don't have a manager because I'm trying to eke out a living after they raised my rent on this place."

"All right, all right, I get it." Meghan had part-time employees, but they were mostly high school students. "Maybe you can make it on a Sunday when the store's closed."

"It's a deal."

The phone rang, so Chloe browsed the romance section, avoiding the front window, while Meghan handled the call. Her books were already face out and there were eight fresh copies.

A moment later Meghan rounded the corner and handed over a Sharpie. "Get to work, lady."

Chloe opened the first book and signed her name on the title page. "Are they still selling well?"

"Like proverbial hotcakes. News of your celebrity relationship sure isn't hurting. It's making people curious about you."

"I never really considered that. But my following on social media has exploded."

Meghan lowered her voice. "Just . . . keep it all in perspective, you know?"

She glanced up at Meghan. "What do you mean?"

"Just remember the relationship's not permanent. It's not real. You know . . . when the film is over he'll be leaving."

"Well, duh. That's been the plan all along."

"I know, but . . . just be careful, that's all. He's awfully charming, and sometimes what we know in our heads and what we know in our hearts are two different things."

Chloe rolled her eyes. Between Meghan and Sean, neither her head nor her heart was likely to forget it. "I'm not about to fall for Liam. He's nice to look at, but he's the opposite of what I'm searching for in a man."

A shuffle sounded, something very much like footsteps coming to a halt. Chloe's and Meghan's eyes widened as they locked on each other. Her friend slowly leaned back and peeked around the row of books. "Oh, hi. Seems like you found some books."

Chloe winced. No doubt he'd heard those last regrettable words.

"Let's get you rung up." Meghan shot a sympathetic look over her shoulder, then headed for the counter.

Chloe wanted to crawl onto one of these shelves and do her best book interpretation. But she couldn't hide back here forever. She crept out from the row and joined Liam at the register.

"What'd you find?" she asked.

"A couple books Spencer recommended. And that Higgins novel you've been wanting to read."

She blinked at the familiar beach cover. He'd remembered. Guilt pinched hard. "Thank you."

She traded a covert glance with Meghan, who rang him up, then stashed his books in a brown-handled bag bearing the store's logo.

Liam ran his credit card. He hadn't so much as glanced at Chloe.

Why had she said those things? She better understood now the way the gossip sites spun the truth. But he'd as much as admitted he'd never had a real relationship. That made him the kind of man she could never be with, didn't it? Nothing wrong with that.

Still, she hadn't had to say it out loud and in such an abrasive way. Also behind his back. She'd obviously hurt his feelings—even if he did place his hand on the small of her back and slide her an encouraging grin as he turned her toward the exit. "Ready for this?"

She was so not ready for this. "Bring it on."

"Good luck!" Meghan called.

Chloe had a feeling her friend's well-wish encompassed more than just their impending showdown with the paparazzi. But she didn't have time to follow the thought as Liam was already reaching for the door.

"Smile," he said.

Oh yeah. She was half of Chliam and deliriously happy. She plastered what was probably a dopey grin on her face, and they exited to a flurry of action and words.

"Liam, how long have you two been dating?"

"How's the filming going?"

"What books did you buy?"

Liam put his arm around Chloe, drawing her close as they came to a halt under the canopy. "Hey, guys. How's it going?"

She slipped her arm around his waist and turned her face up to him, hoping and praying he'd take it from here because she had no idea what to say right now.

"Miss Anderson, what's it like to date a movie star?"

Liam chuckled, gazing down on her like a man madly in love. "Absolutely crazy, I'm sure. But hopefully worth it."

"Definitely worth it." She told her smile to widen. Her eyes to soften on Liam. But his come-hither look had just melted her bones into the sidewalk so she couldn't be sure either of those things actually happened.

Liam turned back to the photographers, holding up the bag. "Two crime novels for me and a beach read for her. Have a great day, folks."

# Chapter 17

It was so quiet in the car, Liam might've been wearing a pair of muted AirPods.

The run-in with the paps had gone pretty well. If Chloe seemed a little dazed, that could easily be attributed to her inexperience in the spotlight. As for Liam, he'd simply gone through the motions, his acting skills coming through for the win because his heart had definitely not been in it.

He hadn't been able to get Chloe's words out of his mind. Still couldn't. *"I'm not about to fall for Liam. He's nice to look at, but he's the opposite of what I'm searching for in a man."* Even the memory of those words made him flinch.

Not that he had any designs on Chloe. They'd only known each other two and a half weeks, and their lives were worlds apart in more ways than one. But they'd spent many hours together during those days. And pretending to be a couple in public and on the movie set had allowed them to bond more quickly than they would've otherwise. He'd started thinking of her as a friend. But just because he'd begun to enjoy her company didn't mean she was doing the same. She was in this "relationship" for her own reasons.

*"—the opposite of what I'm searching for in a man."* He had no reason to feel sucker punched by her words.

And yet he did.

It couldn't be more obvious who Chloe's perfect man was. And it was just as obvious that Liam could never measure up to the paragon she'd created. Not that he wanted to for Chloe's sake, but he did want to be that man for someone, someday.

Didn't he?

"Thank you again for the book," Chloe said quietly from the passenger seat.

"You're welcome."

It was obvious she felt bad about what she'd said and was trying to make up for it. But nothing she'd said was untrue. Tabloid spin aside, his record with women spoke for itself. As for all the doting fans who claimed they wanted to marry him, they wouldn't really want that.

The truth pierced his chest. Deep down he wanted to be the kind of man Ledger was . . . He just had no idea how to get there. Acting like him was one thing; being like him another.

He breathed a quiet sigh as he pulled into Chloe's drive, ready to dispel the awkward tension and get this day behind him.

But instead of opening her door, Chloe turned toward him. "Liam, I owe you an apology. I'm sorry about what I said to Meghan. I didn't—"

"It's okay."

"No, it's not. It was callous and uncalled for and— Would you look at me?"

At her plea he turned and zeroed in on her features. Sadness turned down the corners of her mouth. Regret lined her brow. If that wasn't enough, tears filled her liquid blue eyes. Something inside him went soft.

"I'm truly sorry. You've been nothing but kind to me, and you have some very excellent qualities that, quite frankly, you don't get enough credit for. I'm just getting acquainted with you." She touched his chest. "But I already realize there's a man inside here the rest of the world should know."

His stomach tightened at her heartfelt words. He hoped it was true. He wanted it to be. And he hated seeing her so sad. So un-

Chloelike. He brushed away the tear that trickled down her cheek. "Thanks for saying that."

Her hand patted his chest ever so lightly, her gaze searching his. "Do you forgive me?"

"Yes, you're fine, Chloe. Don't give it another thought."

Her smile wobbled. "Friends?"

"Of course." He offered her a grin. "And hey, let's cross our fingers the paps will give it a rest for a while, huh?"

"Do you suppose it worked? We didn't say much. And I think my smile might've looked kinda goofy."

"You did fine. I'm sure they're happy; they got their money shot."

She glanced down at his chest where her hand still rested. She gave it two awkward pats and jerked it away. "Right. I, uh, should go in now."

"Have a great night at work."

"See you on set tomorrow."

He watched until she slipped inside, then put the Camaro in Reverse and pulled from the drive, the corners of his mouth lifting.

# Chapter 18

The money shot ended up being a fairly adorable picture of Liam and her gazing at each other. Meghan texted the photo to Chloe, who saw it once she arrived home from work. She grabbed a shower and sprawled on her bed, wearing her favorite pajamas.

Buttercup jumped up on the bed, gave her the stink eye, and curled up on the edge of the mattress.

"I'm sorry. I know I've been gone a lot." Even though she'd been at home this week, she was out back where the movie was filming. "At least I've brought friends over for you. Don't act like you don't like all the attention."

Buttercup blinked and glanced away.

"Oh, stop it." She dragged the cat closer, her body a deadweight. "You know you love me." With one hand she petted Buttercup and with the other she clicked on the link Meghan had sent.

The photo was captioned "Life with Liam" and below it was an article expounding on today's outing. Somehow they'd constructed a whole piece about the brief moment, including every word they'd spoken and plenty of speculation about their relationship.

Even though Meghan might be in bed by now, Chloe texted her back. *They got your logo in the photo! And they didn't say anything negative about me. Yay!*

She hopped over to another tabloid site and found a similar picture and article. This one was even more complimentary about her—suggesting she might be a good influence on Liam. Because they'd been shopping at a bookstore? That was a reach. Chloe rolled her eyes.

*Apparently I'm a positive influence on you.* 😇 Chloe sent the text along with the link to Liam, then put down the phone before she was tempted to go poking around the internet for more news.

She gave Buttercup a scratch behind her ears. "Better quit while I'm ahead, huh?"

She hadn't spoken to Liam since he'd brought her home this afternoon. But when she reflected on the way he'd responded to her apology, the day's tension rolled off her shoulders. He could've closed himself off from her. Could've given her the silent treatment—Evan had been a master at that. But he'd forgiven her instead. That said a lot about him.

A text dinged in. Liam. *Our evil plan is working. Bwa-ha-ha.*

She tipped her lips up in what was probably a silly grin. *Oh, the pressure.*

*You've even got the illiterate actor reading books.*

*I'm just a good influence like that.* 😂*Those guys went in the bookshop after we left and tried to extract from Meghan the titles you bought.*

*I'd like to say I'm surprised.*

*You can't even tell by the photo that I'm freaking out.*

*We look like a couple of lovebirds.*

Yep, somehow they'd pulled it off. *I believe that was the goal. I only went snooping around two sites. I hope our strategy will fix your image problem.*

*Don't worry about the gossip. Spencer will keep an eye on it.*

*How will he know if it's working?*

*Because producers will start sending some decent scripts my way.*

She hadn't realized things had gotten that bad. *You haven't had many movie offers lately?*

*Nothing good since yours. I don't have anything on the schedule after Summer Skies. And that stays between us, please.*

Her stomach bottomed out. *Of course. I won't say a word.* She was honored he'd be so open with her—especially after she'd hurt his feelings today. Before he could respond she sent another text. *Again, I'm really sorry about what I said today.*

A long moment passed while three little dots danced in the text box. Maybe she shouldn't have brought it up again.

The phone buzzed with a call. Liam's name appeared on the screen. She hadn't expected that. They'd only spoken on the phone once before. Her pulse raced as she answered.

"Enough of that." The gentleness of his tone softened the words. "You've already said sorry and I've already forgiven you, so you can stop apologizing."

"I know. Sorry."

"I'm frowning at you right now."

Chloe laughed, then a comfortable silence filled the space between them before he spoke again. "I enjoyed having dinner with your family last week. They seem really great."

"Even Sean?" she teased.

"I'm sure he's just looking out for you. If I had a kid sister, I'd do the same thing."

He definitely would. Her lips curled at the thought. "You mentioned you wished for siblings when you were growing up."

"Constantly. Especially after my dad left and it was just me and Mom."

What was that odd note in his voice? She wanted to know but didn't want to pry. "How old were you when he left?"

"Almost six. I'd just started first grade two days before."

You didn't forget details like that. "I'm sorry. I know a little about what that feels like. My father left when I was seven."

"You mentioned he was out of the picture. You don't have a relationship with him anymore?"

Chloe snorted. "When he left the picture, he really left. Moved to Connecticut and never looked back."

"Aw, jeez. What an idiot."

"Can't disagree with you there."

"What was in Connecticut, if you don't mind my asking?"

She wasn't quite ready to go there yet. "A job."

"Wow. That's really sad. I guess I can be thankful my dad didn't move away. Though he did leave for another woman, so there's that."

Her heart squeezed tight for the little boy who'd lost his intact family. "That's hard. I feel bad for your mom."

"Yeah," he said softly. "Like I said before, she never quite got over it."

Since Chloe's dad had also left for another woman—another family, in fact—she could definitely relate. Not to mention what Evan had done. "It's the worst kind of betrayal. Do you have a relationship with your dad now?"

"Not much of one. He's a Realtor in Riverside where my mom still lives, so I see him whenever I go home. But that's only a few times a year."

"Does he have a second family?"

Liam huffed. "Not at the moment. He can't seem to commit long enough to make it down the aisle again."

"And your mom never wanted to remarry?"

He gave a mirthless laugh. "Oh, she wants to remarry, all right. But the man she wants isn't interested. She's a glutton for punishment, I guess." He said the words lightly, but Chloe knew the situation must sit on him like a heavy weight.

"That's gotta be hard. For both of you."

"Well, mostly I just try to stay out of it." His tone hinted he'd appreciate a shift in conversation.

"Sounds like a good move. My mom wasn't single long before she met my dad."

"He seems like an upstanding guy."

"He really is. He and Mom started dating about a year after my father left, but Mom held him off for three years—my father had left her with a few trust issues. She and Dad finally married when I was eleven, and Dad adopted Sean and me right away. He's a pretty mellow guy—even a couple teenagers couldn't shake him up. He just kind of went with the flow. He's good for my mom, I think. Balances her out in a lot of ways. I'm just happy she found someone who loves her so much, loves us all."

There was a beat of silence. Then, "I envy you your family, Chloe."

Was that a lonely note in his tone? But how could a man like Liam Hamilton—a celebrity with fans all over the world and women clamoring to be at his side—possibly be lonely?

"Even though I know the road wasn't necessarily easy," he added.

He didn't know the half of it. But then, things weren't always the way they seemed. "I'm definitely blessed." She smothered a yawn. It was past midnight already.

"Well, hey, it's late. I should let you get to bed."

"All right. I guess I'll see you tomorrow."

"I'm not on the set until two. Wanna run lines in the morning, or are you going to the beach?"

The crew was filming at Holden Beach all day. She'd rather make sure Liam had those scenes down cold. "Sure, yeah, let's run lines."

"Why don't you come over around ten and I'll feed you before we get started."

"Sounds great, but"—she glanced down at Buttercup—"maybe we should run lines here. I've been neglecting a certain feline lately and she's very annoyed with me."

He laughed. "Bring her over here. The rental allows pets."

"But your allergies . . . I don't want to bring pet dander into your space."

"No worries. I've been taking an allergy med every day. You know, just in case."

Sometimes he surprised her in the best of ways. "That's . . . really sweet of you."

"Well, when your girlfriend has a cat," he said playfully, "you do what you must."

# Chapter 19

Chloe knocked on Liam's door for the fourth time. When he didn't answer she cupped her hand on the sidelight and peeked inside. The sun poured through the back of the house, lighting the interior with buttery light. But there was no sign of Liam.

Buttercup meowed pitifully from her crate. "I know, I know. I'll get you out of there as soon as I can."

Chloe set down the crate and whipped out her phone. *Good morning! I'm at your door.*

She waited for those dots but they never came, so she pounded on the door again. Did she have the time right? They had agreed to run lines here, hadn't they?

She was about to call him when the door opened and a tousled Liam appeared, wearing only a pair of pajama bottoms.

*Do not look at his chest.*

His shoulders were broad, his pectoral muscles well defined, and those abs rippled like an undulating wave. Clearly he took his workouts more seriously than she did.

"I'm sorry. I overslept."

Her gaze shot to his face.

He winced against the daylight, and his words sounded as if they'd passed through a wood chipper on the way out. His face (sporting a sexy five o'clock shadow) was flushed—and did his eyes seem a little glassy?

Uh-oh. She reached out for his forehead. "Oh boy, I think

you're sick, Liam. You should go to the doctor. I have a good one I can——"

"It's just a cold. Sorry I didn't call, but we'd better pass on the line reading so I can save my strength for this afternoon."

He seemed about ready to drop. "Liam, you might have the flu or something. We should call Simone."

"I'll make it to set. Gotta keep the film on schedule."

According to the statistics she'd read about the daily cost of filming, delays could wreak havoc on the budget. "Have you eaten this morning? Let me come in and make something for you."

"You don't have to do that." He wavered in the doorway.

"Let me in, Liam."

He didn't seem to have any fight left in him as he opened the door wider.

She grabbed the kitty crate and stepped around him. "Take a load off. I'll go see what's in the kitchen. Have you taken anything for that fever?"

"I don't have anything. And it's just a cold."

"Right. Fever *and* delusions." She kept Tylenol in her purse. And she'd get him his allergy med while she was at it.

A *whoosh* sounded as he hit the sofa. He sounded so weak, poor baby. She scanned the contents of his fridge. Wow, she could cook him a feast with the ingredients in this thing. Well, if she could cook, that was.

She spotted the antihistamine on the counter. So she poured him a glass of orange juice, shook out the allergy med and Tylenol, and brought them into the living room. He was sprawled on the leather sofa, eyes closed. Buttercup had made a nest of his bare chest.

The cat cut her a look. *Jealous?*

Chloe waggled her head at the feline.

"Here you go." She handed Liam the juice and he downed the meds in one gulp. "I should've taken your temp before you drank that. Though your rental probably doesn't come equipped with one." She laid the back of her hand to his forehead. "You're pretty hot."

Humor flickered in his glazed eyes. "Thanks."

Her own skin flushed as she pulled her hand away. "I mean you have a temperature. Jeez, the ego on you."

His lips tilted a bit as his eyes fluttered closed.

She headed back to the kitchen. "How do scrambled eggs sound?" Since he had plenty of eggs and also since it was one of the five dishes she'd mastered.

"'Kay."

Chloe put a small skillet on the stove and got cracking on the eggs. Despite his denial he was clearly in the throes of the flu or something equally insidious. It could take a week or more before he'd have the energy to work. The setback on the film wouldn't be ideal. She itched to call Simone and give her the heads-up, but that wasn't her place.

When Chloe was finished cracking eggs, she searched for a whisk and found it in a drawer. It should feel strange, bumping around his kitchen when she'd known him such a short time. And also because he was Liam Hamilton. She gave her head a shake. Sometimes that still hit her out of the blue.

*I'm in Liam Hamilton's house. I'm taking care of Liam Hamilton while he's sick.*

It was just that he was so down-to-earth, he made her forget he was a big-time celebrity. Until, yeah, the paparazzi came nosing around and the gossip sites posted pictures of them. But other than that, he was sort of an ordinary guy.

A very hot ordinary guy, but still.

The eggs all whipped up, she poured them into a sizzling pan and worked them around the skillet until they were cooked through. She opted against cheese since his stomach might not be ready for that.

She divided the eggs onto two plates, but when she entered the living room, Liam was sound asleep.

Chloe glanced at Liam still sleeping soundly on the sofa. She hadn't awakened him to eat since he needed his rest. Instead, she'd eaten her eggs, then sat quietly in the armchair, immersed in an e-book she'd downloaded a while back and hadn't found time to read.

Buttercup had hopped off Liam's chest a while ago, taking a spot by the patio door where she could scowl at the seagulls and sandpipers scuttling around the beach.

At some point Liam had clutched a pillow to his chest (more's the pity) and reclined lengthwise on the sofa. His lips were parted in sleep, but the flush on his cheeks had abated. Hopefully the meds had brought his temperature down.

As if sensing her perusal, he opened his eyes. He seemed a little dazed as his gaze swept over the room, then settled on her. "You're still here." His tone indicated that pleased him.

"Somebody has to take care of you. Feeling any better?"

"A little. What time is it?"

"Almost eleven thirty."

He eased into a sitting position and winced. "Can't believe I slept that long."

"You need your rest. But you also need sustenance. I'll heat up your breakfast." She headed to the kitchen, microwaved his food, and was back a few minutes later with a steaming plate of eggs.

"Thanks," he said when she handed him the plate. "You really don't have to stay. I feel better and I'm used to taking care of myself."

"You feel better because the Tylenol kicked in. And I'm sure you have plenty of women happy to nurse you back to health."

He slid her a smile that didn't quite reach his eyes. The guy was an enigma. He was photographed with beautiful women constantly, had a zillion zealous fans, and received constant media attention. But sometimes she caught a look in his eyes or heard a tone of his voice that made her think . . .

*Or maybe you just have a great big imagination, Chloe Anderson.*

\* \* \*

Liam shoveled a bit of scrambled eggs into his mouth. He couldn't taste a thing, thanks to his congestion. He swallowed against a scratchy throat.

Chloe had headed to the kitchen to wash the dishes despite his objections. But it was kind of nice having her here. Kind of nice being taken care of a little, even if he didn't really need it.

He coughed, then winced at the pain in his throat.

From her station by the patio door, Buttercup flicked her tail back and forth, condemning him with her eyes.

"It's just a cold." He sounded as if his head was stuffed with an entire cotton field.

A few minutes later Chloe returned to the living room and took his empty plate. "You're looking a little better."

"I feel better. Probably just needed some rest and food. Think I'll grab a shower." He stretched and stood. Maybe the steam would drain this congestion. "By then it'll be about time to head to the set."

"Are you sure you're up to that?"

"Of course. And hey, I don't wanna keep you, Chloe. I'm sure you have better things to do than hang around here."

She hesitated, her feet shuffling as she transferred the plate to her other hand.

"I mean, you're welcome to stay as long as you want. I don't mind the company. I just don't want you to feel obligated."

"I'd actually planned to go straight to set from here since it's on the way."

The pleasure that streamed through him was only because he

didn't want to be alone. "No worries then. Help yourself to the TV. The movie selection is pretty good."

"Are you sure?"

He smiled at her hesitation. "Of course. Make yourself at home." He headed upstairs, his tank emptying a little more with each step. He'd soon feel much better. His morning shower always revived him.

By the time Liam donned a pair of shorts, he was shaking from exertion. Or maybe it was chills. For sure the effort of running a bar of soap over his skin had completely wiped him out. He hadn't even washed his hair.

He staggered to the bed and collapsed like a felled oak tree, wet hair and all, and just lay there breathing. Through his mouth. Because his entire head was congested. His muscles ached, his skull throbbed, his *skin* hurt.

"Oh God, take me now."

He had to face facts. He didn't have a cold. He wasn't making it to set today. He needed to call Simone and warn her he was sick. This would throw off the scheduling. It would be a nightmare for the studio. He mustered the energy to turn his head toward his nightstand. Empty. Must've left his phone downstairs.

He whimpered.

Okay, this wasn't an insurmountable problem. He wasn't helpless. He was sick, not dead. He'd go downstairs and get his phone.

*All right, buddy. On a count of three, we're getting up.*

*One.*

*Two.*

*Three . . .*

He lifted his head. Strained to lift his shoulders. Grunted.

His head fell back to the mattress. Yeah, he wasn't going anywhere. The phone would have to come to him. Thank God Chloe hadn't left.

He rested a moment, his pulse beating out a painful tattoo in his temple. Then he opened his mouth and called, "Chloe!" But the call was more like a whisper.

He'd try again. In a minute. After he took a few more deep breaths and rested up. Called on his reserves. But by the time he caught his breath, he couldn't seem to keep his eyes open another second.

# Chapter 20

What was taking Liam so long? Chloe gave the kitchen counter one last swipe and tossed out the paper towel. Her gaze drifted over the clean dining room table, the spotless floors, and the sparkling windowpanes. Liam kept an immaculate home. There really wasn't anything else for her to do.

She glanced upstairs where he'd disappeared almost an hour ago. Even allowing for Hollywood grooming and hair products (because that hair didn't happen by accident), he should be finished by now.

Was he okay? She hadn't heard him moving around in a while, but then, she'd been making noise of her own. "Liam?" Her call was surely loud enough for him to hear through the cracked bedroom door. But he didn't respond. She tried again, a little louder.

Nothing but silence.

What if he'd passed out or something? She should check on him. She crept up the stairs. The house was built like a castle—not even the stairs creaked.

She reached the landing, approached the door, and gave a little push. "Liam?" she all but whispered. But silence met her call.

She stepped into the room, which was well lit by a wall of windows, and found him face down and sideways on a king-sized bed. Buttercup curled at his side, both of them sound asleep. At least she hoped Liam was just asleep. What if . . . ?

No, that was unlikely. He was young and otherwise healthy. She zeroed in on his back and yes, indeed, his chest rose and fell. He was fine. Well, maybe not fine, but alive.

Being in his bedroom felt a bit intrusive, but man, did it smell like heaven. She took one more deep breath before she checked her watch. He was due on set soon. And he couldn't have called Simone since his phone was downstairs on the coffee table.

She walked toward the bed, noting his flushed cheeks and unshaven jaw. His hair lay damp on his forehead and his lashes were still spiky from the shower.

When she reached the bed she leaned over and touched his forehead with the back of her hand. Still warm.

His lids fluttered open and his eyes locked on hers. "Save yourself," he croaked.

She bit back a smile. Reality had apparently set in somewhere between the shower and bed. "Don't worry about me. I never get sick. But your fever's back and I don't think you'll make it to set today." Or tomorrow or the next, but she probably shouldn't hit him with all that right now. "I'll get your phone so you can call Simone."

"Thanks." His eyes fell closed as if he didn't have the energy to hold them open. His hands lay on the bed like dead fish washed up on the shore, and Buttercup was making a fishsicle out of one of them.

"Want me to put Buttercup downstairs?"

"She's fine."

"Okay, I'll get your phone."

Chloe headed downstairs. She hadn't been that sick for years. Not since junior high. She'd missed cheerleading tryouts because, like the sharing brother he was, Sean had given her a terrible case of the flu.

Chloe felt bad for Liam, away from home and feeling so miserable. Remembering his congestion, she hunted for tissues but couldn't find any, so she grabbed a roll of toilet paper. She grabbed another glass of orange juice and his phone and returned to his room.

He seemed to be asleep again. She set the juice on the nightstand and the toilet paper next to him. Then, catching the predatory gleam in Buttercup's eyes, she moved the roll to the other side and gave the cat a pointed look. *Don't even think about it.*

She shifted her attention to the sleeping man. "Liam? I have your phone."

He grunted but didn't open his eyes.

"Want me to call Simone for you?"

His head moved in what she assumed was a nod. Okay then. She awakened his phone only to find a locked screen. He didn't even stir as she brought the phone to his hand and pressed his thumb on the button.

*Voilà.* It took only moments to open his contacts, locate Simone's number, and place the call. While it rang she composed herself. This would be unwelcome news.

"Hey, Liam, what can I do for you?"

"Oh hi, Simone. It's actually Chloe."

"Chloe! Hi there."

"Sorry to bother you but I'm over at Liam's house, and I hate to tell you this but he's pretty sick. There's no way he'll make it to set today. I couldn't even rouse him enough to call you. He's running a fever and completely wiped out." She couldn't tell if Liam was asleep now or just too tired to open his eyes.

"Oh no. That's not good. I'll call the doctor and have her come right over." The studio kept one on call for just such a crisis.

"Okay, I'll be here to let her in."

"Good. Sounds like he needs to rest, and he sure shouldn't be around the cast and crew with a fever."

"Right, I agree." As if he'd be able to move from his sprawl on the bed anyway.

"We'll have to rearrange the shooting schedule. He was in every beach scene that was filming this afternoon and tomorrow. But maybe we can schedule the flashback scenes while he's under the weather."

Chloe could only imagine the chaos this would cause, but it couldn't be helped. "He feels terrible this is happening right now."

"Not his fault. Hopefully he can kick this virus quickly. I'm sure I don't have to tell you how costly these delays can be. Tell him to rest up and we hope he feels better soon."

"Will do."

Liam opened his eyes as Chloe ended the call. "Thanks."

"No problem. She said to rest up and hopes you feel better soon. Also, the doctor will be coming by."

She took his grunt as consent.

Dr. Angela Borden, who, as it happened, was a good friend of Chloe's mom, came to Liam's house right away.

Chloe tried to read her novel in the living room while the doctor examined him upstairs, but she couldn't concentrate. Buttercup sat at her feet, glancing at her for reassurance every now and then. Funny how her cat seemed to sense when something was awry.

Chloe stroked her soft fur. "He's gonna be just fine, sweetie. You can go sit at his bedside soon."

She still had Liam's phone and had seen multiple texts come in: several from Elliot, his assistant; one from Simone; and another from the director. Everyone was in a dither, no doubt. She could only imagine the scheduling nightmare. The actors who played the younger versions of Ledger and Cate weren't even in town. They'd have to be flown in immediately. New locations would have to be reserved, if they were even available.

Upstairs, the bedroom door opened and Dr. Angela appeared at the top of the stairs with her medical bag. She looked every inch the lady as she descended in her blue linen skirt, white sleeveless sweater, and nude pumps. Her short brown bob flattered her graceful neckline and highlighted pretty brown eyes that were feathered with laugh lines.

Chloe stood as she reached the first floor. "How is he? Or can you not tell me?"

The doctor smiled. "He gave me permission to fill you in, you being his girlfriend and all. He's definitely got the flu, I'm afraid." She reached into her bag. "Here's a sample of the antiviral. It'll get him by for a couple days, then he'll need to fill this. And I can't recommend fluids and rest highly enough."

Chloe took the sample and prescription and followed the doctor to the door. "Thank you. I'm on it."

"Tell your mama I said hello. I haven't seen her since Easter brunch at the church."

"I'll do that. And thank you again, Dr. Angela. We sure appreciate you coming all the way out here."

She turned at the door, her eyes twinkling. "They're paying me quite well. Plus I got to meet a movie star today. Don't worry though. I won't tell anyone where he's staying. The guy's got enough problems at the moment. But he's lucky to have you looking after him. I'll be coming by to check on him. Take care now that you don't get sick."

"Oh, you know me. I never get sick. Have a great day, Dr. Angela!"

# Chapter 21

Liam awoke to a darkened room and a pounding headache. Was it a hundred degrees in here? He pushed off the covers, his arms moving like leaden bricks. Every muscle in his body ached.

*Ugghh.*

He had no idea what time it was, but clearly it was night and time for more Tylenol. Too bad he didn't have the energy to retrieve it.

Chloe was gone now. He had a vague memory of her leaving this afternoon. Bending over the bed, concern lining her face and flickering in her pretty blue eyes. Something about work and keys and the nightstand. Or had he dreamed all that?

He rolled over and carefully felt around his bedside table. There. His phone was on his charger. It awakened as he grabbed it, illuminating the table. A glass of water and the container of Tylenol sat right there.

*God bless you, Chloe Anderson.*

He gulped down two pills, then answered some of the concerned texts that had come in from Elliot, Simone, Spencer, and the studio, letting them know he'd started on an antiviral, even though the doctor had surely already contacted them.

Then he fell back onto the bed like he'd just finished a marathon. His lips were dry from all the mouth-breathing and his brain was filled with a thick fog. Last time he'd been this sick was several years ago in his Santa Monica home. He was between films and suffered in silence for a few days until he ran out of food. Finally he let Spencer know. Liam wasn't about to have a stranger come to his door. His friend kindly brought groceries, leaving them on the porch because he had a newborn at home and couldn't take chances with Liam's virus.

It had taken a week and a half to feel normal again. The hours had passed like a boulder-sized kidney stone. He hated being sick. Trapped home all alone. It reminded him of being sick during his childhood when his mom was too distracted by her own life to do much more than look in on him now and then.

He thought of the movie schedule and felt a jolt of panic. This illness was probably going to leave him useless for a week or so. He vaguely remembered Chloe's call to Simone. The producer was probably frantic about the schedule and budget.

The clock downstairs ticked away the seconds and the dim roar of the surf sounded through the walls. Remembering the way Buttercup had curled up with him earlier, he felt around the bed for the cat's soft fur, then lifted his phone and shone the light. Buttercup was gone with Chloe, of course. Melancholy closed in like a heavy fog.

He checked the time. Ten o'clock. And he was wide awake. Exhausted but unable to sleep. It was going to be a long night.

\* \* \*

Chloe was closing out the cash drawer when Sean emerged from his office in street clothes.

"Busy night," he said. "If you're all set here, I'm gonna take off."

She eyed his black jeans and button-down shirt. "Where you headed so late on a Friday night?"

He adjusted his collar. "Got a date."

"Anyone I know?"

"Is there anyone in this town you don't know?"

"Pretty much just the tourists."

He pushed through the swinging doors into the kitchen.

Chloe finished up at the register and followed him to the kitchen, where he helped himself to a water bottle.

She grabbed a to-go box and began filling it with dinner rolls. "Why do I get the feeling you dodged my question? You're not going out with our new waitress, are you? I've already put a week into her training and she's got real promise."

He leaned against the fridge, wearing a smug smile. "I have to agree."

"*Sean.* We agreed: no dating the staff!"

"No . . . You suggested a no-dating policy and I vehemently disagreed."

She threw her arms up. "Did the fresh-produce fiasco teach you nothing?"

"Annalee is nothing like Haden. She's very sweet—and we have sparks." He winked.

*Eew.* Chloe closed the container and loaded another with leftover fruit. Her brother had sparks with 90 percent of the female species, mostly because he was easy on the eyes. Too bad he was no good on the follow-through.

"When you break up with her, she's gonna quit, and then I'll have to go through the interview and training process all over again."

"Who says I'm gonna break up with her?"

She speared him with a look. "Me and your extensive history of breaking up with every woman you date."

His gaze fell to her take-out boxes and he lifted a sardonic brow. "Hungry?"

"Hush. These are for Liam. And don't change the subject. If she quits, you're hiring another server. It took me weeks to find her."

"I thought Liam was such a *great cook*."

"If you must know, he's down with the flu. Now, do we have an agreement or what?"

"What are you now, his nursemaid? He's a grown man."

"I'm just being neighborly. He doesn't have any family here, in case you forgot." Though he did seem to have a million people checking up on him. "And you haven't agreed to our agreement."

"Because I don't *agree*. And by the way, news flash: you're not his real girlfriend."

She narrowed her eyes. "Thank you, Captain Obvious." She moved to the fridge and waited for him to move. "Do you mind?"

He moved out of her way with all the speed of a drugged snail. "Last thing you need is to get the flu while your movie's filming."

"You know I never get sick." She reached into the fridge and retrieved an unopened gallon of orange juice. Elliot had brought over groceries, but she'd used the last of Liam's, and he needed all the vitamin C he could get.

"I hope you remember to restock that," Sean said as she put the OJ and food containers in a bag and headed for the exit.

"And I hope you remember Annalee is a valued employee." And with that she was out the door.

# Chapter 22

A rattling stirred Liam awake. He opened his eyes.

Chloe set a tray laden with food on the bed beside him. "Morning. How are you feeling today?"

"Fine," he croaked.

She smiled. "Okay, tough guy. I'm sure you're fit as a fiddle, but you have to be hungry. I brought dinner rolls from the restaurant and a selection of fruits. Have you had your meds yet?"

The fog in his brain cleared a bit. "Wait. How'd you get in?"

"I told you yesterday I'd take the key, remember? Oh, you don't remember. Well, I need to check on you and there's no reason for you to drag yourself to the door."

He didn't even have the energy to say he didn't mind at all. That, in fact, he loved having her here. The house was so empty and quiet without her. "Time is it?"

"Almost ten." She pressed her cool hand to his forehead.

He wanted to grab it and hold it there the rest of the day.

But she snatched it away and opened a pill bottle. "Elliot filled your prescription. Everyone's very concerned about you." She handed him the meds and he downed the pills with a glass of OJ. His pulse throbbed in his temples from the minor exertion.

"Is Buttercup bothering you? I can take her downstairs. I was gonna hang out for a while in case you needed anything."

"Aren't you going on set today?"

"They're not filming till later tonight."

His eyelids were growing heavy, but he had to ask. "How bad did I mess things up?"

She patted his arm. "Now, now, this isn't your fault. Simone's working it all out, don't you worry."

He wanted to say something else, but whatever it was slipped away like a slimy fish. His eyelids grew heavy.

"You should eat something. Your body needs the nutrition and calories."

*I will.* But before he could even reach for the food, he lost the battle to sleep.

The buzzing of Liam's phone stirred him awake. It lay beside him, still lit with an incoming text. He picked it up, noting not only the time but the day: Sunday. He was sleeping his life away. The text was from his mom.

*Hi sweetheart. What's all this I'm reading about a girlfriend?? Is love in the air? I can't wait to meet her. Oh, and I wanted to mention that I'm a little short this month. There have been some unexpected expenses. Could you have Spencer cut me a check? Fifteen hundred should do it. Thank you, honey!* 😊

Stomach weighted, he dropped the phone and rolled over, seeking the sweet oblivion of sleep.

A soft *thud* woke Liam. When he opened his eyes Buttercup was slipping out the door, tail fanning behind her. *Come back.*

He felt a familiar weight on his head and reached up. A wet washcloth lay across his forehead. He didn't feel feverish and the rag was lukewarm. But he left it there anyway, remembering the care Chloe took each time she placed it on his brow.

He checked his phone: 2:12 p.m.

*Monday?* Where had the weekend gone?

From downstairs soft voices played from the TV. The sound carried well with the open floor plan and vaulted ceilings. He pictured

Chloe curled up on his sofa with a bowl of popcorn, watching a movie.

*Wait a minute.*

With great effort he lifted his head from the pillow and homed in on the dialogue. The washcloth slipped from his face, but it didn't distract him from his task. He recognized that voice—it was *him*. He couldn't quite make out the words. But a moment later when the movie's soundtrack began playing, he recognized the music from *Valor.*

He fell back against the pillow, breathing hard from his efforts. *Chloe's watching my movie.* A smile curled his lips as his thoughts drifted away.

The ringing of his phone awakened Liam. He reached for it, opening his eyes only long enough to squint at the screen. Spencer.

"What day is it?" he asked in lieu of a greeting. "And why are you calling so late?"

"Wow, you really are sick, buddy. It's Tuesday and it's only nine o'clock your time."

Chloe would be at work. He opened his eyes and got his bearings. Hey, no headache. And only a minor sore throat. Also he didn't feel the immediate need to go back to sleep. "I'm a little better."

"I can tell by your disorientation. Listen, do you need anything? I know Simone and Elliot have been checking on you and that Chloe's over there a lot, making sure you rest up."

"Oh, I'm resting all right. Everyone's been great. Especially Chloe."

"Almost like a real girlfriend, huh?" Spencer chuckled.

"Yeah. I guess the studio's eager for me to get back to work."

"There are only so many scenes they can do without you. How much longer do you think it'll be?"

"Another day or two, maybe." His chest tightened with anxiety even as his gaze fell on the huge bouquet of flowers the production company had sent. "I'm doing the best I can."

"Well, your health comes first, but the sooner the better, if you know what I mean. I also wanted to check in and tell you things are looking positive on the image front. Chloe's been posting pictures from the set—with Patty's approval—and making some kind comments about you. And since you've been laid up, I posted a couple photos of you two on your socials."

"Thanks. What's the scoop?" And what kinds of things had Chloe posted?

"Your fans are curious about Chloe. The gossip sites are mentioning her in a favorable light. This is all good, Liam. We're only a couple weeks into it, and the conversation has already shifted."

"Great news." He sat up in bed. There was a tray of food beside him. Suddenly ravenous, he grabbed a bagel and took a bite.

"Once you're feeling a little better, you'll have to put out some fresh pictures of you and Chloe. Your fans are eating that stuff up."

"Sure thing." He put Spencer on speaker and started to jump over to Chloe's Instagram page, but the sight of his mom's text from the other day stopped him cold. Put that heavy weight back in his stomach. He'd completely forgotten about that. Or maybe he'd thought it was a dream. Wishful thinking. "Hey, could you send another check to my mom? Make it fifteen hundred."

Nothing but silence met him on the other end of the phone.

"Spence, you there?"

"Yeah, I made a note. I'll send it out today." He had that tone he always used when they talked about Liam's mom.

"Don't even give me a hard time right now. I don't have the energy to deal with it."

"You got it, buddy."

A few minutes later they ended the call and Liam clicked over to Chloe's Insta page. She'd posted a close-up of Buttercup curled against his leg and had written, *Looks like I'm not the only one who's smitten.*

She'd also posted a photo of him from the set. The cast and crew had been joking around and he turned to flash a smile at Chloe. He read the caption: *The right man for the job.* 😍

It was possible he had a dopey grin on his face right now. It seemed Chloe was happy with the way he was handling the role of Ledger. Satisfaction swelled inside him at the thought. He'd been working hard to make sure she was pleased.

Also Liam had never asked her to avoid mention of his illness on social media. He'd been too wiped out to even think about it. But somehow she knew he wouldn't want that broadcasted. Instead she kept the dialogue about their relationship fresh while he was under the weather.

He'd always said he would never date someone outside the industry because they couldn't understand his life. But maybe he'd been wrong about that. Of course it was early days and they weren't dating for real. But Chloe had adapted pretty well so far. Not that he was thinking of anything permanent with her. After all, they lived across the country from each other.

He took another bite of the bagel and washed it down with a swig of water. He was definitely feeling better. He didn't want to sleep anymore. He was actually bored. Too bad Chloe was at work.

# Chapter 23

It was official: Chloe was sick.

She'd felt a little sluggish all day, but there were plenty of reasons she might be tired. For the past week she'd been working full-time, taking care of Liam, and appearing on set as much as she could.

But when she walked into the restaurant for her shift, Sean took one look at her flushed cheeks and sent her packing.

"But it's Friday," she said. "We have a band coming. There'll be a crowd and who's gonna run the front? You need me."

"We need you not to share your germs with the staff. Go home." Then, softening a bit, he added, "I'll check on you in the morning."

It was now morning and the filming at Holden Beach started in thirty minutes. Yesterday had been Liam's first day back on set. And now she was stuck at home and feeling worse by the minute.

She rolled over in bed and whimpered. She needed Tylenol and an antiviral, and she'd better get those meds before the weekend rolled around. She didn't have a set doctor and a studio staff at her beck and call. Mustering some energy, she called Dr. Angela, begged for the prescription, and managed to get one without an appointment. Now she just needed someone to pick it up. Too bad she didn't have an Elliot. She grabbed her phone and made the call.

"Oh, good gracious, you sound awful," Meghan said upon hearing Chloe's greeting.

"I'm sick."

"But you never get sick!"

"I know, right? I hate to ask, but can you pick up a prescription for me and drop it by on your way to work?"

"Of course, honey. I'll bring you a few other things too. We'll have you on your feet in no time. Rest up and I'll see you shortly."

Chloe must've fallen asleep because the next thing she heard was the rattle of bags outside her room.

"It's just me," Sean called.

"Don't come in here. Someone needs to run our restaurant."

"Oh, I'm not coming anywhere near you, pal. But I brought some food and Mom sent that tea she swears by. She said to tell you she was knee-deep in cake batter but she'd swing by later this afternoon."

"'Kay, thanks. Bring me the Tylenol. You can just drop it by the door—and some cold water too." Man, her throat was a raging fire.

"Yes, Your Majesty."

She didn't have the energy to respond. Had Liam's head throbbed like this? Had his body felt like one giant ache? No wonder he'd slept his life away. She was inclined to do the same.

"Wow, you look awful." From a safe distance Sean tossed the Tylenol and water bottle onto the bed.

"How'd you get in?"

"Please. Everyone knows where you keep your spare key."

She probably ought to move that now that she had paparazzi in her life.

A knock sounded on the front door, then a voice called, "Chloe? I'm here."

Sean's eyes shot to Chloe's. "You didn't tell me Meghan was coming."

"Meghan's coming," she deadpanned. But why would that matter to Sean? She thought back to that inkling she'd had when Meghan told her about collecting sand on the beach with Sean for her window display.

Her brother had already left, presumably to greet Meghan and, from the sounds coming from the kitchen, help her unload some things. They were conversing too quietly for Chloe to make out the words.

She frowned. He'd better not be leading her friend on. Meghan had been through enough recently. Last thing she needed was another broken heart.

Chloe grabbed the Tylenol, took two, then lay back against her pillows and closed her eyes against the thumping in her temples.

She might have dozed because when she opened her eyes it was nine thirty and Meghan was at her bedside wearing a face mask.

"I didn't want to wake you, but I figured the sooner we get this medication in you, the better. How are you feeling?"

"A little better. Thanks. You're a lifesaver." Chloe took the pill with the orange juice Meghan had brought. "Where's Sean?"

Her friend was suddenly busy with all the vitamin supplements she'd brought. "Um, he had to leave a while ago. Said to tell you he'd check on you later."

Chloe's gaze sharpened on Meghan's face—or what she could see of it. Did her friend have feelings for Sean? Should Chloe warn her off? But Meghan already knew all the gory details of Sean's so-called love life. She would know what she was getting into.

"How would you like some positive news?" Meghan shook vitamins from one of the two hundred bottles she'd brought. "There's an article up on one of the gossip sites I thought you'd like. Want me to read it?"

"Sure. It'll be a great distraction."

Meghan handed Chloe the juice and no fewer than seven pills. Chloe frowned at her.

"Trust me."

Chloe choked them all down and fell against her pillows.

"I'll fill a pill organizer so you know what to take." She whipped out her phone and tapped the screen a few times. "Now, listen to this. The article's called '5 Reasons Liam's New Love Is Good for Him.'"

"Oh brother."

"No, it's good. Listen. 'Number one: she's down-to-earth. Maybe she's penned a bestselling novel and has a movie in the making, but Chloe Anderson is also a restaurant manager who has worked a full-time job since graduating high school. We think she's already having a grounding effect on Liam. Number two: she's a small-town girl. Born and raised in Stillwater Bay, North Carolina. Not only does Chloe have small-town values, but she exhibits southern charm to boot. Her good, old-fashioned virtues will help center Liam.'"

"Great. Now everyone knows where I live."

Meghan pulled a face. "'Number three: she has a close-knit family. Chloe values intimate relationships because it's all she's ever known. Her stable roots have made her into the kind of woman Liam can count on.'"

"That's not even true."

"'Number four: she brings out Liam's lighter side. Since the couple began dating they've been seen laughing and canoodling on the regular. Liam needs a mate who will help him unwind from the rigors of his job. Number five: she makes Liam happy. Our sources say Chloe is positive and fun by nature. We think Liam agrees.'"

Meghan beamed. "Then it has the photo of you and Liam gazing all googly-eyed at each other. Isn't that great?"

Chloe rubbed her temples. "They mentioned sources. What sources?"

"Oh, you know, they've probably interviewed people around town. Or maybe they just make stuff up. They tried to pry information from me, but I decided to stick with 'No comment.'"

Meghan's eyes narrowed on Chloe's face. "I think you need to rest, honey. Is there anything else you need before I go? Here's some crackers and Sean left your favorite muffins and brought Popsicles for your throat."

"I'm good. Thank you for everything."

"Of course. Give me a call if you need anything at all."

She felt a long nap coming on. And sure enough, moments after the front door snapped shut, Chloe drifted into a deep sleep.

# Chapter 24

Where was Chloe?

Liam had been filming scenes with Daisy all morning. The sun was now high in the vibrant blue sky, bright and scorching. The waves rolled into the shore relentlessly, and the wind tugged at their hair and clothes, causing delays.

When it was time for a costume change, he headed for wardrobe, feeling sluggish. It was only his second day back on set and the long hours had drained him. Veronica, the barista to whom he'd offered a set visit, was here today. She'd been a perfect guest, and he'd introduced her around and tried to make her comfortable. But his energy was fading fast.

After he'd donned a pair of trunks he stepped from the trailer, hoping to have a minute to call Chloe. But he was immediately beckoned for the next scene—a picnic on the beach. As he headed that way he ran through his lines quickly, and then it was time to shoot.

Midafternoon Liam grabbed a quick sandwich at crafty with Simone, Rex, and Daisy. They hadn't heard from Chloe today either. Maybe she'd had errands to run before work. After all, she'd had a busy week taking care of him. But it was unlike her to be uncommunicative.

She'd be arriving at work soon, but he sent her a quick text anyway. *Everything okay? Missed you on set today. It's going really well though.*

But soon he got tied up with the next scene and was left to wonder—and maybe even worry a little.

The golden-hour scene, shot as Liam and Daisy walked along the shore, was stressful. Golden hour actually lasted about twenty minutes, and because of the camera angles, the scene had to be shot many times. They finally wrapped for the day just after nine, and that's when Liam was able to check his phone again.

He'd received several messages, but it was the one from Chloe he tapped on first. *Sorry I didn't call. I'm sick and I've been sleeping most of the day.*

His stomach dove for his feet even as guilt settled in. Poor Chloe. She'd been so thoughtful to take care of him, and look what it had gotten her.

*I'm coming over*, he texted.

He said good-bye to the cast and crew, then his driver shuttled him home. From there he headed to Chloe's house. By the time he arrived, she still hadn't responded to his text. But rather than wake her, he hunted for a key—and found one under a gnome statue in her landscaping.

He had second thoughts about invading her space, but she'd been letting herself into his house all week—and he had let her know he was coming.

"Chloe?" he called as he entered the house. "It's just me."

Buttercup met him in the foyer.

"Hey, sweetheart," Liam whispered. "How's your mommy?"

Buttercup meowed and wove between his legs, her tail wrapping around him. Liam stroked her back. That little smooshed face was growing on him.

The house was quiet and lit only by the moonlight coming through the wall of windows at the back of the house. He headed down the hallway where he assumed her bedroom would be. A night-light guided his steps.

"Chloe?"

"Liam?" a scratchy voice called back.

He followed the sound to the second doorway and stopped on the threshold. "Sorry if I woke you. I helped myself to your hide-a-key."

"Hey, Liam." A smile laced her voice this time.

He entered the room. "Mind if I turn on a lamp?"

"Here's one." A rustle sounded. Then a clatter. Something clunked to the floor.

He rushed over. "Sit tight. I'll get it." He flipped on the lamp and took in Chloe. Her cheeks were flushed, her eyes glazed over. He felt her forehead and found her skin warm.

Her bedside table turned up an empty glass, a bottle of Tylenol, and a prescription bottle.

A pill organizer lay at his feet. He picked it up and set it back on the table. "When did you have Tylenol last?"

"Mmm . . . not sure. Meghan was here, and Sean, and that was in the morning." Her forehead wrinkled. "I think it was morning. Is it nighttime outside? It's nighttime inside."

Something was off. Her words were a little slurred and her eyes . . . She seemed kind of out of it. "How are you feeling, Chloe?"

"Head hurts and my throat hurts and my whole body hurts. But I'm kinda floaty too." She narrowed her gaze on him. "Are you moving? No, I'm moving. Am I moving?"

He put his hand to her forehead again. She grabbed his hand and held it there. She was warm, but not alarmingly so. He scanned the pills on her bedside table again and picked up the pill organizer with the hand she wasn't grasping. "What's in here, Chloe? What are these pills?"

"Vitamins from Meghan. She brought them over this morning? I think it was morning." She moved his hand to her cheek and sighed.

Something she'd taken must've had a bad effect on her. "How about we call Meghan and figure this out, huh? I'm gonna need my hand."

She let go but her bottom lip turned out. "Awww."

He grabbed her phone off the bed and found Meghan's number in her contacts. The woman answered on the second ring. "Hey, honey. How're you feeling?"

"Um, it's actually Liam. We met last week."

"I'm not likely to forget," she said with a wry tone. "Is Chloe okay?"

She was currently playing with his other hand. "I'm not sure. She seems . . . out of it. Loopy, I guess. She's slurring her words and seems a little confused. I was hoping you could tell me what's in this pill organizer."

"Oh no. I only brought her vitamins. Nothing that would cause this. And she's taken Tylenol, of course, and that prescription she asked me to pick up. Hang on, let me see what I can find out about that med."

"All right."

Buttercup hopped up on the bed and Chloe beamed. "Buttercup! Come here, my little Butter Butter Boo Boo!" She gathered the cat into an embrace and buried her face in the yellow fur.

The feline's horrified eyes shot to Liam.

*Hang in there, girl.*

"Oh boy," Meghan said. "Apparently, in rare cases that medication can cause some unusual behavior. How many has she taken?"

Liam emptied the bottle on the nightstand and counted. "Just two, it looks like. But I took this same med and didn't have any problems at all."

"Everyone's different though."

"Right, right. Should I take her to the hospital?"

"Let me call Dr. Angela first and then call you back."

"You have her personal number?"

"Small town. I'll call you back in a minute."

They ended the call. Liam scooped the pills back into the container with hands that were now shaking. He pocketed the bottle, then fetched Chloe a glass of water. When he returned she was still doling out affection to Buttercup like she hadn't seen her in a year.

The cat snarled at her.

"Okay here, why don't we give Buttercup a little break." Liam rescued the cat from Chloe's death grip.

She pouted as the cat leapt from the bed and hightailed it from the room as if her tail were on fire.

Chloe stared pitifully up at him from her pillow. "I'm sick."

He eased down on the edge of her bed. "I know. I'm sorry about that."

"You'd better go, mister, or you'll get sick too."

"I've already been sick, remember? I can't get it again."

"Oh yeah." She took his hand again, set it against her cheek, and closed her eyes on a sigh.

Maybe he should give her Tylenol for that fever. But it would probably be better to wait and sort out this other situation.

A few minutes later a call came in on Chloe's phone. He picked it up, letting her keep his hand since she seemed so attached to it. "Hey, what'd she say?"

"She's on her way over. How's Chloe doing?"

The woman in question blinked up at him as if she were working out a puzzle and whispered, "Liam Hamilton."

"Um, much the same. Doctors do house calls here?"

"No, but Dr. Angela is good friends with Chloe's mom and also my godmother. She's worried Chloe's having a bad reaction to that medication."

"That can't be good."

# Chapter 25

Liam closed the door and sagged against it. Dr. Angela had said Chloe was experiencing a rare side effect to the prescription and told him to discard the pills. Her vitals were normal though, and the effects would wear off as the medication cleared her system. Once she'd made the diagnosis, she allowed Chloe to take the Tylenol for her fever and sore throat.

The doctor had also recommended that someone stay with her until she returned to normal. And since he was here anyway . . .

He pushed off the door. "Looks like it's you and me keeping watch tonight, Buttercup."

The cat purred as Liam swept her up in his arms and went to check on Chloe.

She was blinking at the ceiling and reached a hand up as if to touch it. "Hi there. I come in peace. Or you come in peace." She caught sight of Liam. "There's a UFO in my room. See it?"

His lips twitched. "That's a ceiling fixture, sweetheart."

"You sure? It's all spacey and it's moving. See it moving?"

He set Buttercup beside her and her face brightened. "Butter Butter Boo Boo! Come to Mommy."

Liam grabbed Chloe's phone and called Meghan back.

She answered on the first ring, concern in her rushed tone. "What did Angela say?"

"She'll be fine." Liam passed on the information the doctor had given him and assured Meghan he'd stay with her until morning, when he had to go on set.

"Are you sure? I could come and stay with her. Or I could call Sean or their mom."

"Probably best I do it since I've already had the virus."

Chloe was trying to catch Buttercup's thrashing tail, but her reactions were too slow to keep up.

"If you're sure. But if she's still loopy tomorrow, call me. I can come stay with her. I'll close the shop if I have to. I'll also call Sean in the morning and let him know what happened. No sense in worrying him this late."

"Sounds good. Thank you for your help, Meghan."

They ended the call and Liam eased onto the edge of the bed. Since Chloe's cheeks weren't flushed anymore, he pulled the covers to her chin. "Dr. Angela said you're gonna be just fine. But I'll stay here tonight just to make sure."

Chloe grabbed his hand and laid it flat against her cheek.

Her temperature had definitely gone down. "How are you feeling? You look a little better."

"Mmm . . . better." She petted his hand. "Nice hands. Big 'n' strong 'n' tan. I like being your girlfriend, Liam Hamilton."

"Is that so?" Now that he wasn't so worried about her, he smiled at her antics. Even though she was sick and her hair was sticking up in all directions, she was cute as a bug, those luminous blue eyes full of wonder.

She was gazing at him now with those eyes. "Know what, Liam Hamilton? You're very, very, very handsome. Even your scar is handsome. Can I touch it?" Before he could answer she pointed, not at the scar by his lip but at his eye, her fingertip two inches from its target. "Those eyes are silver and blue. Not just plain ol' gray."

"Oh yeah? Good to know." For the first time he noticed the slogan on her tee: *I'm not short, I'm fun size.* No doubt.

As if suddenly remembering she still had his hand, she brought it to her mouth and pressed a kiss to his palm. ". . . make you happy, grounded," she murmured.

"What was that?"

"That's what they said." She gave him a dopey grin. "I can help you unwind."

He chuckled. "Oh really?" He was tempted to see what would come out of her mouth next. But he probably shouldn't bait her when she was clearly delirious.

"Listen, I should get ready for bed now." He'd done a little snooping while the doctor examined Chloe. There was a spare bedroom right next door. He should be nearby in case she got up and started wandering around. No telling what she might do in her current state.

"'Kay." She closed her eyes. Her dark lashes feathered her cheeks and her full lips were parted slightly. She looked so sweet lying there, holding his hand to her face.

His heart softened. He leaned over and pressed a kiss to her forehead. "Get some sleep, sweetheart." He tried to get up but she grasped his hand for dear life.

"Don't leave!"

"Um . . . I won't go far but I'm gonna need my hand, okay? I'll bring it back in the morning." Of course she probably wouldn't want it then.

"Promise?"

"Yes, Chloe, I promise."

She finally released his hand, rolled over, and grabbed Buttercup in a death grip.

The cat slid him a pitiful look that screamed, *Save me.*

Liam quirked a brow. *You're on your own, pal.*

Before Liam left the room he cleared the nightstand of all pills, leaving only the glass of water. And before he went to bed he set his alarm to wake him every four hours.

# Chapter 26

A thump woke Chloe. Only half aware, she kept her eyes closed and let the fog lift slowly. Her head throbbed dully and her throat hurt. Oh yeah, she was sick with that awful flu.

She'd missed being on set yesterday. She had a vague memory of Meghan and Sean stopping by in the morning. Something about that triggered a memory. But the thought was gone before she could grasp it.

The smell of coffee beckoned her and she pried her eyes open. Early morning light filtered through her blinds. Sean or Meghan must've stopped to check on her. She felt like death. She wanted that coffee like she wanted a hair serum that kept its promises.

"Sean?" Her voice was a two-decibel croak. She cleared her throat and tried again. "Sean, can you—?"

Liam walked into the room.

She blinked to clear the delusion. But no, it was still him.

"Morning." His hair was sleep-tousled, a five o'clock shadow covered his jaw, and he wore a pair of jeans and a wrinkled tee. He had no business being so handsome first thing in the morning.

"Hi." She ran her tongue across fuzzy teeth, imagined what her hair must look like, and winced. Also, she had no memory of removing her makeup last night. But wait, she hadn't even put on makeup yesterday. *Ugh.*

His head cocked sideways as he approached the bed, wariness lining his eyes. "How are you feeling this morning?"

"What are you doing here?" But even before she finished the sentence, a sudden memory flashed in her mind.

*He was sitting on the edge of her bed.*

*She pressed his hand to her face.*

*Held it to her cheek.*

*Petted it.*

"Chloe? You okay?" His brow furrowed as he pressed the back of said hand to her forehead.

She clenched her fist to keep from accidentally grabbing his hand in some kind of sick replay.

"I gave you Tylenol a few hours ago. Fever's down."

When he drew back she hiked the covers to her chin, those vague memories trickling like water into a sinking boat. But maybe they weren't memories at all. Maybe they were just dreams. Fever-induced nightmares.

She cleared the frog from her throat. "Were you, um, were you here last night?"

"I was. It was quite the night. You had a little reaction to the prescription you were taking. Do you remember anything?"

"A . . . a reaction?"

"The pills made you a little . . . loopy. I called your friend Meghan and she got Dr. Angela over here to check you over. You seem to be feeling much better today though."

Was she? Because she was kind of flipping out actually. Since she had *petted* Liam's hand. Unless it had only been a dream. *Please, please, let it be a dream.*

She mustered up the courage to ask. "I didn't by any chance, uh, play with your *hand*, did I?"

His lips twitched. "Um, possibly you did . . ."

She closed her eyes. "Oh my gosh." She'd held his hand to her cheek. Petted it. Another memory trickled in. *Kissed* it. "Oh. My. Gosh."

He chuckled. "It's okay. You were a little disoriented, that's all."

"Did I say things? What did I *say*? No, don't tell me. I don't wanna know."

"You didn't say much at all."

"Thank God for small favors."

"You were just . . . um, very affectionate with my hand. And there was that little bit about the UFO . . ."

Afraid to ask, she opened one eye.

His gaze drifted slowly to the light fixture. "It was very spacey and mysterious and kept hovering over your bed."

She groaned and pulled the sheet over her face.

He laughed as he pulled down the sheet. "Chloe, it's fine. It was kind of cute, actually." A twinkle of amusement appeared in his eyes. "Do you have a raging fever right now, or are you just blushing really hard?"

She swatted his arm. "Stop it. I am completely humiliated. And I'm sick! You should be nice to me." The last came out as a whimper.

His laughter faded away, leaving only a shadow of a smile. "All right, all right. I'll be nice. Want me to make you a mocha?"

"You have no idea." She was never gonna live this down. The caffeine would help her feel better. Too bad it couldn't erase the past twelve hours. Speaking of . . . she hoped someone had fed her cat. "Where's Buttercup?"

"In the living room. She might be a little, ah, traumatized by all the hugging last night."

Chloe had a vague memory of some unreciprocated affection—and something else . . . "Did I say 'Butter Butter Boo Boo'?"

He burst out laughing as he eased off the bed. "One double-chocolate mocha coming right up."

# Chapter 27

Liam was adding chopped onion to the Crock-Pot when Chloe's front door opened. It was almost ten o'clock and he had to leave for set soon. "Hello?"

Chloe's brother, grocery bags in tow, came to a halt on the threshold of the living room, scowling. "What are you doing here so early?"

"Didn't Meghan call you?"

"No, why? Is Chloe okay?" Sean set the bags on the dining room table.

"She is now. Last night she had a reaction to the prescription medication. Dr. Angela checked her over and said it would wear off—and it did."

Sean's lips flattened. "You should've called me." He took off for Chloe's room before Liam could explain.

Seemed he couldn't do anything right where Sean was concerned. Oh well.

Liam washed and chopped a couple of carrots, then added some celery to the broth. He'd placed a grocery order late last night and it had arrived early this morning.

He must've left the front door unlocked when the groceries arrived. His gaze drifted to the hallway and the quiet buzz of conversation.

After he'd added all the ingredients to the soup, he checked the chicken breasts, which were baking in the oven. Another few minutes.

While he waited he put away the groceries Sean had brought, then cleaned up the mess he'd made in the kitchen. By the time he finished, the chicken was good and tender.

He was removing it from the oven when Sean entered the room. "She seems fine now, other than the virus."

Though you wouldn't have known it by the frown on the man's face.

Liam began shredding the chicken. "I'm glad. She gave me a scare last night."

Sean moved into the kitchen. "Thanks for your help, but I can take it from here."

This guy really rubbed him the wrong way. "Good. I have to be on set soon anyway." He finished shredding the chicken, dumped it into the pot, and set it on Low. "This should be ready by dinnertime. I'll go say good-bye to Chloe."

He brushed past Sean and headed to her room. But when he reached the door, her eyes were closed and her chest rose and fell with deep breaths. He didn't want to bother her when she needed her rest. Buttercup glanced at him from the other side of the bed, tail twitching. Liam smiled as he left the room.

But his lips fell quickly at the sight of Sean waiting for him in the foyer, arms crossed over his chest. Liam braced himself for confrontation.

"What's your game, man?" Sean asked quietly.

"What are you talking about?"

"You and Chloe have a business arrangement that hardly includes overnight stays and chicken noodle soup."

He'd had about enough of Sean's attitude. "What's your problem exactly?"

"My problem is that you show up over here and suddenly Chloe's delirious? She's never reacted to any kind of medication like—"

"You think *I* gave her something? Why would I do that?"

"I don't know—same reason other guys do that kind of thing."

Like a roofie or something? Wow. Sean's opinion of him couldn't be lower. Liam tamped down the rage that swelled inside. He wanted to slug the man's smug face. "I would never do that to anyone, much less Chloe."

Sean lifted a shoulder. "I don't know you. And what I do know about you isn't very flattering."

"If I'd done something like that, why would I have called Meghan or anyone else for that matter?"

"Why did you call Meghan? Why not just take Chloe straight to the hospital?"

"Because Meghan had left a bunch of pills for Chloe, and I was trying to figure out what they were. Is it so impossible to think I might actually like your sister? Want to help her?"

"She really doesn't need another guy coming around making promises he can't keep."

"As you said, we have a deal. That's all." But he'd been here all night, taking care of her. Even he could admit that was beyond the confines of their arrangement. Was he starting to have feelings for her? He flagged the thought for later.

"Just remember when your so-called deal is over, you—and your bad reputation—will go back to your Hollywood life."

From what Chloe had told him, Sean had his own issues with commitment. It took the control of a saint to keep that thought to himself.

"You'd better not be leading her on."

"Chloe's a good person. I'd never do anything to hurt her."

Sean's gaze burned into Liam for a long, tense moment. "See that you don't."

Liam pressed his lips together. He was done with this guy. He reached for the doorknob.

"You can leave the key with me."

What did he think Liam was going to do? Break in at night and make more soup? "It's on the table."

He was so irritated he didn't notice a third car in the driveway until he was off the porch.

Chloe's mother stepped from the white Chevy Malibu, aiming a warm smile his way. "Hey, sweetheart, how's our girl?"

He shook off the confrontation with Sean and returned her grin. "Hi, Millie. She's much better today, thank God. Back to normal— except for the flu, of course."

Millie rested her hand on his arm. "That was so kind of you to keep watch over her all night. I'd have been happy to come over and stay with her myself."

"I know you would've, but it's a nasty virus and I've already had it."

"Well, you're an absolute angel."

"Hi, Mom." Sean lounged in the doorway.

"Hi, honey. I'm glad you're here. You can help me squeeze these oranges. There's nothing like fresh orange juice to perk up your immune system." She shifted the bag and addressed Liam. "We'll get her back on her feet again. I know she hates missing the filming. Such terrible timing."

"She's blessed to have so many people who care."

"The church already has a meal train in the works. And hopefully she'll be back to her usual peppy self in a week or so, just in time for the Fourth. It's a big to-do around here with a parade and fireworks. I hope Chloe invited you to our cookout. We do it every year—though now that I think of it, it's usually here at Chloe's, and I'm not sure if the filming schedule will interfere. The county sets off fireworks from a barge, and she has a lovely view from her pier."

"I'm not sure of the schedule either—sometimes they change things last minute. But you're all welcome to come out to my rental. It's on the beach so I should have a nice view, and it has a huge deck and a top-notch grill."

Millie beamed. "Well, aren't you just so sweet. We'd love that, wouldn't we, Sean?"

"Love it," he deadpanned.

"It's settled then. But we'll bring all the food." Millie patted his arm. "You won't have to worry about a thing."

"Sounds like a plan."

# Chapter 28

The Fourth of July dawned warm and sunny. Chloe and Liam arrived downtown bright and early to set up their chairs on Main Street along the parade route. She couldn't believe he'd never seen a parade in person. But then, he wasn't from a small town and she didn't reckon Hollywood folk had much appreciation for the simple things.

It was fun watching him take in the fanfare. The local bands marching past, blaring out "You're a Grand Old Flag." Ellie's Dance Academy sashaying by, starting with the adorable preschoolers in their tutus and transitioning to their older, more skilled counterparts. When he caught a piece of taffy thrown from the fire engine, his eyes lit up like a child's.

They'd gotten coffee early on, then stopped by Henry's Hardware to pick up their free flags, which they waved as the parade passed by. Throughout the morning they'd run into just about everyone Chloe knew, and she introduced Liam to each of them. Most of the townies knew exactly who Liam was, but no one begged for a photo or singled him out. She was so proud of her town for letting him enjoy the holiday like an ordinary citizen.

Chloe didn't mind the arm he kept around her chair throughout the parade. Or the hand that settled at the small of her back as they milled around the crowded sidewalks.

When they reached the clothing boutique where he'd first spotted her, he leaned down and whispered in her ear, "If you feel the need to hide, there's a clothing rack right over there."

Her cheeks went warm at the memory. "I wasn't hiding."

"Oh, you were definitely hiding."

"I was shopping."

"You wouldn't be caught dead in that bathing suit."

She aimed her index finger at his ribs. "I know your ticklish spot, Liam Hamilton."

"And I know yours, Chloe Anderson."

She considered. "Good point."

She'd felt closer to him since their illnesses. There was something about seeing a person at his weakest—and being seen at your most vulnerable—that lowered a person's walls. She thought he might feel the same. There was a new easiness to their relationship. When they were in public, the affection, the physical touch felt more natural somehow.

So natural that when they were alone Chloe had to remind herself: *No touching.*

That thought gave her pause later that evening as she searched Liam's kitchen for salad tongs. Liam and her dad were on the deck grilling steaks, and Sean and Meghan were helping Mom set the outdoor table. Chloe had insisted her friend join them. The bookshop was closed for the holiday and her family lived in Florida. She didn't want Meghan home alone, ruminating about her ex-husband and playing mind games with her remote thermostat for entertainment.

Once Chloe located the tongs, she grabbed the salad makings from the fridge. Liam's boisterous laughter carried through the screen door. There was no doubt she enjoyed his company. He was kind and thoughtful and funny. He enjoyed teasing her and making her blush, but he never pushed too far. He'd taken such great care of her when she was sick, and she was pretty sure Buttercup now preferred his company to her own.

He was not at all who she'd expected him to be. He wasn't entitled or standoffish or arrogant. There were times she thought he might even be a little wounded—but he had yet to open up about anything personal.

Sometimes running lines with him was a moving experience. He got so into the character, sometimes she felt she was actually with the man she'd created. If she was maybe developing a little crush on Liam, that was the reason why. He was playing the part of her ideal man—and doing it quite convincingly.

The patio door opened and Liam slipped inside, looking like a swimwear model in a snug gray tee and board shorts. "Everything all right in here?"

She afforded him a wry grin. "Even I can toss a salad."

"I didn't doubt it for a minute. You didn't warn me about Jerry—he takes his grilling pretty seriously."

"It might be best to just hand over the spatula."

"Yeah, I kinda figured that out."

"And you should know he's never satisfied with the outcome, no matter how delicious it is or how much we rave over it."

"Good to know."

She glanced at Liam as he opened the fridge and retrieved the steak sauce. "Is my brother behaving himself out there?" He was so surly around Liam she wanted to throttle him. She'd never seen him like this.

"Don't worry about me. I can take it."

"He's probably just grumpy because Annalee broke it off after only three dates. He usually has the gratification of ending relationships."

Maybe Sean and Liam should get together and compare notes. She got a little aggressive with the tongs. "What is it with men and commitment anyway? Don't you guys want a family someday?"

The cautious look he gave her revealed he knew to tread carefully. "Um, sure. Of course."

"Just not till you're fifty or something?"

"I can only speak for myself, but I'd definitely like to settle down before I'm eligible for AARP."

"But you've never had a serious relationship."

He set the condiment down and settled back against the counter beside her. "I guess I've just never found that special someone. It's hard when people have preconceived ideas about you—not to mention agendas of their own."

He'd mentioned that before. She tried to put herself in his shoes. It would be hard to open up if you couldn't trust the motives of the person you were dating. "I guess that would complicate things."

"Women sometimes view me as a character from their favorite movie. But those were just roles I was playing, not *me*."

And sometimes he didn't feel that he was enough? "If they can't see you for who you are, that's their loss."

Those gray eyes searched hers as if hungry to believe her words.

What did he see when he gazed at her that way? What was he thinking? His nearness, his scrutiny, made her skin tingle. She was intensely aware of the heat radiating from his sun-warmed skin. Of the way her arm brushed his. And those eyes—so attentive.

"What about you?" he asked. "Just haven't found the right man yet?"

Was it just a simple question? Or was he intrigued by her the same way she was by him? "I thought I did twice over. But one of them moved away and the other broke it off after a year."

After he'd been caught cheating. Evan's final jab replayed in her head. *"Maybe I wouldn't have had to find someone else if you didn't make me feel so alone. You're so closed off, Chloe. You never let me in."*

*Phooey.*

She shook the memory from her head, not wanting to think about his troubling accusation.

Liam seemed to drink her in. "Well, they're both crazy if they didn't see what they had in you."

She fell into the warm depths of his eyes. His words touched someplace deep inside her. Someplace soft and achy. She pulled her gaze away and resumed tossing the salad. "Yeah, well, after being abandoned by my father, I guess I'm not too keen on being left behind."

"I'm sorry that happened to you. You deserved better."

Remembering his own childhood, Chloe said, "So did you. I guess love can be complicated no matter who you are."

"We can definitely agree on that."

Fifteen minutes later they gathered on the deck in the twilight, the savory scent of grilling steaks filling the air. Dad hovered over the grill while Liam engaged him in conversation. Chloe stood at the deck rail between Sean and Meghan, enjoying the view of the endless blue sea.

"Turn around, kiddos." Mom aimed her phone toward the three of them and snapped a few pictures. "Oh, this light is so beautiful. Let's not waste it. Liam and Chloe, you first."

They followed her down the steps where a white Adirondack chair sat facing the ocean.

"Sit right down," Mom said. "This lighting won't last long."

Liam sank into the chair and Chloe lowered herself onto its wide arm. Liam put his hand at her waist.

Mom held up the phone. "Oh, come on, you two, act like you like each other."

Chloe leaned closer, holding her expression. But Liam grabbed her around the waist and pulled her into his lap. She squeaked in surprise and was vaguely aware of her family's laughter as she settled in his lap and met his twinkling eyes.

Their gazes held. And as the moment lengthened, his smile faded.

Chloe became hyperaware of his sturdy arms locked around her. Of the way the breeze ruffled his hair. Of the clean scent of him washing over her like a cool wave. The moment hung suspended like a mist over the water.

His eyes dropped to her mouth, making her lips tingle. If they'd been alone, if this had been a date, he might lean down to kiss her next.

"Now that's more like it!" Mom said.

Chloe jerked her attention forward and lifted her lips as Mom took more photos. All the while Chloe's mind spun.

*What was that?*

Had she imagined that moment of . . . what? Attraction? Or had Liam only been pretending—playing his part for the camera? If the latter was true, he was a better actor than she'd ever given him credit for. It had felt so real. The goose bumps on her skin were certainly real. As were her racing pulse and fluttering stomach.

Her thoughts were disrupted by Dad's call from the deck. "Come and get it!"

Five minutes later Dad said grace and the meal was underway. Chloe hadn't had time to analyze that moment in the yard. Instead she tucked it away for later.

"The steak is delicious, honey," Mom said.

"I cooked them a little too long."

"It's just the way I like it." Mom turned to Meghan. "How's your bookshop doing, sweetheart? I'm sorry I haven't been in for a while. I keep meaning to get over there and pick up the newest Debbie Macomber book."

"The store's been pretty steady. I think you'll like her new novel. I would've brought it with me had I known you wanted it."

"I'll grab it for you next time I'm in," Chloe said.

"Is everyone's steak okay?" Dad asked.

"Mine's perfect."

"Just right."

"Delicious."

"I met the nicest guy at the restaurant," Mom said. "He's new to town and works at the marina, comes in for supper a couple times a week. James Whitley. Have you met him yet, Chloe?"

"I don't think so."

"He's single, about your age, Meghan—very handsome." Mom winked. "If you should happen to stop in for supper on a Tuesday or Thursday night, I'll make sure to introduce you."

Meghan's attention flickered to Sean—who suddenly seemed very intent on forking his green beans. "Oh, thank you, Millie, but I don't know about that. I'm, uh, not much for fix-ups, I guess. And I'm not dating just yet anyway."

"Give it some thought, honey. He seems like a really great guy, and you'd make such a nice couple."

As Mom went on about the guy, Chloe's gaze toggled between Sean and Meghan, whose neck was now mottled pink. Her friend wasn't particularly shy and she was probably ready to move on romantically. What was going on between the two of them? They would've told her if they were dating, wouldn't they?

The tension in the air dissipated when Mom changed the subject.

"How's filming going, Liam?" Mom asked. "It must be very interesting, the work you do."

Dad's brows pinched as Mom added steak sauce to her plate. "I should've added more seasoning."

"You know I like my A.1., sweetheart." She turned her attention back to Liam, waiting.

"Filming's going well, I think. Everyone's getting along great. The cast and crew are friendly and easy to work with—that's not always the case. My illness set us back a bit, of course, but we're working some long days to make up for it."

"Is it hard to get into character when you're filming?"

"Not usually. Having a skilled costar is helpful though."

"Yeah, Daisy's really talented," Chloe said. "They both are. I can't believe we're almost halfway through filming already."

"That's amazing," Mom said. "So, Liam, you'll be heading back to LA then?"

"Uh, yeah. Once filming wraps."

An awkward silence ensued, Mom and Dad no doubt wondering how this relationship of theirs would work long term, Sean and Meghan knowing the whole thing was bogus.

It *was* bogus, wasn't it?

Mom beamed at Chloe and Liam. "Well, long distance is so much easier these days what with FaceTime and all."

"Of course," Liam said. "Lots of people do it."

Sean scowled at Chloe from across the table. *Shouldn't be keeping secrets from your family.*

Chloe quirked her brow. *You're one to talk.*

Sean glanced away.

Yep. Just as she'd thought. Something was going on between Sean and Meghan, and she would get to the bottom of it before the night was over.

The sky was starting to darken, so Liam turned on the deck lights. They glowed amber so as not to misdirect the sea turtles that hatched on the beach in the summer.

Meghan addressed Liam. "What's next for you after Chloe's movie?"

"That's a good question. I'm still weighing my options. I have time to decide on my next project. It's more important to get the right movie rather than rushing into something that won't be a good fit for my career."

"It must be hard to determine what that is," Meghan said.

"It can be. I rely heavily on my manager, Spencer. He's the one who talked me into Chloe's movie."

"And see how wonderfully that turned out," Mom said.

Chloe and Liam exchanged what she hoped was an infatuated look. But the questions roiling inside left her worried. Was she getting in too deep? Had Liam wedged his way into her heart? And if he had, what was she going to do about it?

"Yeah." Sean smiled glibly. "See how that turned out."

# Chapter 29

When Chloe found Meghan loading the dishwasher, she shoved aside her concerns about Liam. She had another matter to attend to right now. Entering the kitchen, she grabbed a rag and began wiping down the counters. "Fair warning, they're setting up Poetry for Neanderthals outside."

"Ugh," Meghan said with a wry grin.

The game was a family favorite, but her friend wasn't great at giving one-syllable clues. "Good news is, it'll be a short game. The fireworks start in half an hour."

"Speaking of fireworks . . ." Meghan flashed a grin at Chloe. "Is it just me or are there some *real* sparks flying between you guys?"

Chloe's cheeks warmed. She hadn't yet processed her feelings on the matter. Anyway, Meghan had offered the perfect segue for the conversation she'd planned. "Funny you say that—I was about to ask you the same thing."

Meghan let out a nervous chuckle. "What do you mean?"

She decided on the direct approach. "Is there something going on between you and Sean?"

"What? *No.* Of course not."

But Meghan's sudden lack of eye contact, added to the laser-like attention she gave the already-clean plate, tipped Chloe off. She tossed the rag into the sink and crossed her arms, giving Meghan a pointed stare. "This is me you're talking to. Your left eye is twitching like mad and you're avoiding eye contact. On top of that, you got all squirrelly when Mom mentioned that guy from the restaurant, and Sean looked like he was chewing on sawdust at the idea of you dating someone else."

Meghan's shoulders sagged. "All right, all right. I'll admit I've been having some—I guess I'm attracted to him, that's all. So sue me, he's an attractive guy."

*Attracted.* Chloe's tension eased. Didn't sound as if she'd acted upon that attraction. Yet. "Okay . . . but you wouldn't go there, right?"

Meghan put the last plate in the dishwasher and swung the door closed. "I know all about Sean's track record—you've regaled me with all the stories. Believe me, that's the last complication I need in my life."

Relief bloomed inside Chloe. "I'm glad to hear you say that. You know I love my brother like mad, but he seems incapable of settling down. He goes from one woman to the next—"

"I know, I know. You don't have to spell it out for me."

The problem wasn't that Meghan was attracted to Sean. The problem was that the attraction went both ways. And there was no way they didn't recognize the electricity sparking between them. Mutual attraction could be a powerful thing. "He's a great guy. He really is—but I don't want to see you hurt."

"I don't want that either, believe me."

The patio door eased open, ushering in the sounds of surf and chatter. Mom poked her head inside. "Time-to-play-fun-game. Leave-plates-and-come-out-on-deck."

Chloe laughed. "All-right. Be-there-in-a . . . bit."

Mom slipped back outside as Meghan groaned. "Isn't there a deck of Uno cards around here somewhere?"

"Come on, girl. Put away those big fancy words and let's have some fun."

After a lot of verbal stumbling and raucous laughter, they ended the game a few minutes before the fireworks were to begin. The women had lost, due in large part to Meghan, though no one made her feel bad.

Dad helped Liam arrange the chairs in the sandy yard while Mom went to the kitchen for a drink and Meghan hit the bathroom.

It was now or never. Chloe cornered Sean in a shadowed corner of the deck. "I want you to leave Meghan alone."

"What are you talking about?"

"Don't play dumb with me. I can see you're attracted to her."

He frowned at her. "And how's that any of your business?"

"She's my friend and you're my brother. Come on, Sean, can't you see this is a train wreck waiting to happen?"

"Says who?"

Just the fact that he asked the question ratcheted up her tension. He was obviously entertaining the idea. "You know she just got out of a bad marriage, right? She's only now beginning to feel like herself. I don't want to see her hurt again."

"I would *never* hurt Meghan."

The sheer intensity of his declaration would keep her awake tonight. But his fervent expression also softened something inside her. "You wouldn't mean to, pal, but you would. You just can't help yourself."

He flinched.

Chloe set her hand on his arm and he shrugged it off.

"I'm not trying to be mean, Sean. You're a good guy and you know I love you. But you have a short attention span where women are concerned, and Meghan is in a vulnerable place right now. Surely you can see that. She's been through a lot and she deserves someone who can—"

"Know what, Chloe? You're hardly qualified to dole out dating advice. You're trapped in a fake relationship with a celebrity—and *you're* the one heading for heartache. If you can't see that, then you're blind as a bat."

Like a punctuation mark on the end of his sentence, the first *boom* of fireworks sounded and color bloomed across the night sky.

* * *

Liam watched a red firework burst overhead. Somehow Chloe had ended up in his lap again. Okay, so he'd pulled her down as she'd been passing by. Could he help it if they were one chair short? But she seemed comfortable leaning back into the curve of his chest, his arms encompassing her waist. She was so tiny. He usually dated tall women, but he was finding he liked her compact size. It made him feel protective somehow.

He rested his chin on the top of her head. Relished the soft weight of her body against his, the scent of fireworks in the air, and the muffled sounds of exclamations on the beach. He'd had fun tonight, hanging out with her family. And despite Sean's attitude toward him, Liam had shared in the camaraderie and laughter naturally. He felt like one of them.

Sitting here, watching the fireworks bloom overhead with Chloe in his arms, he couldn't remember ever feeling so content. How odd. If anyone should feel content with his life, shouldn't it be him, with all his fame and money and success? What more could a man want?

But the way he felt in this moment somehow surpassed all that other stuff. Made all the other things seem meaningless. And he couldn't help but attribute it to Chloe.

Something had shifted inside him the past few weeks. There

was a softness to her. A vulnerability that drew him. But he didn't have to remind himself what happened to the moth when it got too close to the flame.

Nonetheless, that knowledge never seemed to stop his heart from thudding in his chest when she gazed up at him. Or keep his insides from clenching when those wide eyes, full of questions, met his. He had those same questions running through his mind. Was there something here? Was she feeling it too? What would it be like to kiss her?

As of today they'd been fake dating for almost five weeks. Just the fact that he hadn't kissed her yet was noteworthy. He kissed women all the time in the process of his job. This PR relationship was an extension of his work. If he didn't have feelings for Chloe, he'd have no trouble laying one on her for the cameras.

He was avoiding kissing her because he was afraid where it might lead. Anything real between them would be a dead-end relationship. She lived clear on the other side of the country. There was no point in traveling down that road.

Something deep inside flagged the convenient excuse. But he didn't care to explore the thought further.

Whatever he was feeling for Chloe, he needed to pretend it wasn't there. Pretending was what he did for a living, after all. Once the filming was complete, they'd fake their breakup and he could go back to his regular life, hopefully with a promising movie offer.

And just like that, a heavy shadow loomed over the sense of contentment he'd felt only moments before.

# Chapter 30

One of the photos taken on the Fourth went viral after Liam posted it on his socials. Mom had captured the moment just after Liam pulled Chloe onto his lap. They faced each other, laughing. His fans loved it. And her social media following climbed to new heights.

"Spencer says you're the new media darling," Liam told her a week later as they sat in the coffee shop, running lines for the day's shoot.

"Is that so?" Chloe could hardly fathom such a thing. But as long as it was good for both their careers, she was happy.

"Can't say I blame them. And, uh, according to Spencer, they're crying out for more PDA."

Chloe glanced away as her face warmed. She gave a put-upon sigh. "Suffering for the cause."

"Somebody's gotta do it."

He held her hand as they exited the coffee shop and kissed her cheek when they parted ways.

Over the next week there was a lot of hand-holding, hugs, and kisses on the cheek. The media showed up at the restaurant, and Chloe began getting used to the public life. But most of their time was spent on set. During breaks they ran lines or Liam lingered in the video village, hands on her shoulders, sometimes offering a mini-massage as he stood behind her. A peck on the cheek as he went back to work.

What came next started small. A gentle hand on her back in the privacy of his home. A quick touch on her shoulder when they were reading lines in her living room.

Their public relationship was creeping into their alone time— and Chloe wasn't altogether unhappy about it. Maybe he simply carried over the intimacies by habit. Or maybe he was just affectionate with his friends, and familiarity allowed more demonstration.

Or maybe the same feelings growing inside her were also growing inside him. The thought stirred something deep down. Was it possible? He seemed to enjoy her company. He sought her out sometimes when there were no lines to run or gossip to generate. He shot her random texts and called her up just to chat. Their relationship had clearly expanded beyond the boundaries of their bargain.

In mid-July she had a rare Saturday night off, and Liam took her to Main Street Grill, the nicest restaurant in town. She curled her hair and added a touch of makeup. Her pale yellow sundress complemented her small waist and bronzed skin. Liam was handsome in khakis and a button-down shirt the same gray-blue shade as his eyes.

They marveled over their perfectly cooked steaks and a sweet potato casserole that could've been served as dessert. They talked about the filming, which was only a month from wrapping, and about Liam's upcoming movie offers—he had two potential scripts, though he wasn't sold on either. They talked about Docksiders and Chloe's ambivalence about the restaurant business. About her desire to write a novel set during the World War II era and the lack of inspiration about the same.

They chatted and laughed, lost track of time, and, except for the fangirling hostess at the beginning of the evening, forgot they were even in public.

Sometime during the meal it had begun raining, and by the time Liam ushered Chloe out the door it was pouring. They stopped under the canopy, staring at Liam's Camaro across the street and down a ways.

Feeling nothing but joy after their wonderful meal, Chloe laughed. "Where's an umbrella when you need one?"

"I'll pull the car around for you."

"That's okay." She was loath to leave his side—and besides, what was a little rain? She linked arms with him. "Let's do this."

His eyes lit up. "Really?"

She shrugged. "I won't melt."

When the traffic cleared they darted across. They hunkered together, jogging down the street, splashing through puddles like a couple of kids. She squealed as rain pelted her bare shoulders and they laughed like maniacs.

When they neared the car she called, "Unlock the doors!"

He went for his pants pocket.

The rain was relentless. Her feet were already soaked, sloshing around inside her sandals.

"I can't find them!" he called over the maelstrom.

They'd reached the car and stopped at the passenger door. Liam frantically patted down his front pockets, his back pockets. "Where are they?"

Under the glow of a streetlamp, wet strands of hair hung over his forehead like seaweed. His lashes clumped together as he blinked rapidly. Rain streamed down his neck and under the collar of his shirt. Speaking of his shirt. He was soaked to the skin. And still searching desperately for his keys.

Laughter bubbled up and spilled over.

Liam, still patting his pockets, stared at her as if she'd lost her mind even as a grin tugged his mouth. "Have you gone mad, woman?"

"You look like a drowned rat. Anyway, what's the rush at this point? It's not as if we can get any wetter."

He paused his searching, seeming to take her in: soggy hair, drenched dress. Even though she must look a wreck, she couldn't stop grinning.

Movement over his shoulder, back toward the restaurant, caught her eye. But it must've just been the flashing red light on the corner.

Their gazes connected again, the moment lengthening as their smiles fell away. Something passed between them. Something momentous. Something beautiful. Something *real*. All those intimacies they'd been sharing flowed naturally into the next logical step.

Chloe reached up and brushed Liam's wet lips with her own.

\* \* \*

It might've ended right there. But Liam had waited too long for this. He framed Chloe's face and kissed her with all the passion that had been building over the past two months. All those touches and brushes. All those searching glances and sultry smiles. He was a man who'd restrained himself—but for what he couldn't seem to remember just now.

He forgot about his reasons, forgot about the rain, and homed in on her lips. So soft and warm and responsive. When her mouth parted on a breath he took full advantage. She emitted a soft mewling sound that lit a fire inside. He turned her back to the car. He'd wanted her like this forever it seemed.

And here was the kicker—she wanted him too. And she didn't just want Liam Hamilton the actor. Or Liam Hamilton the famous rich guy who could pull strings, pave an easy path, or bail you out of trouble.

She wanted *him*.

And he was downright heady with the knowledge. Chloe had never asked him for anything outside of their mutual bargain. But their relationship had quickly progressed from business arrangement to friendship and now to so much more.

She liked him for *him*.

The fulfillment of something long denied stirred a place deep inside. He hadn't realized how desperate he'd been for that validation.

For the confirmation that he was more than his fame or his money or the heroic parts he'd played. He was downright drunk on the feeling of being the object of her affection.

"Liam, over here!"

The voice jarred him from his thoughts. From the kiss. He straightened and searched over the top of the car. Through the torrential downpour. To the cameramen across the street.

The buzz he'd been feeling evaporated. He glanced down at Chloe's shadowed face. It was impossible to read her expression.

Liam suddenly wanted to be anywhere else. On a whim he grabbed for the door handle and found it unlocked. When Chloe slipped inside he spied the keys on the console. He shut the door. And as he jogged around the car he remembered that moment just before the kiss. When Chloe had glanced over his shoulder.

Had she spotted the photographers? Spencer had suggested more PDA—had she taken up the challenge?

Maybe the kiss hadn't been real.

Liam wiped his face with his hand, gathering himself before he opened the door and sank into the seat. The engine started with a roar as the wet cold lifted gooseflesh on his arms.

Unwilling to lay his heart on the line, he tested his theory. "Couldn't have planned that any better." His voice betrayed no hint of the disappointment that threatened to swallow him whole. He pulled from the curb, narrowly missing a photographer who'd closed the gap. "That'll be all over the sites in the morning."

"Perfect timing," Chloe said.

He turned on his wipers, wishing he could so easily wash away the past few minutes.

# Chapter 31

Liam cradled Chloe's face, his gaze intent on her, eyes smoldering. "You've come back into my life, and I don't know how I lived, how I breathed, without you. You've captured a piece of my soul and I don't want it back. I don't want anything but you." His eyes dropped to her lips. His Adam's apple bobbed.

Chloe's heart skipped a beat. She fisted her clammy hands. She'd known rehearsing this scene would be difficult. Not to mention awkward after last night. But it was crucial he get it right.

Awareness crackled between them as tension wove a web around them, cocooning them in a sensual haze. The memory of that spectacular kiss sent her airborne, rising, floating. Until she recalled the pinprick of his words afterward that had sent her plummeting back to earth.

He cleared his throat. "This is where you push me away. I mean *Cate*. Cate pushes me away."

Chloe blinked. "*Oh*. Right." Belatedly Chloe shoved his shoulder. A half-hearted attempt that barely budged him.

Their gazes held. It wasn't the end of the scene. Not hardly.

Liam delivered the next lines. It was practically a soliloquy.

Her mind drifted for the millionth time to last night when he'd melted her knees with that kiss. But the moment, the way he'd stared down at her, had been calculated. Maybe he and Spencer had even arranged for the photographers' appearance as they'd done at the bookshop. She went cold inside.

She should've known better than to believe it was real. Her brother had warned her not two weeks ago what was happening. His words now buzzed in her ear like a pesky mosquito. And she had listened to him! She'd been so careful to keep her guard up—no easy feat with those smoldering glances Liam aimed her way in public.

"Chloe?"

Oh. He'd stopped speaking. His last words rang in her head. He stared down at her uncertainly.

Time for the kiss.

"I, uh, I think we're good," she said.

"Yeah." He eased away from her. "We're all set."

"Right." She grabbed Buttercup off the couch, and the cat yowled at having been snatched from slumber. *Be still, you ingrate.* The feline settled in Chloe's arms—her furry, if begrudging, shield.

"Any suggestions?" he asked.

"Nope. Nailed it." She tried for a big smile. She was so full of it. She hadn't even heard that last part. "You've got this." Of course, with his scorching looks and tender phrases, Cate would be a fool to deny the man anything.

"Great. Good." He checked his watch. "I should be going anyway. I have—uh—errands. And stuff."

They still had a good hour before they had to be on set. Apparently she wasn't the only one eager for escape. Did he feel it too—that electric tension that connected them like a power cable? Was that why he'd seemed so distant since last night? She sensed the potent connection even in the moments when no one was around. When it was just the two of them talking, laughing, just being together. Or maybe he was just that good an actor. Maybe it was all in her head.

*You're an idiot, Chloe.*

She avoided eye contact all the way to the door, all the way through their awkward good-bye. Then she closed the door and sank against it, her heart giving one final shudder as Buttercup leaped from her arms and scampered away.

The bay was beautiful tonight. The sky was an inky canvas sparkling with a million diamonds. The pinpricks of light reflected off the sea, dazzling the surface. A warm breeze blew across the beach, carrying hints of salt and woodsmoke from a nearby fire.

The area was deserted except for cast and crew. Chloe settled on a chair in the video village. Her heels bounced on the footrest. Ledger and Cate would be at the waterline for most of the scene. The lighting crew had the area lit with an ethereal glow.

She spotted Liam and Daisy walking from the wardrobe trailer, unspeaking, their expressions serious and focused. There was no levity to the atmosphere tonight. They were behind schedule, they were filming a crucial scene, and no one wanted to mess it up.

Chloe tucked her trembling hands beneath her and watched the TV screen as the two actors took their places. Elliot relayed a message to them from Rex, then scurried off on some other errand. Simone and the others joined her in the video village some distance from the shore.

"I'm glad you could make it tonight," Simone said to Chloe. "Critical scene."

"Nice of you to schedule it for when the restaurant was closed."

"I do what I can," she said wryly as she put on her headphones.

Chloe did the same. Now she could hear the director giving final instructions to Daisy and Liam before stepping out of the shot.

A few minutes later the assistant director called, "Picture's up!" The set went quiet. "Roll sound, roll camera."

"Speed."

"Rolling."

The clapper sounded and the scene began.

Chloe's eyes were glued to the screen in front of her. The wind toyed with Daisy's long blonde hair. Liam's shirt glowed white under the mellow lights. Even without the movie magic that happened postproduction—angles, timing, music—Chloe fell into the scene. She felt the tug of emotions: one of them was fighting for love, the other fighting against it. The push and pull of their words, their tones, and their expressions had a visceral effect.

Cate pushed Ledger away and anger flared in his eyes. "That's right. Keep pushing me away. We both know that's not what you really want. You're just afraid. You're afraid to feel what I make you feel. You're scared to death and all you want to do is run. But I'm not gonna let you do that this time, Cate. You're gonna stay and face this once and for all."

He took her in his arms and kissed her.

The moment their lips touched, the couple ceased to be Ledger and Cate. They were Liam and Daisy. The Liam she'd come to know and care for. The Liam who teased and flirted and charmed. The Liam whose mouth had been on *hers* last night.

Chloe tensed as coldness swept through her, chilling her to the bone. Jealousy took root and sprouted tendrils that squeezed and strangled.

The kiss went on for hours.

Days.

Eons.

The light smattering of applause broke her train of thought. The embrace had finally ended, and the crew showed their appreciation for the actors' skills.

The script supervisor patted Chloe's leg. "Don't worry, sweetheart. He's just acting."

She must be so transparent. She tried for a smile. "Of course." Liam didn't really want to kiss Daisy Hughes. It was his job. He was only pretending.

The same way he'd pretended with Chloe. The thought made her stomach shrivel to the size of a bean.

The crew was already setting up for the next take. Sophía removed red smudges from Liam's mouth and touched up Daisy's lipstick. Powdered their noses. "There, *mis queridos*, pretty as a picture," Chloe heard through her headset.

If she was lucky, she'd only have to watch that kiss a dozen or so more times.

# Chapter 32

"How's filming going?" Spencer asked.

Liam set the phone to speaker, sprawled on a deck chair, and closed his eyes against the afternoon sun. "Great. We filmed a critical scene last night. Simone's very happy with it." They'd gone through twenty takes. The wind had wreaked havoc with Daisy's hair.

"Glad to hear it. The other project seems to be coming along nicely too. The photo of that hot kiss in the rain is going viral. Your fans are eating it up."

Liam clenched his jaw. "Good to know." He'd done a lot of thinking since that kiss three nights ago. It seemed pretty obvious now that she'd seen the photographers and staged the moment. She was the one who'd kissed him, after all.

His presence in her life boosted her exposure, gained her followers. She'd become a media darling. Her publisher was happy. People were reading her book. Sure, it had already been a bestseller, but there was always room to grow an audience. One could never sell too many books or have too many fans. Maybe it was about the movie too. The film was obviously important to her. Did she seek celebrity status?

Fame was addictive. One little taste and people got hooked. Did Chloe relish her newfound fame? Was she craving more? It didn't seem like the Chloe he knew. But then, he'd only known her a couple of months. And sometimes people surprised you. He'd been on the wrong end of that kind of revelation more than once.

"Liam? You still there?"

He'd completely missed that. "Sorry, what were you saying?"

"I said I sent out your mother's regular check. Have you heard from her lately?"

"Not really." That wasn't such a bad thing. Mom didn't communicate much unless she needed something.

"That's good, I guess."

He didn't want to talk about his mom. "How's Gwenn feeling? She's gotta be due soon."

"Not soon enough for her. She's still a few weeks away."

"You ready for that—two kiddos?"

Spencer chuckled. "Can't wait. Nolan's eager to meet his new sister. He keeps talking to her through Gwenn's belly. It's the cutest thing."

Liam's chest constricted at the image. What a life his friend had. Liam wasn't jealous of Spencer exactly. But he envied the place where he was in life. His obvious contentment. Liam had a feeling if Spencer's career was stripped away, he'd still be content with only his little family.

Liam wasn't sure he'd ever have that. He didn't even know how to go about getting it. He'd started thinking he might be able to have that kind of life with Chloe. And look how wrong he'd been. He'd begun entertaining those feelings. Had thought she was falling for him—the real him. He'd held out his heart and Chloe had stomped on it—albeit unknowingly. There was a reason he avoided relationships. He needed to remember that—especially where Chloe Anderson was concerned.

\* \* \*

The kiss had somehow changed things between them—and not in the ways Chloe had hoped. Liam hadn't called all week and they hadn't hung out except to run lines. There were perfunctory texts to handle details. And beyond that . . . radio silence.

When they ran lines she got the focused, businesslike Liam who appeared on set. No, not even that. After all, he joked around with the cast and crew between takes.

There was no joking between Liam and her. Not anymore. Chloe wasn't sure what had happened. He was getting exactly what he'd wanted. That kiss, as he'd no doubt planned, had certainly furthered his cause. His fans were swooning over Chliam, and their fake relationship was changing the narrative about him on the gossip sites.

Now he was depicted as a warm, caring man in a steady relationship. She had helped create that image, but now it only ticked her off. Because she hadn't seen hide nor hair of that warm, caring man since that stupid strategic kiss. Never mind that she'd initiated it.

He must be avoiding her because he'd seen through her. They both knew she was no good at hiding her feelings. He'd deduced she actually wanted the kiss and pulled back. Her cheeks burned.

The whole thing left her feeling like a fool.

So it was no surprise she was feeling a little testy as she approached him Friday morning at Waterfront Park. Because yes, since that uncomfortable kissing scene they'd rehearsed at her house, they'd only run lines in public.

He lounged in the freshly mown grass, knees up, arms resting on them, staring toward the sea. He wore sunglasses and a red ball cap pulled low. A script and water bottle sat beside him. Was he going over his lines in his head or plotting their next phony kiss?

She crossed over to the shaded patch of grass. The park was deserted this time of day, and the sun, hiding behind fluffy clouds, hadn't yet hiked the temperature. A squirrel scrambled across the sloped lawn, scaring a pair of seagulls into flight.

He straightened as he spotted her. "Hey." A week ago he would've stood. Maybe taken her hand or hugged her.

"Hey." She settled on the grass a safe distance away, trying to think of something to say. The next scenes, filming tonight, were from earlier in the script. They took place at a street fair, which unfortunately Chloe wouldn't witness since she had to work.

She cut him a glance. He was too handsome for his own good with his unshaven jawline and lips that were made for kissing. She didn't want to notice any of those things. She didn't want to feel the things he made her feel. Or remember the way his mouth had felt on hers, demanding yet reverent.

She shook the thoughts from her head.

He grabbed the script and opened it. "This one's fairly straightforward, I think."

He was doing perfectly fine with these scenes. She rarely had constructive criticism for him anymore. He had the part of Ledger down cold. Why was she putting herself through this? Oh well, she was here. They might as well run through it.

"Let's start at the top." She opened her script to one of the scenes that would film today. It was between Ledger and his brother. Liam began, playing off the complex family dynamics with target precision. Chloe did her best to match his skillful reading, but of course his performance outshone hers. He was Ledger in all the ways that mattered. He could put on the part and take it off again like a T-shirt. But that's what actors did.

It was a long scene, and Liam, unhappy with the first reading, wanted to run through it again. Chloe acquiesced.

In the middle of the scene he interrupted his own dialogue. "What's wrong?"

She blinked at him. "Nothing."

"We've been working for fifteen minutes, and you haven't made a single correction or so much as a comment."

"Because you're doing fine."

He smirked. "I'm doing fine."

What was his problem? "Yes, you're doing fine."

"That first read-through wasn't fine. It was mediocre at best."

"And we're running through it again. At least we were until you stopped to argue."

"I'm not arguing. I'm just asking why you're not giving me any input."

She huffed. "Because you're *fine*."

His lips tightened. His eyes probably snapped closed with frustration, but the sunglasses hid them. He glanced at the script. Took a moment to get into character and picked up where he'd left off.

She went through the rest of the scene mechanically. What was going on with him? Why was he so touchy? She was the one with feelings. The one who'd made a complete fool of herself. His mood impacted his reading. He was tense and the delivery sounded forced, even to her untrained ears.

He delivered the last line, then glanced her way, his expression unreadable.

"That was . . . fine."

He scowled. "That was terrible. Why don't you just say it?"

"Fine, it was terrible. Try it again."

He tossed the script to the grass. "What is going on with you?"

"With me? You're the one who's been so distant."

"*I've* been distant? You won't even tell me when my acting's bad. I thought you cared about this movie and your precious *Ledger*."

She saw her own eyes narrow in the reflection of his glasses. "Now you have a problem with the character? If you find him so ridiculous, why'd you even take the part? And would you please take off those stupid sunglasses?"

He ripped them off and tossed them onto the script. A storm was brewing in his eyes. "I have no problem with the character, but if you care so much, why aren't you critiquing my performance? I thought that was the whole point of this?"

"Not the *whole* point. We're also working on your little image problem, remember?"

He gave a mirthless chuckle. "Oh, you're definitely doing your part there."

A blast of heat erupted, spreading into her limbs, into her neck. "What's that supposed to mean?"

"Not a thing. You're right. We're working on my image and you're doing a bang-up job of it. You learn fast, I'll give you that."

She flinched. "Why does that sound like such an insult?"

"It's fine. I guess there's nothing wrong with being an opportunist. God knows I've been surrounded by them all my life."

She was on her feet before she even thought about it. *"Opportunist?"*

He rose to his feet, their gazes clashing as they faced off.

She wished she hadn't worn flats because he towered over her, and she hated giving him the advantage. She tried for a deep breath, but her lungs felt tight and rigid. "What are you talking about?"

"Come on, Chloe. I know you saw the paps the other night. And that's fine—it benefited me too."

Chloe froze. Her lungs hardened like cement. He thought she— Wait a minute.

"I know how this works. You're growing a readership, you're selling books. And now you're a media darling. You made a deal with me and it's working out for you in ways you hadn't expected. Hey, that's great."

He didn't sound like it was so great. And she didn't care for what he was insinuating. But apparently he hadn't called the reporters, and he hadn't been turned off by her obvious feelings for him. Yet that happy realization was offset by his accusation, and it somehow gave her the courage to admit the truth. "I didn't see the photographers, Liam."

He searched her face for a long moment.

She shelved her hands on her hips. "I thought *you* called them. And for the record, I don't have any desire to be in the spotlight, and enhancing my career or whatever else you're accusing me of was the last thing on my mind that night. I was just having a nice evening out. I was having fun and enjoying your company—and I thought you were enjoying mine too."

# Chapter 33

As Liam held Chloe's gaze, the air around them drained of tension like a balloon emptying of air. Her words reverberated in his head. *"I was having fun and enjoying your company—and I thought you were enjoying mine too."*

He had enjoyed her company that night. So much that if she hadn't leaned in for that kiss, he would've. And it had been amazing. The best kiss he'd ever had. Then the photographer called out.

And Liam made some assumptions.

He studied Chloe's features. Her eyes, even wider than usual, filling with tears. Her trembling chin.

Realization dawned. This was a terrible misunderstanding. He'd put all kinds of false motives on Chloe.

She wore her heart on her sleeve, a trait he'd always appreciated until now. Until it put tears in her eyes. Tears he'd caused. He should've known better. She was thoughtful and sweet, not manipulative and opportunistic. She wouldn't have crossed the kissing boundary for publicity.

Was he that jaded that he'd put such selfish motives on her? Had he been in Hollywood too long?

Apparently.

His lungs emptied and he closed his eyes in a long blink. "I am such an idiot. I'm sorry, Chloe. I don't know what I was— You're not an opportunist. I know that and I'm sorry I said it." He gave his head a shake. "That kiss was . . . It took me by surprise—in the best of ways. And then that photographer called out, and I thought you'd seen him before you kissed me. I thought——"

"That I saw him and used the moment as a photo op."

"I guess I was . . ." Wounded. Heartbroken. "Disappointed."

She gave him a long, searching look, her eyes softening to denim blue. "You were hurt."

She was right, but he was loath to admit it. Doing so made him vulnerable in a way he didn't exactly enjoy. But after making those accusations, the least he could do was give her the truth. "I was hurt." He held his breath, waiting for her to use his honesty against him.

"I thought *you* had staged the moment. After the kiss, you acted as if you'd known they were there all along."

Heat worked its way up his neck. "I was trying to save face—trying to see if you'd known they were there. But I shouldn't have done that. I'm sorry." He'd never been so honest in all his life. Apparently she brought this out in him. He hoped he didn't regret it.

Her gaze sharpened on him, and as the moment lengthened, her posture lost some of its rigidity. She tried for a smile. "I guess we both made some assumptions. I'm sorry too."

He wrapped his brain around the misunderstanding and came to a logical conclusion that buoyed his spirts. He took a step toward her. "So . . . just to be clear, when you kissed me, you actually meant it."

Her cheeks bloomed pink. "And when you kissed me back . . . you meant that too?"

"I wasn't pretending." His hands framed her face as he stared into those luminous eyes and told her the biggest truth of all. "I've never meant a kiss so much in all my life."

Her gaze fell to his mouth.

He leaned forward and brushed her mouth with his. They came together like magnets. His arms went around her. His hands mapped the curves of her shoulders, the small of her back. The indentation of her waist, the gentle swell of her hips.

Her fingers cut paths through his hair, knocking off his hat. Bringing every follicle to life. Her lips gave way beneath his and he feasted on them.

He couldn't believe she would forgive him so quickly, so easily. No silent treatment or guardedness. He wasn't used to this. The emotional honesty, the raw communication, the forgiveness, the closure. But what a fine ending to the suffering he'd endured the past week—all of it needless, as it turned out.

His previous relationships had been shallow, but he hadn't realized just how superficial until now. But there was a cost to this kind of intimacy. Laying his feelings on the line was terrifying. But Chloe hadn't taken advantage of his vulnerability. She would never. He didn't know her well, but he knew her well enough to know that. She brought out the best in him. Made him want to be a better man, a better person. And he wanted more of that.

More of her.

A squirrel nattering overhead interrupted his thoughts, reminding him they were in public and he was all but mauling her. She made him lose his mind.

Slowly, he ended the kiss.

Chloe gazed up at him. "Please tell me you didn't see paparazzi in the bushes."

He chuckled. "All clear." He couldn't care less who had seen their display of affection. He'd been so miserable all week, and now he was almost dizzy with relief. "I'm so glad we had that conversation."

"Apparently communication is key. Who knew?"

"We should definitely do more of that."

Her eyes twinkled. "I understand communication can come in many forms."

Of their own volition, his hands found the curve of her waist again. "Is that so?"

"That's what I hear."

"I look forward to exploring them all." And then he kissed her again.

# Chapter 34

The next three weeks Chloe floated on a cloud. Whenever she wasn't working or on set, she and Liam were together. They had coffee downtown or donuts at the bakery on the weekend. They had a picnic at the park. When they wanted privacy, they hung out at Liam's place or took the boat out on the creek.

There was a world of difference between fake dating and real dating. The fluttery feelings he stirred up in her never went away. She thought about him constantly. When she wasn't with him, she wished she were.

He was attentive and affectionate, always holding her hand or touching her face. Smiling with his eyes and his mouth. Chloe still kept up her end of the bargain, posting photos to her social media accounts. It felt so much different, so much better, now that the emotions behind them were real.

But according to Liam's manager, the media seemed to have moved on from Chliam. Now that Liam was in a settled relationship, he was no longer top billing. She hoped that wasn't a bad thing.

Chloe had quickly come clean to Meghan and Sean about the change in their relationship status. Meghan reacted with excitement. But it was no surprise when Sean did not. She told him one night before supper service started when he was prepping salads in the kitchen.

"You should probably know that Liam and I are in an actual relationship now."

He spared her a look. "As opposed to a fake one? How do you even know his feelings are real? He's an actor. Faking it is what he does for a living—and apparently he's pretty good at it."

Her chest tightened at his words. At the insecurity they stirred up in her. She shoved it into the box where she stuffed all her self-doubts. "He makes me happy, Sean. Maybe you don't think I'm enough to hold his interest—a big celebrity like him—but he makes me feel like I'm the only woman in the world."

Sean scowled. "That's not what I think at all. You're too good for him, not the other way around."

"You don't even know him."

"And I won't really have the chance, will I?"

Because yes, the movie would wrap soon. It wasn't as if the thought didn't plague her late at night. The feelings his departure conjured reminded her of when she'd been afraid of the dark as a child. She always slept with her bedside lamp on. But one night she awakened and her room was pitch black. Her heart raced and felt as if it would explode. She couldn't even gather breath to call out for her mom as panic slammed into her like a tidal wave.

She'd overcome that fear as she grew older. But oddly, she still had that same sensation whenever she felt especially vulnerable. Like when she told a boyfriend how she felt. Or the times she'd tried to tell Evan why her father had left. Or when she thought of Liam leaving. That same feeling of panic, of breathlessness, consumed her.

"He's gonna go back to Hollywood, back to his fancy life and his old ways, Chloe. And then what?"

Geography would be a challenge, but they'd figure it out. Wouldn't they? She tied her apron strings with more force than necessary. "I'd appreciate it if you'd just support me, Sean."

"Like you support Meghan and me? Your thoughts on that couldn't have been clearer."

She snorted. Meghan was only Sean's flavor of the month. "Please. That's hardly the same thing."

"Sure, Chloe. Whatever."

Her brother was the farthest thing from her mind as she sat across from Liam over coffee a week later. The shop had emptied of its early morning crowd, so they'd had their pick of tables. Chloe had always loved the eclectic feel of the place with its mismatched furniture and twinkle lights strung across the ceiling.

They sipped their drinks and worked on an enormous cinnamon roll as they chatted. Liam looked handsome, if a bit tired from their late nights. He no longer wore his ball cap in public. Townsfolk usually respected their privacy, though occasionally a tourist would recognize him. He was always gracious, stopping to chat, take a selfie with them, or sign something.

But there was no fear of a scene this morning as they were tucked away in a corner and the place was practically empty. Liam had to be on set at eleven. The filming was going great and was expected to wrap in a week.

She eyed his lovely hands as he took a bite and set down his fork. Then she laced her fingers with his, reveling in their size and strength. "I've always liked your hands."

His eyes smiled just before his lips. "I know."

Remembering her medication episode, she felt heat bloom in her cheeks. "A gentleman would forget such things ever happened."

"Now, now. You also told me you liked being my girlfriend, and I kept that all to myself, didn't I?"

She gasped. "I did not say that."

"You most certainly did."

"You never told me that."

He gave that low, sexy chuckle. "I didn't want to embarrass you."

Well, that was kind of sweet. Her heart swelled a size or two. "Trust me, I was already plenty embarrassed."

"You were pretty darn cute that night. Those pills were like truth serum." His eyes twinkled. "Maybe I should keep some on hand."

"Hey!" She tapped his hand with her fork. "I was having a health crisis."

"And believe me, I was plenty worried until the doctor eased my mind."

He really was sweet. How else would he surprise her? She wanted to know everything about him. "What do you do for fun back in LA when you're not filming movies and attending premieres?"

"Well, let's see. I like to read. I enjoy a game of hoops now and then. There's a youth club nearby that's sponsored by my foundation. I like to hang out with the kids there sometimes."

She stopped chewing. "You have a foundation?" She hadn't read anything about this on the gossip sites.

"It's called At Risk Youth of California—ARYC for short. We've opened up seventeen centers across the state so far. It gives teens something to do after school and during the summer. We have volunteers who help with homework too."

He seemed to be downplaying his role. "Wow, that's amazing. What got you interested in that?"

He lifted a shoulder. "I had too much time on my hands growing up. Not that I got into major trouble, but I was bored and a little lonely. There are a lot of kids out there going through that and worse. What about you? What do you like to do when you're not working?"

She was still taking in the fact that he'd started his own foundation. "Well, like you I like to read. As I mentioned before, I also like to kayak a lot. Hang out with Meghan. Eat chocolate. That's really about it."

Liam's phone buzzed and he checked the screen. "Spencer, reminding me of my phone interview with *People* magazine tomorrow night."

"That's a pretty big score, isn't it?"

"It's significant. And it's always good to keep my name out there, especially since I haven't had a film release in over a year. I'll plug the movie too, of course. Things have been a little too quiet for Spencer's liking the past couple weeks. He has some publicity planned for me once I'm back home."

And there was that awful pit in the center of her chest. What would happen to them once he left? Was Sean right? Would Liam just go back to his old ways? She'd hinted at the subject of their impending separation, but they hadn't really talked about it. Maybe it was time. If nothing else, perhaps it would set her mind at ease.

Chloe plunged in. "Have you scheduled your flight back to LA?"

He gave her a wan smile. "I'm flying back the day after filming wraps. I have an event to get back to, unfortunately, so I can't hang around any longer than that." He forked a bite of the roll and stuck it in his mouth.

"I see. Have you, um, thought about how things might look, you know, once you're back home?"

"You mean with us?"

She nodded as she picked at the pastry. Tried her best for a casual expression even as she reminded herself to breathe and tried to ignore the way her heart palpitated in her chest.

He waved his fork. "Plenty of ways to stay in touch these days. And my schedule is somewhat flexible, so that's good."

"Yeah, sure." What did that even mean? That he would fly here occasionally? He seemed kind of vague about their future. But maybe it was too early in their relationship for permanent plans. Never mind that her feelings had grown deep roots over the past few months. Or the dawning realization that she just might be falling in love with him.

He squeezed her hand. "You're important to me, Chloe. We'll figure out the distance thing. I'm not worried about it."

She could see that. But if she were important to him, wouldn't he want some kind of plan in place? His response did nothing to assuage the panicked feeling swelling inside her.

Liam's phone buzzed on the table and he checked the screen again. "Spencer again?"

"No. It's my mom."

She took in his crestfallen expression. "She okay?"

He met her gaze, then his lips twisted. "She's never really okay."

He hadn't talked much about his parents and she hadn't pried. But they were opening up to each other more and more. "What do you mean?"

He picked at the roll a moment before answering. "I mentioned a while back that she never got over my dad. And she used to have a job at the bank to pay the bills. She did all right. But over the years her drinking has gotten out of control, and she's had trouble holding down a job. Then my career took off and now she kind of . . . depends on me, I guess."

"Financially, you mean?"

Liam gave a nod. "Partly. She checks in on me and she loves me and everything, don't get me wrong. But you know, I have plenty of money and she is my mom. I don't mind helping her out."

Which one of them was he trying to convince? And it sounded as if he was doing a lot more than just helping her out. Her heart clenched. "That's very generous of you, Liam."

"Not a big deal. But she's been asking for more lately—on top of the usual bills." He made a face. "I feel like an ingrate for even mentioning it. She raised me as a single mom. Maybe she wasn't, you know, that attentive and stuff, but she took care of me in her own way."

Chloe studied his expression and saw the little boy who perhaps didn't get all the love and affection a child should receive. It put a pinch in her chest. Boy, people's lives were not always the way they appeared from the outside. "If you're feeling used or taken advantage of—you have a right to your feelings."

He offered a smile. "Still, she's my mom."

"It sounds as if she needs more help than you can give. Do you think she's an alcoholic?"

"I do and I've said as much. But she either doesn't believe it's true or won't admit it. Whenever I try to talk to her about quitting, I never get anywhere. If she could just get over my dad and move on . . . I feel like she wouldn't need the alcohol. It's just a Band-Aid for her broken heart."

"That's really sad. Maybe a steady job would be good for her. She wouldn't have so much time on her hands. Pursuing other interests could open up a new world for her. Allow her to meet new people, not to mention make a little money."

"No doubt. But whenever I mention applying for another job, she— Well, it's not like I don't have the money to help her out. And being generous never hurt anyone."

She put her hand on his. "It sounds like it's hurting you." And enabling his mom's addiction. But it wasn't her place to say so.

He laced his fingers with hers, gazing at her with affection. "You're really sweet, Chloe. I'm sure it'll work itself out. Thank you for listening."

"Parent-child relationships can be pretty complicated sometimes."

"That's true." He tilted his head, studying her. "Your parents seem pretty awesome though."

"Mom and Dad? Sure." She took a sip of her mocha. "My real father's another story, however."

"You haven't told me much about him. Just that he's out of the picture."

She'd never told anyone except Meghan what had happened all those years ago. There were times she'd wanted to tell Evan, but that terrible suffocating feeling always stopped her from laying herself open that way. But now, gazing into Liam's earnest eyes—and knowing a little of what he'd endured—she felt the courage to tell him.

"My dad was a sales rep for some pharmaceutical company, so he was gone a lot. I remember being excited every time he came home. Sean and I would wait in the picture window for him to pull into the drive. Mom let us stay up late sometimes, waiting for him. Sean always gave him one of his stuffed animals to take along on his trip. Being a little older, he has more memories of our father than I do.

"Anyway, one day after he came home, Mom found an airline ticket stub in his pocket—it was for a flight to Hartford, Connecticut, and he'd told her he'd gone to Indianapolis. She confronted him and there was a big fight, and he convinced her it was all a misunderstanding. Sean and I didn't know these details then—Mom told us when we were older.

"A few days later he left for another trip, and by then Mom had a gut feeling he'd lied to her. She started doing some research. Long story short, she discovered he was married to someone else. That he had another family in Hartford: a wife and a daughter."

"Oh no. How awful."

"Needless to say, Mom was completely shocked, not to mention devastated. According to public records he'd married this woman a few years before he'd met Mom on a business trip here. I guess he fell in love with her, and they married less than a year later. Never mind the wife he already had."

"So your parents' marriage wasn't even legal."

"Nope."

"Man, your poor mom. I can't even imagine."

"She pulled herself together and when he came home she confronted him. There was no denying it—she had public records as proof." Chloe smirked. "He actually begged her not to tell his other wife. Can you imagine? Apparently that was his only concern. Talk about a final death blow to my mom."

"What nerve. I assume she didn't give in to his pleas."

"Oh no. My dad packed up his things. He said good-bye to Sean and me—I vividly remember that. I thought he was just leaving for a business trip, but his eyes were puffy and red-rimmed. I knew he'd been crying, but I didn't understand why he was so upset. And I sure didn't realize it would be the last time I'd see him."

"Oh, Chloe." Liam pressed a kiss to her hand. "That's awful. I'm so sorry that happened to you."

The memory always left her feeling so ashamed. Like there must be something wrong with her if even her dad didn't love her. If he left her and never came back. After all, he had no problem being a father to his other daughter. Her eyes stung with tears, and her face filled with heat. The shame still held her in its grip all these years later. Good grief, maybe she needed therapy to resolve this.

She swallowed back the lump in her throat and shifted her thoughts. "Looking back now, I'm so proud of my mom. She was downright stoic. She picked up the pieces and went on. And yes, she did call that other wife—Maeve Daniels. But apparently the woman somehow forgave my father because they're still married. Or they were last time I heard."

"So there was no need for your mom to divorce him or anything. Was your father held accountable legally? He broke the law."

"Bigamy is a felony but it's rarely prosecuted. However, he cared deeply about his reputation and his career, so my mom decided to use that in her favor. Since our financial well-being was about to take a big hit, she threatened to sue him in a civil case. He decided it was in his best interest to settle. That's how she got the funds to buy and renovate Docksiders."

Liam grinned. "Good for her. She must be one strong woman."

"She is. But as you can imagine, she didn't particularly want word getting out around here. Small town and all that. The scuttlebutt was that she'd kicked him out for being unfaithful and they divorced and he never returned."

"He got off pretty easy to my way of thinking. And I can't imagine how a man could desert his kids like that. You must've been so confused."

The pain of her father's abandonment never quite left. "Honestly, it's still baffling. I remember him as being an involved dad when he was home. He'd make pancakes in funny shapes. He taught me to swim and took us fishing." She'd thought he loved them. But love didn't run away. It didn't desert. She blinked against the swell of tears in her eyes. "Sorry. It was all so long ago. I don't know why this is hitting me fresh."

Liam took hold of her chin. "You don't have anything to be sorry for. As for your dad, he has no idea what he's missing out on. I almost feel sorry for him."

Chloe gave a mirthless laugh. "Almost but not quite?"

"He doesn't deserve you. But you and Sean sure deserved a lot better."

Chloe took his hand and pressed a kiss to his palm. "I think that might be something we have in common."

# Chapter 35

Liam closed his eyes as Sophía powdered his face between takes.

"Why are the good complexions always wasted on the men?" she asked.

"If I have such a good complexion, why are you always covering it up under layers of makeup?"

"I have to at least act like I am earning my wages." She tsked. "This sun is ruining my good work. I will be glad to return to the dry California climate. This heat and humidity is for the birds. There, the shine is gone—for all of two minutes, I am sure."

When she moved on to Daisy, Liam chugged from his water bottle and glanced at Chloe in the video village. She tossed her head back, laughing at something Simone said. The sun hit her brown waves, bringing out copper highlights. Her smile dazzled. *She* dazzled, from the inside out. She lit him up and he was finding he couldn't get enough of her. He'd never felt this way about another woman. The thought struck him like a punch to the gut.

He was in love with Chloe.

This wasn't an emotion he'd experienced before, and still he somehow knew with every fiber in his being that he felt it now. The realization left him breathless. As if a cement block were sitting on his chest, inhibiting its rise and fall.

He was flying back to LA in a week. He hadn't let himself think about it much, not even when Chloe had brought it up. Because every time he did, he got this terrible ache inside as he imagined hundreds of miles separating them. He hadn't meant for this to happen. Hadn't meant to fall head over heels for Chloe—or for anyone for that matter. The fondness he'd felt for certain women in his life had been easy and comfortable.

This love left him feeling dizzy and heady and somehow completely out of control. Daunting. He wasn't sure he liked feeling this way. Which was weird, right? People loved falling in love. That's why so many writers penned songs and stories about it. But the realization that he'd lost his heart to Chloe left him shaken.

"Looks like you two are getting pretty serious."

Daisy had approached while he'd been staring at Chloe like a lovesick teenager.

"She's something else." An understatement. She'd been through a lot—her whole family had—and yet she'd managed to grow into a strong, capable woman. A loving woman. It only made him respect her more.

Daisy's eyes twinkled. "She must be special to have turned your head. When do you return to LA?"

"Day after we wrap. You?"

"Same, but I'm flying to New York—that's where David lives. We have some final wedding plans to go over, then we'll fly to Malibu for the big day."

"That's right. It's just a couple weeks away, isn't it?"

"Two weeks from tomorrow. I can hardly wait. David said you RSVP'd, so I guess we'll see you there. I hope Chloe can make it."

He hadn't even thought to mention the wedding to her. "I'll check on that. But it's hard for her to get away because of the restaurant."

Later, after they wrapped for the night, he thought about those words on the short drive home to do the phone interview with *People.* It might be hard for Chloe to get away from the restaurant. He wouldn't mind coming back here—it would be worth seeing her. But if he was the only one making room in his schedule, that wouldn't give them as much opportunity to be together.

And the thought of how much he would miss her between visits made him ache inside. Made him wonder if he could do this. If he *wanted* to do this. For some reason the image of his mom, wasting away for want of his father, stole into his mind like an audacious intruder. The thought made him squirm in his seat until he shoved it far away.

* * *

Saturday night Docksiders was hopping. A local country band blared cover songs for the lively gathering. Even at ten o'clock the savory smell of grilled steaks and seafood gumbo wafted in the air. A light breeze blew off the bay, fluttering the umbrellas on the deck.

It was the last day of August and the summer crowd had already begun to thin. Soon fall would usher in cooler evenings, and the beaches would grow quieter. The downtown shops would move their wares off the sidewalks and shorten their hours.

Perhaps Chloe could take a few weeks off during the winter and fly to LA, depending on Liam's schedule. She had trouble even envisioning his life there. Envisioning herself there. All she knew for certain was that in six days he was leaving, and she didn't know when she would see him again.

"Sweetheart, could you help Stella with her order, please?" Mom called as she passed with a tray of desserts.

"Sure thing, Mom."

The new server hadn't adapted to their on-screen ordering system. Chloe headed over and helped her get the order in. Then she stopped by a table that had just received their meals. "How does everything look, folks? Is your steak cooked to order?"

The middle-aged woman frowned at her rib eye. "Would you mind putting mine back on for a few minutes?"

"Of course not. I'll get this right back to you." Chloe carried the plate to the kitchen, where Sean put it back on the grill.

Before she could make it far, the hostess called her to the stand, where a couple waited for a table. "There's a call for you on line two, Miss Chloe."

It was too noisy for a phone conversation. "Thank you. I'll take it in the office."

Once she arrived at her office, she picked up the phone and hit the button.

"Docksiders, this is Chloe."

"Hey, Chloe, sorry to bother you at work."

Meghan's delivery was rushed—and she never called the restaurant's landline. "What's wrong? Are you okay?"

"I'm fine, but I'm afraid I have some upsetting news for you."

"That doesn't sound good. Let me get the door." Chloe closed it, ushering in relative silence even as she braced for bad news. "Okay, what's going on? Are you all right?"

"I'm fine. But I was poking around online, reveling in your new-found fame, and I came across something disturbing. Seems like it just posted this afternoon. Chloe . . . they know about your father."

Chloe froze, the phone plastered to her ear. "What do you mean?"

"They know everything. His illegal marriage to your mom, his name, the fact that he has another family, that he left and never returned . . ."

Dread weighted her stomach. "That's—that's not possible."

"I'm so sorry."

The whole world was now privy to her private business? Her deepest wound and hard-won scar was now exposed for a bunch of nosy fans to pick at? Not to mention how this might affect Mom and Sean.

How had this happened? It was all her fault. She was the one who'd stepped into the spotlight. Chloe cupped her forehead as she grappled for a solution. "If it was just posted, maybe we can get it taken down."

"I've been looking around. The story's already been picked up by a few sites. People are talking about it on social media."

"*No.*" There was no pulling something back once it went viral. Her eyes stung with tears. How could this be happening?

"I know this is upsetting, honey. But you didn't do anything wrong. It was your father's problem, not yours or your mom's or Sean's. The comments have been mostly sympathetic toward you guys."

"Oh great, they feel sorry for us. How did this happen?"

The door opened, music blaring, and Sean shoved his head inside. "Mom wanted to know if you can— What's wrong?"

Chloe was at a loss for words. And so many emotions were roiling through her that she didn't know which one to focus on first. She put Meghan on speaker. "Sean's here, Meghan. Can you tell him what happened? For heaven's sake, shut the door."

Sean did as she asked, his gaze sharpening on her. It wasn't like her to snap.

"I was looking around online," Meghan said, "and I came across some unfortunate information. The media knows about what your father did to you guys. They know his name and everything, and the story's being reported on multiple sites."

Sean pinned Chloe with a stare. "What? How did this happen?"

"I know, I can't believe it myself. I just don't understand how—" Chloe cut off as Sean's eyes narrowed on her.

"I'll tell you how it happened. You put yourself in the spotlight. You made yourself a household name. Now those vultures are crawling all over, pecking away at any carcass they can find."

"I couldn't have known this would happen, Sean." Still, a wave of shame washed over Chloe. Because he was right. It didn't explain how they'd discovered the skeleton in their closet, but she'd all but begged for their interest by entering Liam's world.

"What site did this start on, Meghan?" Sean asked in a much gentler voice. "Can you tell?"

"Let me see. Give me a second."

"There's no way a reporter could've found this on his own, is there?" Chloe said. "There would've been no record of divorce. Their so-called marriage wouldn't still be on record."

"Mom told us she'd had it annulled, and that would've removed the marriage entirely from public records."

"Then how could they have found out? Have you told anyone at all?"

"No, never. I think Mom only told Aunt Sharon and Uncle Ernie, and they would never divulge this."

Chloe agreed. They would never humiliate Mom this way. "There's only a handful of people who know." She'd only ever told Meghan—and then Liam two days ago. A sick feeling stirred in her stomach. But he would never . . .

Sean's gaze sharpened on Chloe's face. "What? What are you thinking?"

"Nothing," she said weakly.

"Guys," Meghan said, "I think it was *People* magazine who reported the story first."

Chloe froze. Liam had had an interview with *People* yesterday— the day after she'd confided in him about her father. Bile rose to the back of her throat. She put her hand there as if she could stop the burning sensation. It couldn't be true. He wouldn't do that to her. He had to know what a sensitive subject this was, and he cared about her. Didn't he?

"Great," Sean said. "They'll probably put it in their magazine, too, the filthy vipers." His attention flittered to Chloe and stuck there. "What? You're holding something back. What aren't you telling us?"

She couldn't seem to control her shallow breaths. And her heart felt as if it might leap from her chest. "I—I might've told Liam about our father recently."

Understanding dawned in Sean's eyes. Then they went deadly narrow. "I'm gonna kill him."

"That doesn't mean he did it. He wouldn't do that."

"Oh really? Seems pretty obvious to me that he would—and *did*."

"Chloe," Meghan said, "I don't mean to pile on, but didn't Liam have an interview with *People* recently?"

Chloe's eyes locked on Sean's. Admitting it would damn Liam in Sean's eyes. But it was obvious he'd already made up his mind anyway. She released the words reluctantly. "His interview was yesterday."

"You've gotta be kidding me!"

"That's not proof, Sean," Chloe said. "It's possible the marriage record is still out there somewhere, isn't it? Or—or that someone else knows and told the media."

"Why are we even discussing it?" Sean barked. "We all know who's responsible for this."

"We don't know for sure. You never liked him to begin with." While Chloe might be reluctant to admit Liam would do something like this, Sean's opinion was subjective.

Her friend, however, was more objective and she'd always been a voice of reason. Chloe glanced at the phone, her left eye twitching. The seafood gumbo she'd had before dinner service roiled in her stomach, threatening to make an appearance. "Meghan . . . ? What do you think?"

There was a long pause. "I'm sorry, honey. I know you care about him, but I don't know how else they could've found out. And it's a little too convenient that you just told him and that he interviewed with the magazine yesterday."

Chloe didn't want to believe it could be true. But the evidence was strong, and she was no doubt blinded by love. She remembered the things he'd said recently about needing to stay on the media's radar. And how noncommittal he'd been about their long-distance relationship. Was that because he knew it was about to end?

This didn't seem consistent with the Liam she'd come to know and love. But people weren't always who you thought they were. Sometimes they failed you. Caring fathers left. Loving boyfriends cheated. Somehow she'd forgotten that.

She had to face facts. Liam had betrayed her. How ironic that the first man she'd trusted with her deepest wound was the man who'd least deserved that trust. She blinked back tears.

Sean's expression softened. "We need to tell Mom what's happened before she hears it from someone else. I hope this doesn't cause bigger problems."

"What do you mean?"

"She signed an NDA with dear old Dad. He won't be happy about this getting out. What if he sues her and the courts make her pay back all that money she won in the civil suit?"

"Can they do that? She didn't reveal anything. This isn't her fault."

"I don't know. I guess we'll find out."

This situation just kept getting worse. Chloe had to get it together. One way or another this was her fault. She was the one who'd brought this media attention—and Liam—into their lives. And she was the one who'd take responsibility for it.

"I'll tell her," she said.

# Chapter 36

Liam should've gone to bed an hour ago. He set his phone on the nightstand and turned out the light. It had been a long day on set, but now they were running a day ahead of schedule. Which meant filming would wrap in four days. It also meant he'd have a whole day free to spend with Chloe before he flew home. That was something to smile about.

Tomorrow at sunrise they'd shoot the last chronological scene of the movie. It would show Ledger and Cate's future together, giving moviegoers a chance to savor the characters' happily ever after. Liam had taken special care with his lines since the timing would be critical—sunrises didn't last long.

A text buzzed in and he considered ignoring it. Four a.m. would come early. But it was just after eleven and Chloe would be getting off work. He grabbed his phone and opened the text. It was from Chloe.

*Just tell me why you did it.*

He frowned at the message. Read it again. Maybe she'd intended to send this to someone else. He replied, *What?* After sending it he waited for her to acknowledge her mistake. But that's not what happened.

*Don't play dumb. Just answer the question.*

The text hadn't been a mistake. A terrible dread slithered up his spine. His blood pressure shot up by fifty points as he sat up in bed. He reread the texts. What was he missing? He gave his head a sharp shake.

He was done with this texting nonsense. He tapped on her contact number and soon the phone began ringing. He waited for her to answer, his pulse thumping in his temples, but it rang until voice mail picked it up.

Seriously? He disconnected the call and texted her. *Pick up the phone, Chloe.*

He called again. But it rang through to voice mail. He gritted his teeth. What was going on? This wasn't like her at all. He sent another text. *Why won't you answer the phone?* The temperature in his room seemed to have risen by ten degrees. As he shoved off the covers, a new text appeared.

*I don't want to talk to you. I just want you to answer my question.*

His thumbs shook as he tapped the virtual keyboard with more force than necessary. *That's kind of hard when I don't know what you're talking about!* He stabbed the Send button and waited.

And waited.

What could he have done to upset her like this? She'd been fine this afternoon on set before she'd gone to work. What could've happened between then and now?

Another text appeared. *Maybe you haven't seen your handiwork yet. But don't worry, I'm sure you'll get everything you wanted. And in case I haven't been clear enough, we're done.*

Adrenaline pumping through his veins, he jumped from the bed and paced as he read her text once. Twice. He couldn't make sense of it.

What was she talking about? He reread the entire thread.

"Seen my handiwork?" he muttered. "Get everything I wanted?"

He was at a loss. Could this have something to do with the media? Where else could he "see his handiwork"? Maybe one of the sites had posted some old picture of him with another woman and claimed he was cheating on her. But Chloe now knew better than to believe something like that, didn't she?

He did a Google search using his name, something he never did. But there were too many hits to wade through. After a minute he figured out how to narrow them down to the past twenty-four hours. Quite a few hits appeared, including *People* magazine, which was right at the top.

He clicked on it, mentally reviewing everything he'd said in his interview yesterday. He couldn't think of anything that would warrant Chloe's anger though. He'd talked about the movie and—

His thoughts came to an abrupt halt at the headline: "The Scandalous Scoop Behind Liam's Lover." His stomach dropped as his gaze fell to the photo, a zoomed-in photo of him and Chloe at the Fourth of July parade, happy and cozy as they waved their flags. He skipped to the article.

*"It turns out Liam Hamilton isn't the only part of Chliam with a scandalous past. Chloe Anderson, the wholesome author who recently captured Liam's heart, also has a shocking past. It appears her mother's marriage to her pharmacy-rep father, Ted Daniels, was annulled because he'd already been married when he met her. The bigamist left Chloe's family when he was exposed and, according to our source, has never contacted them again. Though bigamy is a felony, Daniels was never prosecuted; however, Chloe's mother had her day in court. She was later awarded damages in a civil suit to the tune of half a million dollars."*

A fist tightened in Liam's gut. He could only imagine how Chloe felt to have this painful experience exposed for public consumption. But why would she believe he was responsible? Yes, he'd been interviewed by *People*, but surely she knew he'd never betray her confidence like this.

He glanced at the short scoop. There was nothing in here that related to yesterday's interview. Someone else, some "source," had apparently preempted his article. After all, this story was more salacious than anything he'd revealed.

*I just saw the article. You cannot believe I would do this to you! I would never betray your confidence like that. You have to know that. I never told the guy from People anything about your family.* He sent the message and started to type more.

But beneath his text bubble the red words "not delivered" appeared. Frowning, he tried to send the text again.

The same message popped up.

He let out a huff of disbelief. Had she blocked him? She must've. He'd taken so long to respond that she'd given up on him. He wanted to throw his phone across the room.

He had to do something. He had to convince Chloe he had nothing to do with this. But what could he do? Go bang on her door?

Something gave him pause. He tossed his phone on the bed and planted his hands on his hips as he paced the room. He couldn't believe she thought he'd do this. What had he ever done to make her think he was that kind of person? She should know him better than this.

But maybe she didn't know him at all. Maybe he'd only been kidding himself. Maybe she only saw him as Liam the Hollywood celebrity the way everyone else did. This was certainly something a celebrity might do to capture the spotlight. To make himself relevant. Never mind that Liam would never.

She had to be deeply hurt that this private thing was now public. And he'd been in this business long enough to know the story had already gone viral. Other sites would've quickly picked it up; his fans would be tweeting about it.

His heart squeezed in sympathy. He wanted to hold her and assure her it would get better. That her father's duplicity had nothing to do with her, that what he'd done was on him.

At the same time, everything in him wanted to go over there and defend himself. But should he really have to? Shouldn't she believe him innocent until she had some kind of proof? Or at least offered him the chance to explain? Anger flared up, tensing every

muscle in his body. She hadn't even asked him if he'd done it—
she'd accused him.

He wanted to tell her he'd never hurt her like that. Never betray
her. That he loved her. But what was the point? Did he really want
to be involved with someone who would so easily believe terrible
things about him? The media printed lies about him on a regular ba-
sis. Would she just believe them all? Would he come home to accusations of infidelity simply because some journalist thought it would
make a good story?

She obviously didn't fit into his world. Hadn't he said all along he
should stick to someone in the industry? He should've listened to his
gut. There was a reason celebrities married other celebrities.

He sank onto the bed, willing his heart to slow down before it
burst from his chest. But it felt as if it had already shattered into a
million pieces.

# Chapter 37

Chloe's alarm blared at o-dark-hundred. She groaned as she turned it off and rolled over. She couldn't bring herself to get out of bed and go to set. Couldn't bring herself to face the man she loved—the one who'd betrayed her so cruelly, so publicly.

Who did that?

A person who put his career ahead of everything and everyone else, that's who.

She'd hoped for an answer to her question last night—something less painful than what she'd come to believe. And when he called her, she was so tempted to answer. But she knew herself. Liam could be very convincing—he was an actor for heaven's sake—and she was afraid she'd be susceptible to his lies. God knew she wanted to believe he was innocent.

She just had to get through the next few days and then he'd go back to Hollywood. Back to his regular life. And she could go on with hers. Maybe she wouldn't even return to the set; it wasn't as if they needed her. She didn't make any real decisions, and the filming was pretty much in the bag anyway. She sure didn't want to face any reporters who might be hanging around town. She'd already received two voice mails in the night asking for interviews. She'd blocked them too. But tabloid reporters were like roaches—where there was one, there were a hundred. She might have to change her phone number before all was said and done.

She thought back to last night when she'd had to break the news to her mom. She took it with grace and focused on comforting Chloe and Sean and assuring them everything would be okay. Clearly she'd recovered from Ted Daniels's abandonment in ways Chloe hadn't. Just what she wanted to lie here thinking about at four in the morning.

Sunday and Monday dragged by. Since the restaurant was closed she hid out at her house. Monday night she heard from Sean. He'd consulted a local attorney about their mom's NDA. Their father would have no case since Mom hadn't been responsible for the leak. Of course, their father couldn't know that. But he'd find out quickly enough if he dared to file a lawsuit. Now that they'd had time to digest the information, they doubted he would. It would only bring more attention to what he'd done.

On Tuesday Meghan stopped over. It was past noon and Chloe was still in her pajamas when she answered the door. She hadn't showered or even combed her hair.

Meghan took one peek at her and frowned. "Come on, friend. You can't hole up here forever. You need to grab a shower, then I'm taking you for coffee."

Losing the fight with gravity, Chloe plopped on the sofa, disturbing Buttercup, who gave her a sour look. "I have coffee here." She hadn't made any, but still.

"That's hardly the point. It's been three days and you need to start getting on with your life."

"Two and a half. And I'll do just that as soon as there's no chance of running into He Who Must Not Be Named."

Meghan stood in front of her, arms crossed. "This isn't like you. You're missing the last days of the filming of your movie! Where's your pride? Your fighting spirit? You have more heart than anyone I know."

Meghan became hazy as Chloe's vision blurred with tears. "My heart's been smashed to smithereens."

Her friend's expression softened. She sagged onto the sofa and gathered Chloe close. "I'm so sorry, honey. He's a real jerkwad for what he did."

That was about as malicious as Meghan ever got. Chloe leaned into her friend and let the tears come for a few minutes.

"It's not just what he did," Chloe said once she'd gathered herself. "Though that's bad enough. This whole thing has triggered all the pain from my father's rejection. Like it's compounded because now I'm dealing with two betrayals."

"That makes all the sense in the world. But you know what your father did was no reflection on you, right?"

"I know that in my head. I can reason like an adult now, and I know sometimes parents mess up because *they're* messed up. But deep down I'm kind of afraid there's something wrong with me. My father left and never came back, Meghan. Yet he stuck around for his other daughter. What did she have that I didn't have?" Pain unfurled in her chest. More tears prickled her eyes.

"Oh, sweetheart, not a single thing. I can't explain how a man could do that to his child. I just know it's nothing to do with you. Because you are a wonderful person and you make my life so much brighter. He left Sean, too, you know. Do you think there's something lacking in him? Or in your mom?"

"Of course not."

"There you go, then." She threw a hand up. "Clearly your biological father is a whackadoodle."

Chloe huffed a laugh.

"Plus I'm always right about these things."

Chloe sniffled. "That's true, you are."

"Then be smart and listen to your friend." She kissed the top of Chloe's head and pulled back. "I'm also right about you needing to get out of the house." She wrinkled her nose. "And about that shower. So off you go. I'll be waiting right here for you."

*I'm gonna kill Meghan.*

Chloe sat in the video village the next day, watching on-screen as the crew began yet another take of the last scene they'd film. Her friend had talked her into coming today. *"You'll feel better if you face this head-on. You have nothing to be ashamed of—quite the opposite! And you shouldn't let him rob you of seeing your movie's last day of filming."*

From the moment Chloe had spotted Liam on the end of the marina's pier, she'd felt awkward and uncomfortable. She'd come today perfectly prepared to be cordial despite the terrible turn their relationship had taken.

But as far as Liam was concerned, she wasn't worthy of so much as a glance. She might as well be a production assistant. No, not even that. Liam was friendly with everyone on set no matter their place in the crew hierarchy. It was as if she were completely invisible.

Watching Liam in action was hard. He was obviously doing just fine without her instruction. She thought back to the first days of filming when she was so concerned with his portrayal of Ledger. That all seemed so meaningless now. Who cared about her perfect book boyfriend when her actual life had become so complicated and messy and painful?

The scene ended. There was a pause. Then the assistant director called, "It's a wrap! Good job, Daisy and Liam. Thank you, everyone!"

A ripple of applause sounded. Then the crew went into action, cleaning up the set and storing the equipment, eager to be on their way.

As she stood, Chloe caught a glance of Liam embracing Daisy. She jerked her gaze away.

Simone nudged her. "Well, we've done all we can. Now it's time for postproduction to do their magic."

"Everyone did an amazing job."

"I'm so glad you're pleased. Rex is a genius, isn't he?"

"He certainly is." She'd been intimidated by the director at first, but he'd turned out to be a big teddy bear. A seriously talented teddy bear.

"You're coming to the wrap party tomorrow, aren't you?"

After the awkwardness of today, it was a hard pass for her. "Unfortunately, I have to work. But you have a great time. You certainly earned it. And thank you so much for all the work you've put into this movie. I know it'll be wonderful."

Simone hugged her. "It was a pleasure. Keep in touch. And if you ever get that second book written, I'd like to take a peek. You do good work, Chloe."

That was nice to hear, but after all the havoc this movie had brought into her life, the idea was less than appealing. "Thank you. You'll be the first to know."

Chloe shook hands with the director on his way off set and everyone who lingered in the video village. And by the time she'd finished saying her good-byes, Liam was nowhere to be seen.

# Chapter 38

Liam was unpacking when he got the call.

He'd returned home two days ago to a clean, cool house, thanks to the service he paid to keep it up while he was away. He told himself he was glad to be here, back in the familiar surroundings of his cliffside home, which offered stunning views of the sunset over the Pacific. Everything was better here. His skin didn't bead with humidity the moment he stepped outdoors, and the heat didn't suffocate him with each breath. His mattress was like a cloud and his steam shower rivaled the finest spas in Europe.

Even so, leaving Stillwater Bay had gutted him. He'd slumped in that window seat, watching the shoreline grow distant and thinking only of the miles that would soon separate him from Chloe. Even now his chest tightened at the memory of her: laughing at herself when she tripped over air, peeking out of that clothing rack the first time he'd seen her, hair askew, a blush blooming in her cheeks. She'd grown on him over the past three months.

Liam gave a grim laugh. "Grew on me?"

What a joke. She'd broken his stupid heart. He used to scoff when he saw such cheesy lines in a script. But he understood it now. His chest ached as if there was something actually wrong with the organ. And the only thing wrong was that it missed Chloe.

He thought of the way his mom had mourned the loss of her husband all these years. Was that what his future held?

It was his worst nightmare.

He pushed away the thought as he gathered the pile of clothes from the suitcase. Cat hair clung to most of the items. He tossed them in the hamper for the housekeeper to handle.

There at the bottom of the suitcase was the well-worn script he and Chloe had pored over together. The miniature flag he'd waved on the Fourth. And one of the books he'd bought at Meghan's bookstore but hadn't had time to read. The reminders were like a sucker punch. He should just toss them. But he couldn't bring himself to do it. Instead he shoved them into the back of his closet where he wouldn't have to see them. But hiding the mementos didn't keep the memory of Chloe from playing in his mind.

Being on set with her Wednesday had been difficult and painful. He felt bad about what she was going through. The media was no doubt hounding her and her family about what they'd revealed. But he was also angry with her.

What happened to all that communication she'd advocated during their first misunderstanding? She wouldn't even take his call. She'd blocked him! He'd never in his life been blocked by anyone.

Fine, let her be that way. It never would've worked anyway. This whole situation only proved she didn't have what it took to be his partner. The thought weighted his chest, because before all this he'd begun thinking she just might be the perfect fit.

When his phone vibrated in his pocket, his first thought was *Chloe.*

Scowling at his reaction, he checked the screen. Spencer. They hadn't spoken for a couple of days. "Hey, buddy. What's up?"

"I have some bad news."

"No 'Welcome home, Liam. Let's grab a drink and catch up'?"

"Welcome home, Liam. Let's grab a drink and catch up. Now can I get on with the bad news?"

Oh, why not? "Proceed."

"The media got wind of your PR relationship with Chloe. They're all over it. I got a bunch of Google alerts a few minutes ago."

Liam shut the closet door as his stomach dropped to the floor. "How is that possible?"

"I don't know, but it's happened. We need to figure out how to deal with the fallout. This will set you right back to where you were in the fall."

"If not farther." Liam palmed the back of his neck. No doubt. "My fans won't be thrilled I tried to pull a fast one."

"That's already happening, unfortunately. They really got on board with the whole Chliam thing."

"Who could've tipped them off?"

"You probably don't want to go here, but . . . could Chloe have done this? To get back at you? She had to know how bad this would look and the effect it would have on your career." Liam had told Spencer about their real relationship and subsequent breakup—including all the details.

But Liam's heart refuted the idea. "That doesn't sound like Chloe at all. Besides, this will only bring her more media attention, and she doesn't like the spotlight—of that I'm certain."

"What about her family?"

"They signed nondisclosures, remember? And anyway, this doesn't reflect well on Chloe either. And this is only going to keep her family's past in the headlines. They wouldn't want that."

"I suppose. I guess it doesn't really matter how they found out. We need to decide how we should handle it. Should I contact Chloe and let her know what's happening so she isn't blindsided?"

She'd made it pretty clear she wanted to cut all ties with him. She'd find out soon enough on her own. "No, I don't think so. I'm sure I'll be absorbing most of the damage on this one anyway."

"I'm afraid you're probably right. Let's do a conference call with Patty in the morning and discuss how to move forward. Be thinking about it."

"All right." They made plans, then Liam disconnected, his

thoughts whirling. The last thing he'd wanted was another scandal. And this one was already blowing up in his face. Since he was back to square one with his reputation, he could probably kiss those recent script offers good-bye. He resolved to stay off social media and let Spencer read the situation for him.

He glanced around his room. Might as well get a few things done around here. He approached his bed where his suitcase lay. But all that was left inside was a dusting of sand.

\* \* \*

Liam was officially gone.

Since filming had ended a day early, he'd apparently moved up his departure. Chloe couldn't miss the in-flight selfie he'd posted on his Facebook page, along with his new dating status: single. He must've changed it sometime over the past several days.

Since the last thing she needed was to deal with daily reminders of him, she'd unfollowed him and vowed to stay off social media for a while. People had been privately messaging her since her family's story broke. Most of them were sympathetic, and a few had even experienced something similar. But Chloe didn't want to rehash her tragic past with strangers.

Pushing away the negative thoughts, she began clearing a table to help the busboys. The restaurant had technically closed and only a few patrons lingered. Soon she'd go home and curl up with her temperamental cat and bittersweet memories. She rolled her eyes at her maudlin thoughts.

Sean flagged her down from the kitchen door. Chloe finished clearing the table and headed that way. Her gaze zeroed in on his somber expression, then the phone in his hand.

*What now?*

Rather than tell her, he turned back into the kitchen and she followed him inside. The back of house was already closed up and the crew had left it sparkling clean.

"What's up? Who's on the phone?"

"Meghan called a few minutes ago."

She started to ask why her friend was calling Sean on a busy Saturday night. But because of the recent article and media circus surrounding it, they'd both stopped taking calls from the restaurant's line.

"She got one of those Google alerts tonight," he said. "It isn't good."

She laughed wryly. "Well, it's not like we have any more family skeletons they can drag from the closet."

Sean gave her a grim look. "They know you and Liam were faking your relationship."

Her stomach dropped like an anchor even as her pulse sped. *Liam.* This could have a terrible effect on his career. Did he know? "When did this release?"

"The alert came in this afternoon, but she didn't check her phone until tonight."

"So it's been out awhile." Spencer surely would've alerted Liam by now. He hadn't bothered to contact her. But then, she'd made it perfectly clear she didn't want to hear from him.

"She said his fans are pretty upset. And they're not too happy with you either."

Chloe's publisher wouldn't love this. And she hoped the bad publicity wouldn't tank the movie. But the film release was a long way off. The dust would settle and people would forget.

She hoped.

"What do you want to do?" Sean asked.

"What can I do? The secret's out. People are going to form opinions—and voice them, I'm sure. There's no stopping that."

Sean blinked. "So you're just gonna let it happen?"

"What choice do I have?"

"I don't know. Maybe you could . . . make a statement or something. Defend yourself."

"And say what, Sean? I *did* enter a fake relationship with Liam. They're not going to care why I did it, only that it was done." They were already talking about her anyway, though the thoughts would surely be less sympathetic this time.

"What about folks around here? You know this news is gonna fly around town."

He was right. Gossip spread like wildfire around here. Facing the people who knew her would be embarrassing. Somehow they'd actually believed a celebrity like Liam could care for her. But they'd soon learn it had only been a ruse. Heat traveled up her neck and scorched her cheeks. How humiliating.

But it couldn't be much worse than the shame that had been revealed this past week. "It is what it is. Answering questions will only add fuel to the fire. If we ignore it, the story will blow over eventually. Until then I'll just go on living my life."

Sean gave her an incredulous stare. "Wow. All right. Whatever you say." Noise sounded out front as the last of her customers were probably leaving.

"You need some help out front?" he asked.

She drifted her gaze over the kitchen. "No, I got it. I'd rather stay busy anyway. You know?"

"I hear you. Call me if you need to talk about anything. And stay off social media," he called over his shoulder as he exited through the back.

"Oh, believe me," she muttered, "I will."

Chloe returned to the dining room. The last customers had cleared out and the waitstaff had left for the evening. Chloe turned the Closed sign and locked the door, then went about the last of her duties, her mind laden with worry. What was Liam dealing with? Maybe she shouldn't care after what he'd done to her, but she couldn't help it.

This was his career. He'd spent years building a fan base—would it turn against him? Would this scandal jeopardize the parts he'd already been offered? Surely it would since their efforts to salvage his reputation had exploded in their faces.

She turned the chairs up on the tables for the cleaning crew that would come in later, then she closed out the register. Her steps felt heavy as she locked up and left. Her feelings for Liam clearly hadn't gone away, that much was clear. Had she thought they'd shut off like a spigot just because he'd hurt her? She should've known better.

She started her car and pulled from the lot, her thoughts again turning to the repercussions Liam would face. If he didn't already regret his relationship with her, he surely would now. He was probably ruing the day he'd ever met her.

She should probably be doing the same thing. But even after all she'd been through and all she was still going through, she couldn't quite get there. Maybe she was hurting, but she was also learning things about herself. Coming to grips with what her father had done and the shame it had left her with.

*God, why does growth have to come with such pain?*

Her eyes prickled with tears. She swiped them away as she turned onto the main road and said a prayer for Liam. Then she came to the four-way stop where she'd turn right and head home. On a whim she turned left instead. She needed to talk to someone and Meghan would still be up. Her friend was probably poking around online to see what people were saying.

Meghan lived a ten-minute walk from downtown on a residential street lined with cute one-story bungalows. Golden porch lights lit the neighborhood as Chloe headed down the road, careful of the cars parked at the curbs.

When she reached Meghan's drive she slowed and pulled in. But when her headlights swept across the drive, they revealed far more than she'd expected.

Sean and Meghan were wrapped up like a burrito, making out at the side of Sean's truck. They jumped apart, squinting against the lights.

Nice that neither of them had bothered to mention to Chloe that their relationship had escalated. She considered pulling right back out of the drive, then decided no. She was going to face this head-on. Face *them* head-on.

Her anger faded as she zoomed in on Meghan's worried expression. At the slumping of her shoulders. Chloe couldn't help but fast-forward to the moment when Sean inevitably broke her friend's heart. She didn't want Meghan to go through another heartbreak. She deserved so much better than that.

Still, Chloe had already warned them both. They were adults and it seemed they were determined to take this road even if it was destined to end in a terrible crash.

As she stepped from her car, Sean said something to Meghan. She answered and he replied back. Then her friend headed up the porch steps, turning to offer Chloe a guilty smile.

By the time she reached Sean, Meghan was inside.

Her brother crossed his arms. "It's me you're mad at. No reason she has to stick around for this." His hair was in complete disarray as if . . .

Well. Chloe didn't want to think about that. "You're just determined to see this through then? You're gonna win her over and make her fall for you, then you're gonna break her heart just like her ex did? I can't believe—"

"I *love* her, Chloe."

She froze. Took in her brother's earnest eyes, the fervent frown between his brows, the ardent expression on his face. She'd never heard Sean use that word in reference to a woman outside the family.

"I know you think this is just my usual fleeting interest, but this is different. Meghan is different. I won't hurt her. And I won't give her up, not even for you."

Her mouth fell open. This was a side of Sean she'd never seen. Was it possible he actually had fallen in love with Meghan? "Does she feel the same way?"

"I think so. She's just afraid to tell me. I hope."

"How long has this been going on?"

"We've been dancing around it since spring when I helped her gather sand for her display window. I tried to stay away, I really did. She wasn't exactly open to the idea of the two of us." He scowled at Chloe. "She was convinced I was 'emotionally unavailable' because of all the things you'd told her about me."

Chloe opened her mouth.

"I know, I know. It was true. But this is different. I have feelings for her—real feelings. It's taken me months to convince her of that, and you just interrupted our first kiss, so thanks for that."

"I don't know what to say. I'm still a little . . . concerned about this."

"Will it help to know I've been in counseling all summer?"

She blinked. Her brother wasn't exactly the touchy-feely sort. "Why didn't you tell me?"

He gave her a sheepish glance. "It's kinda personal. I felt stupid paying someone to listen to me whine about my life. But I have to admit it's helped. I've figured out a lot of things, like why I jump from one woman to the next."

"Well, don't keep me in suspense."

He drew a deep breath. His jaw flexed as he struggled with some emotion. Then he met her gaze. "Long story short, I was afraid I was just like our father."

*"What?"* Nothing he could've said would've shocked her more. "You are nothing like him, Sean. You're warm and caring for starters, and you don't desert people when they need you most. You're one of the most loyal people I know."

His eyes took on a glossy sheen. "With family, yeah, maybe. But with women . . . not so much. So I just kept ending relationships before they got too serious."

Her lungs emptied. She grabbed her brother and wrapped him up in her arms. "That could never be true. But I'm glad you're figuring things out." She had another thought. "You were already dealing with these daddy issues when our family's story broke. I'm sorry. That couldn't have helped matters."

"It hit you pretty hard too. I'm determined to fix my issues—I want this to work with Meghan more than I've ever wanted anything."

He must if he was willing to go through therapy. She gave him a hug. "I love you, Sean. I'm sorry I gave you such a hard time about Meghan."

He drew back, a smirk lifting one side of his mouth. "Sorry I gave you such a hard time about Liam. My therapist says I've been projecting my emotions about our father onto you. That wasn't fair."

"Wow, that's deep. And hey, turns out you were right about Liam after all."

His lips went flat as his eyes bored into hers. "And I'm really sorry about that too, Sis. You deserve better."

"Thanks."

Her gaze drifted to the door where Meghan reappeared wearing a sheepish expression. "Is it safe to come out?"

Chloe extended her arms. "Come here. I promise I'm done butting in."

Meghan took the steps and slid into Chloe's embrace. "Thanks for not hating me. I tried to stay away . . ."

Chloe snorted. "It's okay. You guys have my blessing—not that you need it." She pulled back to see happy tears in her friend's eyes. Who knew her brother would be the one to make Meghan happy again? "I think I'll take off and let you two get on with your evening."

Sean's eyes twinkled in the night. "I won't argue about that."

"Eew, stop." She sent Meghan a little wave and a smile, then gave Sean a pointed look. "Be careful with her heart."

Sean turned to Meghan. "You should probably tell *her* that since I'm already a goner."

Somehow, despite the fact that she'd just been outed by the media, Chloe was smiling as she got in her car and drove away.

# Chapter 39

Tuesday morning Liam received a text that rearranged the rest of his day.

He'd planned to meet a few friends for lunch and attend another friend's premiere tonight. But maybe it was best to avoid the public eye right now. Unsurprisingly, his fans felt betrayed by his deception. He could only blame himself. He could justify it all he wanted, but faking a relationship with Chloe had been dishonest.

He and Spencer had decided to take a wait-and-see approach. Likely another story would come along soon and hopefully people would forget what he'd done.

How was Chloe faring? Maybe the news hadn't hit Stillwater Bay quite the same way. Who was he kidding? It would've traveled through the small town in record time. But she had a loving family and good friends. She was well liked and admired by all. Of course, that might've changed now that she'd attempted to deceive them. He hoped not.

He was answering questions for an online interview with *Spotlight* magazine when his mother's text came in. *Hi son. I guess your dad changed his number. I need the new one, please. Have you heard from him? Also, the money you sent last month is already gone. I've had some unexpected expenses. Big ones. I should've written earlier but I was hoping to get by. Three thousand would go a long way toward helping me out of debt. Thank you, honey. It means so much to me.*

As usual, she hadn't asked how he was doing. Wasn't aware he faced a scandal that might permanently cripple his career. And if he told her, she would care mostly because he was her primary source of income. She also seemed unaware that her ex-husband had likely changed his number to avoid her calls. And Liam suspected the unexpected expenses involved cases of liquor.

He remembered what Chloe had said when he confided in her about his mom. She was right. It wasn't healthy for his mom to rely on him financially or to sit around drinking all the time. He had to face facts. He'd only been enabling her. She needed real help even if she couldn't see it.

Controlling the purse strings gave him leverage, and it was high time he used it. He closed the document he'd been working on and opened his browser. An hour later he was on his way to Riverside.

Beverly Hamilton lived in a two-story Mediterranean-style home in one of Riverside's nicest neighborhoods. Mom had sold his childhood home soon after Liam's career took off. She hadn't been able to afford the giant step up to this gated community, but Liam had been happy to subsidize the move. Back then it had felt rewarding to provide something nice for his mother, even if the home was far too large for her. He hadn't realized he was creating a monster.

He turned into the drive, pulling close to the beige stucco house with its terra-cotta roof. It had taken almost three hours to get here thanks to the traffic on 91. He'd had plenty of time to work out what he'd say. But times like this he wished he had a sibling or two with whom he could share the burden. Like Chloe. She and Sean might not always see eye to eye, but they were close and they loved each other. They had each other's backs.

He pushed the thought aside. He had enough to deal with at the moment without remembering how empty his days were without Chloe or how lonely his life sometimes felt.

He took the porch steps and rang the doorbell. After the second ring his mom answered. She wore a red jogging outfit that complemented her dyed-black hair. Even in full makeup she appeared at least ten years older than she was. Hard living and heartbreak had taken their toll.

"Liam!" She embraced him. "Honey, what a nice surprise. Why didn't you tell me you were coming?"

Phoebe, her Yorkshire terrier, yapped at their feet.

"I wanted to surprise you." He wrapped his arms around her, catching a whiff of whiskey on her breath. It was barely midafternoon.

"Well, mission accomplished." Her words weren't slurred yet, so maybe she'd have enough cognitive skills for the conversation they were about to have. "Come in, come in."

Cool air wafted over his skin as he entered the house. It smelled pleasantly of lemon and books. On the coffee table sat a pair of red readers and the *Press-Enterprise* opened to the real estate section. His gaze stopped on a glass tumbler sitting on the end table with two fingers of amber liquid.

"Hush now, Phoebe! What brings you to Riverside? Are you visiting your dad? Can I get you something to drink?"

"No, thanks. I actually just came to see you."

Her eyes lit at his words. "Isn't that nice."

Finally calming down, the dog jumped onto the couch and curled up at her side.

"Have a seat, honey. I was hoping to go to the grocery, but money's a little tight right now."

"Yes, I got your text."

"And you drove all this way. You're so good to me."

Liam took a deep breath, gathering his courage. "You might not think so when you hear what I came to say."

"Well, that sounds foreboding."

"We have a situation here, Mom. It's obvious you're not doing so well, and I want to help you."

"That's awfully sweet of you, honey. But once I get my finances squared away, I'll be just fine."

He pinned her with a look. "You're not fine, Mom."

She chuckled nervously. "Is this about my drinking again? Adults drink, Liam. For heaven's sake, don't be such an alarmist. I've got it under control. I only drink when I'm stressed or sad."

His gaze flickered over to the glass on the table. "Which one are you right now?"

Her lips pressed into a hard line. "I'm stressed about my finances, as I already told you."

"So if I just cut you a check, you won't need to drink anymore?"

"There's no need to be sarcastic."

"You do realize that drinking to numb your pain is exactly how people become alcoholics."

"Oh, lighten up! I don't drink all day. I don't even drink every day."

He found that hard to believe. "I didn't come to argue with you, Mom."

"Well, that's a relief."

"I came to offer you a deal."

Wariness shadowed eyes that were the same color and shape as his own. He braced himself for battle.

"What kind of deal?"

"I've done some research and I've found a very nice recovery center that will make room for you."

"Recovery center? Is that like *rehab*?" She scoffed. "How many times have I told you—"

"The money stops, Mom. I won't give you another dime unless you go."

"What kind of deal is that? How do you expect me to live without an income? That's just cruel. This isn't like you at all! Did your father put you up to this? If he'd just wise up and come back to me, everything would—"

"Dad knows nothing about this." Liam steeled his resolve. "The recovery center has an excellent thirty-day treatment program. They can help you. When you get out you'll be able to—"

"I'd have to *stay* there?" She gave her head a sharp shake. "No, absolutely not."

"That's the way the program works."

"I don't belong with those people! I'm not like them."

"That's the deal, Mom." If there was a clincher, this next part was it. "It's a luxury detox center in Beverly Hills. It's where all the stars go, so you'll be in good company. And I'll be nearby and will visit as soon as I'm allowed." He leaned forward. "Just think about how much better you'll feel when you get out. You'll be able to hold down a job—you used to like working at the bank, remember? You liked being around people. You can get back to that. I want that for you."

A veil of fear fell over her eyes. Then the tears began to fall. "I—I can't do it. I just can't."

"Why not?"

She gestured wildly. "The house. The bills. I can't just leave it all for a whole month. Who would take care of Phoebe?"

He glanced at the dog. "I'll take care of her. And I'll handle your bills while you're away and even until you get back on your feet, as long as you stay clean."

"You talk like I'm some sort of lowlife addict."

"That's the deal, Mom."

"Stop saying that!"

"It's your choice. I'll handle your finances while you get this under control. But the deal's only good today. You can pack a bag and

get in the car with me, or I leave and no more checks are coming."
It would be hard to carry out that threat, but he was determined to
follow through.

"You'd really forsake me like that? I'm your mother! I raised you
single-handedly."

"I wouldn't forsake you. I'll always love you and be here for you.
But I won't support this lifestyle."

"How could you do this to me?" Her voice was shrill. "You're my
son! You're supposed to love me."

A dull ache spread through his chest. But he wouldn't back down.
"What's it gonna be, Mom?"

"You're pressuring me! I need some time."

He settled back in his seat. "Take all the time you need."

She wrung her hands. Her eyes darted around the room. Long
minutes passed while he waited. Finally she gazed at him with eyes
full of terror. "It's a nice place?"

"It's top of the line. Only the best for you, Mom."

She gathered the dog close. "And you'll take good care of my
Phoebe?"

"Of course. She can stay at my place."

Mom seemed to weigh that out. Her throat dipped as she swallowed. Her lips turned down in a pout. "All right. I'll go then. I
don't see as I have much choice since I can't make it without those
checks."

Good enough. She didn't have to be excited, just willing. Liam
exhaled, a weight falling from his shoulders at her acquiescence. "Go
pack a bag. Here's a list of what you're allowed to bring."

Twenty minutes later they left the house, but not before his mom
drained the two fingers of whiskey. Liam let her do it. She would
need all the courage she could muster to walk through those doors.

# Chapter 40

On Wednesday Chloe braved the coffee shop—and soon wished she hadn't.

From behind the counter, Veronica's forced smile told her everything she needed to know. The other baristas barely glanced her way. Chloe's stomach shriveled up like a raisin.

She'd planned to sit and enjoy her mocha with the newspaper, but now she couldn't get out of here fast enough. "Could I get that to go, please?"

Without a word Veronica marked up the cup and took the next customer's order.

Chloe moved to the other end of the counter. Back in June when she'd agreed to that deal with Liam, she'd only been thinking about her own needs. She hadn't considered that she would be deceiving her friends and neighbors. That they might feel betrayed by her dishonesty. What had she been thinking?

When Liam had approached her that day, she'd believed his proposal was the solution to both their problems. Now she was the town pariah. But at least she'd achieved her objective with the role of Ledger.

Liam, however . . . His fans weren't happy and she feared his career was on the verge of collapse.

When her drink came up, she grabbed the cup and slipped from the shop. She needed to see a friendly face, so she drove to Sean's apartment, hoping to catch him at home. He lived in the top of a new four-unit building near the marina that had two things going for it: an ocean view and a cook's kitchen.

When she pulled in the lot, she saw his car was there so she took the stairs and knocked.

A moment later he swung the door open. "Hey. What's up?" He glanced down at her cup. "You shouldn't have."

"Sorry. This was an impromptu visit but you're welcome to it."

"Think I'll pass on the double-chocolate mocha." He stepped aside to let her in. "I'm just glad you're finally braving the public. Very courageous of you."

"It wasn't fun." The cool air felt good as she stepped into his cluttered living room. A pair of socks lay balled up in the corner, and at least three days of newspapers were scattered over the coffee table. Stacks of pots and pans filled the sink. Since he always kept his kitchen spotless, that meant only one thing. "You've been cooking."

"I'm making truffles. Want a sample?"

"Do seagulls poop on picnic tables?" She headed into the kitchen. The chocolates looked divine.

"They're not quite—"

She snatched one and plopped it into her mouth.

"—dry yet."

The texture was silky smooth and the dark chocolate and tart raspberry flavors burst on her tongue. "Mmm." She swallowed it and grabbed two more pieces. She could eat about a dozen of these. Why couldn't she be one of those people who starved themselves when they were stressed instead of eating everything in sight?

"I said a *sample*. And that's gourmet chocolate you're scarfing down."

"I'm drowning my sorrows."

Sean took the pan away. "Maybe I could offer you some M&M's instead."

"Sorry. They are delicious. Are you thinking of offering them at the restaurant?"

"No, I made them for Meghan."

"She'll love them. She adores chocolate almost as much as I do." Chloe finished the second piece and popped the third in her mouth, letting this one melt on her tongue. According to Meghan, she and Sean were giving their relationship a chance. Chloe hadn't gotten her brother's take on things since she'd interrupted that kiss a few days ago. But she could hardly miss his wistful smiles and head-in-the-clouds distraction at work.

"How's that going anyway—you and Meghan?"

"As if you don't already know. We're taking things one day at a time." Though his response was tempered with caution, the smile curling his lips was not.

She licked the melted chocolate from her fingers. "I have to admit you seem pretty happy lately."

"Well, I've never felt like this before."

Her heart warmed at his honesty. "I'm pulling for you guys. Meghan's a wonderful person." Chloe took in the joy that lit his eyes and the goofy expression on his face. She knew just how he felt. She'd been feeling that way herself less than two weeks ago. And then the bottom had fallen out.

She shook away the negative thought. "I'm truly happy for you both."

"Thanks." He handed her a water bottle and she followed him into the living room, where they sat on opposite ends of the sofa. "So things were pretty rough at the coffee shop, huh?"

"The baristas gave me the cold shoulder. And I'm positive Joy Geiger and Wanietta Stuckey saw me and just pretended not to. I'm afraid to get online. I don't want to see what people are saying about me . . ." Not to mention how many followers she'd probably lost.

"Yeah . . . don't do that."

She darted her gaze his way. "You've been looking?"

"I've poked around a bit."

"What are people saying about Liam? Are his fans still upset with him?"

"Seriously? It's *him* you want to know about?"

Her face heated. She must be a slow learner because she couldn't seem to help worrying about him. She lifted a shoulder.

"It's died down a bit on his end from when the story first broke." Sean glanced away. His lips pressed together.

She knew that expression. "What aren't you telling me?"

"I thought you didn't want to know."

"I do want to know—in a curated, carefully worded kind of way."

"The censored version?"

"Exactly." Her poor, shattered heart couldn't take much more. She waited with her stomach in knots for him to spill it, which he seemed in no hurry to do.

"In the past couple days the focus seems to have switched from Liam to you. It's like people initially blamed Liam, but now they're shifting the blame your way."

Her way? For what reason? "What are they saying? Why are they shifting the blame to me?"

He studied her as if trying to ascertain whether he should tell her.

"I *could* just get online and see for myself, you know."

"No, don't do that. The gist of it is, there are some people who think you took advantage of him instead of the other way around."

"How?"

"Some people are saying you're a gold digger or a wannabe or something and others are piling on. The whole thing is stupid. There's a lot of speculation about what you got out of this deal— everything from a big payout to—well, you can imagine."

His words punched her in the heart. "Nice." That's not at all who she was, and she hated that people were assigning such terrible motives to her. She made enough money of her own, thank you very much, and she actually hated being in the spotlight.

But at least they were letting Liam off the hook. If they were angry with her, they might forgive Liam and not boycott him and his movies.

"Everyone who knows you knows none of that's true."

She gave a mock laugh. "Yeah, it's just the other three hundred million people I have to worry about."

"This will pass in due time, you'll see. Some celebrity will go on a drunken rampage any minute now."

"No doubt. Yeah, you're right. I just have to ride it out."

"I get it though. Can't be fun having your name dragged through the mud. Ticks me off. I want to call up every tabloid I can find and set the record straight."

"It would only fan the flame."

"That's the only reason I haven't done it."

She asked the question she'd been dying to know. "How has Liam been handling all this? Has he addressed the situation publicly? Made a statement or anything?"

"Not that I can tell. Seems like he might be hoping it'll die down on its own too."

She nodded. So he was hunkering down and weathering the storm just like her. At one time they would've done that together. This wouldn't be nearly so bad if she wasn't going through it alone. She rubbed the center of her chest where that stupid ache resided. How long would it take for these feelings to fade? For the hurt to stop?

"I hope you're not feeling bad for him. He deserves everything he's getting."

She should feel the same way. But she couldn't quite convince her heart. "I was just hoping this scandal doesn't impact the book sales—or the movie for that matter."

"Sometimes controversy actually helps. I mean, people are talking about it and that's half the battle, right?"

"I hope so." Her phone buzzed. Chloe was reluctant to check it. She was tired of blocking media calls. And the hope of hearing from Liam always made her heart palpitate—which was stupid since she'd blocked his number.

"Aren't you gonna check that?"

She pulled out her phone and peered at the screen. The foreign number on the phone had her ready to block the call. But a second glance revealed the call's origin: Hartford, Connecticut.

She glanced up at Sean. It couldn't be . . .

"What?" he asked.

It had to be a coincidence. Or a reporter calling from the same city where her father lived. But what if it wasn't? Should she answer? If it was just a reporter, she could simply say, "No comment," and hang up.

With trembling fingers she accepted the call. "Hello?"

The line filled with five full seconds of silence.

"Hello?" she repeated, her voice trembling on the word.

"Is this—is this Chloe?" It was a woman's voice.

"Yes . . ."

"This is, um, this is Tiffany. Tiffany Daniels?"

Chloe blinked at Sean.

"I don't even know if you know about me. I'm your half sister."

A sudden coldness spread through Chloe's core. This was the girl who'd stolen her father's affection. The daughter he'd chosen. Her brain scrambled for a hold. "I—I know who you are."

Sean frowned, mouthing, *What?*

"I'm sorry to reach out like this, so out of the blue. I hope you won't be upset that I called. But I just had to talk to you, and I couldn't see showing up on your doorstep."

"No, this is fine," she said rotely. But was it fine? Part of her wanted to hate the woman. The other part was curious about who she was—and why she might be calling.

Sean leaned forward. "Who is it?"

She covered the speaker. "Tiffany Daniels."

His head jolted back even as his eyes went wide.

Tiffany was talking, but Chloe interrupted. "Sorry, uh, Tiffany, but I actually have Sean with me right now. My brother. Can I put you on speakerphone?"

"Yes. Yes, absolutely. I couldn't find his number."

Chloe tapped the button. "You're on speaker now."

"Hi, Sean."

"Hey." His voice sounded dazed. Chloe could hardly blame him.

"So just a few days ago," Tiffany said, "I found out about that article online—the one about my dad. *Our* dad. I can't tell you how shocked and horrified I was. I couldn't believe he'd done something like that all those years ago. It seemed so contrary to everything I've known about him, I thought it had to be a lie. But since then I've talked with my parents, and I know now it's the truth. Honestly, I think I'm still in shock."

Chloe's gaze clung to Sean's. "Are you saying you didn't know about us?"

"I had no idea you even existed until that article." Truth rang through in her tone. "I can't believe I have a brother and sister I didn't even know about. I've been a mess since then. I'm so angry with my parents for keeping this from me."

Chloe set the phone between them. Tiffany would be about thirty. That was one long-buried secret her parents had kept. "I always wondered if you knew."

"Does your father know you're calling?" Sean asked.

"I told him I'd be reaching out to you. I didn't want another day to pass with silence between us."

Sean leaned forward. "And . . . ? What did he say?"

There was a long pause. "To be honest . . . he wasn't thrilled about it. He's embarrassed by what he did. Ashamed. But I'm a grown adult with a mind of my own. He made his mistakes, but that doesn't mean I have to follow in his footsteps."

Her anger with their father was apparent in her tone. But she seemed nice. Normal. Not the daughter of some bigamist. Then again, Chloe was also the daughter of that bigamist.

"I guess I'd hoped . . ." Emotion swelled in her voice. "I'd hoped you could tell me a little about yourselves. I'd like to know you better if that's okay with you guys. I don't want to be pushy or anything, and I understand if you—you don't want anything to do with me. I'll go away quietly if that's the case. But I'm an only child. I always longed for siblings. I just think . . . well, we weren't raised together, but that doesn't mean we have to be strangers, does it?"

A knot swelled in Chloe's throat as she searched Sean's face. This woman seemed like a decent person. She seemed like someone worth getting to know. And she was their sister. Was there room in their lives for a sister?

Sean's expression softened. He raised his brows in question to Chloe.

He was letting her take the lead here. Chloe's heart swelled twice over at the thought of another sibling. "I think I'd like that."

Sean smiled, their gazes holding. "Me too."

# Chapter 41

On Saturday the doorbell woke Chloe from a deep sleep. She opened her eyes to the sunshine streaming through her windows. It was almost ten. Lately she seemed to be sleeping the mornings away.

Buttercup peered at her through the bedroom doorway, wearing a judgy look.

"For your information, I haven't been sleeping well."

The doorbell pealed again. She threw off the covers and went to see who was here. Her hair was probably sticking up in all directions, and her face no doubt sported pillow creases. Oh well. She reached the sidelight and peeked out.

As Chloe opened the door, Meghan's gaze swept over her and she frowned. "I thought we were beyond this."

"I haven't been sleeping well."

Meghan's expression turned solicitous. "Well, never mind. Here." She shoved a to-go cup at Chloe. "Your favorite. And here's a few homemade truffles—raspberry and dark chocolate."

Chloe frowned. Her friend turning up unexpectedly with . . . "*Two* gifts? This can't be good."

Meghan's expression fell. "I'm not gonna lie; it's pretty bad."

What was it now? Chloe closed her eyes briefly, then turned for the kitchen. Then again, how could it get much worse? She'd already lost the man she loved. And gossip about her had only ramped up over the past couple of days. She'd stopped checking her social media pages after receiving vicious messages and confirming that her following had plummeted. She'd officially been canceled by the masses. Oh, and her dissenters now had their own hashtag: #fakedategate.

Chloe offered Meghan a seat at the bar. "Don't tell me . . . they've pinned JFK's murder on me. I mean, I wasn't even alive at the time, but the way my luck's going . . ."

"There's nothing new floating around, and it's nothing like that. Well, it is, but it's not." She grimaced. "Oh man, you're gonna hate me."

"Not possible." Chloe snagged a chocolate. "Anyway, you softened me up with coffee and chocolates. Very wise of you. Just spit it out. You'll feel much better."

"It's my fault everyone knows about your fake relationship," Meghan blurted. "And I'm indirectly responsible for the scandal about your father too."

Chloe swallowed the bite of chocolate, which now tasted like sawdust. "What?"

Meghan covered her face. "You're wrong, I don't feel better. If anything I feel worse."

"Wait. Back up. What are you talking about?"

Meghan lowered her hands. Her eyes were bloodshot and she looked miserable. "It was Kyle. He's the one who told the media everything. I could just throttle him!"

Meghan's ex-husband? Chloe's head was spinning. "How is that even possible? And why would he—?"

"When we were married I told him about your family's history. I didn't think any harm could come of it. And I forgot that I'd even told him until last night. He called me about a pair of heirloom earrings he'd given me—he wanted them back. I couldn't find them and then he accused me of lying about it, and one thing led to another and then we were yelling at each other. That's when he told me what he'd done."

"He admitted it?"

"More like taunted me with it. I'm so sorry, Chloe. He actually sold the information to *TMZ* and then *People* picked it up from there."

"How'd he even know how to do that?"

"I wondered the same thing. There's a contact form online. I guess any old idiot can pass along celebrity gossip—if the price is right."

Chloe's breath froze in her lungs. If Kyle told the tabloids about her family, that meant . . .

"So Liam isn't the one who betrayed you. Kyle is."

*Liam didn't do it.*

She closed her eyes against the sting of tears. What had she done? She'd accused him of spilling the beans about her family. She hadn't even given him a chance to refute the accusation.

Oh, this was terrible! She palmed her forehead.

"I'm so sorry. This is all my fault. I'll call Liam and explain what happened. I'll make this up to you."

If only that would fix the problem. "That's not your place. And he's not gonna care after I treated him like that. I'm the one who jumped to conclusions. How could I have been so stupid?" She gave her head a shake. "Wait a minute. You said Kyle told the tabloids about the fake relationship, but he couldn't have. He didn't have any way of knowing about that."

Meghan made a pained face. "Actually . . . he did. He was quite pleased to inform me he's privy to all my texts. They appear on our old iPad and he's been reading them all these months. That's how he saw the texts about you and Liam. He saw another opportunity and took it. Anything for a quick buck."

To think Chloe had once liked the guy. He'd cost both her and Liam so much. "He really is a schmuck."

"If it's any consolation, the temperature in his house is going to be quite uncomfortable for the foreseeable future."

Chloe breathed a laugh. But this situation was hardly a laughing matter. What she'd done to Liam was unforgivable. What he must think of her. She groaned as she lowered her head to the island. "I'm so stupid. I ruined the best thing that's ever happened to me."

"You're not stupid. This is my fault—the scandals and your breakup. I'm so sorry."

"Why did I jump to such a hasty conclusion about Liam? I should've known better."

Meghan set her hand on Chloe's head. "There was plenty of circumstantial evidence, and I'm afraid Sean and I didn't do you any favors."

"But I'm the one who knew him." Chloe raised her head. "I should've believed in him. I should've stood up for him."

"Aw, honey." Meghan's eyes softened. "You love him, don't you?"

Chloe's heart contracted painfully as tears sprang to her eyes. "Why was I so quick to believe the worst?"

"I don't know." Meghan glanced down. Pressed her lips together.

Chloe knew that look. "If you've got something for me, go for it."

Meghan wore a sheepish expression. "I think I've done enough already, don't you?"

But her relationship with Liam had held so much promise. And Chloe was tired of repeating history. This was the third time she'd had a long-term, happy relationship come to a sudden halt. Though this was the first time she'd ended things. Her other boyfriends had just found her lacking.

Just like her father, come to think of it. A tear spilled over. "If you have any clue what's wrong with me, I want to know."

"Oh, honey . . . there's nothing wrong with you."

"Then why do I feel like there is? Two perfectly nice men have left me, and even though I was the one who spoiled things with Liam, he didn't exactly put up a fight. Maybe it's not them. Maybe it's *me*. Nobody wants me, Meghan."

"That is *not true*. And let's not forget, Evan cheated on you."

Chloe snorted. "I probably drove him to it."

"Hey. Stop accepting responsibility for his behavior. That was his choice."

"But he was always complaining that I didn't open up. That I didn't let him in. And I guess it was true—I never told him about my dad. And I didn't exactly open up about how I felt about certain things."

"Well, no one's perfect. And it's not exactly a fatal flaw. You can always work on being more vulnerable."

Just the thought sent a bolt of panic through her. "I don't know if I can. It's so scary."

Meghan gave her a sympathetic smile. "Believe me, I know it is. Especially for you, I'd guess, because your dad abandoned you and that left you with some scars. But people can't love you until they know you. And they can't know you until you open yourself to them and show them who you are."

She was right. Except . . . "But what if I open myself up and they don't like what they see? What if they leave me just like—?" Her voice broke.

"Like your dad?"

Chloe blinked back the tears. Then she gave voice to her deepest fear. "If my own dad can't love me . . . who can?"

"Oh, Chloe, who couldn't? You're a wonderful person who's worthy of love. Your father is flawed and his inability to love you in the right way is on him, not you."

"I know you're right, but . . ." She gave her head a shake. "Why does love have to be so scary?" And so painful. The thought of opening herself up to someone, of falling in love only to be rejected, was overwhelming.

"When you let the right person in, he's gonna love you as much as I do."

She'd thought that person might be Liam. In their short months together, she'd let him in more than any man she'd ever been with.

She'd told him about her father. And he'd done nothing but support her. She had a suspicion he might've even loved her if she'd given him half a chance.

Chloe wiped her tears away. "The last few weeks Liam was here, I knew I was falling for him. But deep down I was so afraid of what would happen when he left. What that would feel like." She swallowed against the knot in her throat. "I think maybe I sabotaged our relationship. I've never blocked anyone in my life."

Meghan gave a sympathetic smile. "That makes sense. You were afraid he'd hurt you, so you left him first."

The comment hit its target. That was exactly what she'd done. So much for avoiding pain. She hadn't avoided it at all, only hastened its arrival. "How did I not see that?"

"You were too close to it. Love is complicated. It's hard. But maybe it's not too late to fix things with Liam. Maybe you can have this conversation with him."

Chloe wished that were true. But she'd completely shut him down. He already had difficulty believing in people and she'd trampled all over his trust. "I think there might be too much water over that dam."

But she did owe him an apology.

She couldn't believe this was how her big summer had ended. "These past few months have been such a whirlwind."

"No doubt—you had a movie made, fell in love with a celebrity, faced two public scandals—"

"And broke my own heart." She couldn't speak for Liam. Maybe he was glad to be rid of her at this point. Maybe he felt like he'd dodged a bullet.

"But you got a new sister out of the deal . . . And you learned some important things about yourself. Or as we say in fiction, you had an epiphany."

Chloe froze in her seat as an idea lit up her mind like a spotlight.

Meghan's eyes lit. "You know . . . you wrote a novel about the perfect hero—"

"Maybe now I can write one featuring the perfect heroine!" The words sank in soul-deep. Not the perfect heroine—but a flawed one. A character who wanted to love and be loved, but deep down she was too afraid to be vulnerable. Maybe the heroine needed to learn she was actually worthy of that love before she was ready to accept it.

*Yes.*

She didn't know if her publisher would allow her to write it as a historical now that she'd lost her following. But maybe a contemporary could work too. Chloe's heart palpitated in her chest, leaving her breathless. Her gaze flew to Meghan and locked there for a long moment. "I'm think I'm gonna write another book."

A smile stretched across Meghan's face. "Well, it's about time."

# Chapter 42

The Malibu mansion was the perfect setting for a private wedding. A couple hundred guests gathered on the pristine property owned by Daisy's grandfather. The weather had cooperated on this Saturday evening, and the shimmering Pacific Ocean provided a dazzling backdrop for the event. A cellist played from the makeshift stage, the haunting melody drifting on the breeze.

A tuxedo-clad usher led Spencer and Liam to a wide, gently sloped lawn facing the ocean. White chairs had been lined up with military precision, facing a low stone wall and a huge archway, resplendent with flowers and gauzy white fabric.

They took their seats among the elite crowd. This was Liam's first public event since fake-dategate. Normally he would've had a woman on his arm, but he couldn't stand the thought when his heart still belonged to Chloe. The intoxicating joy she'd initially engendered in him might be gone. But the love was still there, residing in him as a dull, ever-present ache.

Yeah, his mood was a little morose for a wedding.

He turned to Spencer for a distraction. "How's Gwenn feeling? I expected her to come with you tonight."

"She was supposed to, but her back's killing her. Also she claims she doesn't have a 'barn-sized dress.'"

"To which you said she'd look amazing in anything she wore."

"It happens to be true." Spencer waved at someone on the other side of the aisle. "Any word from your mom?"

"She's not allowed phone calls just yet." It had been only four days, but as far as Liam was concerned, no news was good news. "But I'm hopeful."

"Well, she agreed to go and she hasn't checked herself out. That's something. You did the right thing."

"I hope so. If she gets sober, it'll all be worth it."

"I'm proud of you for facing it head-on. Giving your mom an ultimatum couldn't have been easy, but you did it. How's it going with Phoebe?"

Liam gave him the side-eye. "She's pooped in every room in the house."

"Thank God for hardwood floors."

Liam scowled. He was tired of cleaning up the messes, but Phoebe was an anxious dog and she was in a new place. At least she'd settled down the past couple of days.

"Listen, are you really doing that interview tomorrow? For what it's worth, Patty and I still aren't sure it's the right move for your career."

That might very well be true. But the gossip about Chloe and their fake dating had gotten out of hand. The rumors hadn't faded as he'd hoped. Instead, his fans had turned on Chloe, making her out to be some kind of gold digger who'd taken advantage of him. Liam couldn't sit by and let people bad-mouth her. The live interview with *Celebrity Today* would allow him to set the record straight. "I'm going through with it."

"Well, let the record show I'm not in favor."

"I appreciate your looking out for me, but this is just something I have to do."

Liam had gotten her into this mess and he would get her out of it—or die trying. Chloe didn't deserve to be disparaged like this. Even if she had broken his heart.

"Maybe you should've invited her tonight," Spencer said.

"Who?"

Spencer smirked. "Phoebe. Who do you think?"

"In case you forgot, she accused me of betraying her, then blocked my calls."

"Yeah, I know, but . . . she's the one woman who's gotten under your skin. There must've been something there. Something pretty powerful for you to lower your very high walls."

"I don't have walls."

"Please. You're practically Fort Knox."

Liam pinned him with a look. "I don't have walls."

"You're sitting here at thirty-two with zero long-term relationships in your rearview mirror."

Liam gritted his teeth. This was what happened when your best friend had an underutilized psych degree. "So . . . what? You think I don't want the whole marriage and family thing? I do, actually."

"I believe you. But you've been so busy trying not to become your mom . . . Liam, I hate to tell you this, but I think you've become your dad instead. And you can't even see it."

Everything inside Liam went hard. As if he'd been filled with cement that instantly solidified. "What did you just say?"

"Fine, get mad. But you need to hear this. You've watched your mom all these years pining for your dad. Seen her begging and desperate and pitiful to the point of becoming an alcoholic. You didn't want to be anything like her—who could blame you?—so you accidentally became your dad instead."

That wasn't true. Liam was nothing like his dad. Was he? Sure, maybe Liam dated around a bit, but Chloe was proof he was open to something long term. Something permanent. "Explain Chloe then. Maybe you weren't around to see it, but I was all in with her."

"I think you were—right up until something went wrong. Then you hightailed it out of there."

"I had a flight scheduled. She blocked my number!"

"Who'd let a little thing like that stand in the way of true love?"

Liam threw his hands up. "I'm supposed to stalk her or something? I won't be like my mom, begging for another chance."

Spencer rolled his eyes. "This is hardly that. You could've given her a little time to cool off and reached out to her again via email or even gone old school with a letter. But as soon as the relationship hit the rocks, you bailed. You think Gwenn and I haven't hit the skids a time or two? You've gotta work through that stuff. You've gotta get good at forgiving. 'Cause believe me, brother, you'll be the one needing it next time, and you'd better hope she's better at it than you are."

Liam opened his mouth, a ready defense on his tongue. But the melodic strains shifted into a new song and the attendants started down the aisle.

He snapped his mouth closed. Settled back in his seat and attempted to slow his breathing. His thoughts whirled. He wanted to tear down every point Spencer had made, one by one. It was true he wanted to be nothing like his mother—not when it came to love. But the thought of turning into his dad gnawed at him. He didn't want to be like his father either: never content, always seeking something different or better.

But had Liam inadvertently followed in his footsteps?

A quick review of his dating history supported the claim. If he was honest with himself, the thought of losing his heart to someone put the fear of God in him. Because no, he didn't want to end up the pathetic puddle on the kitchen floor his mom had once been. He'd learned early on that love could bring a person pretty low.

And maybe Liam had given up on Chloe pretty easily. But the truth was, days before her family's story had broken, he'd been worried about navigating their long-distance relationship. Afraid that he'd ultimately lose her. Had that played into the way he'd responded to Chloe's accusation? Was that why he hadn't defended himself? Why he'd given up on her so quickly?

None of this was pleasant to think about. But it was something he should consider if he wanted to figure this out. If he wanted to have the kind of love he hoped for someday.

Liam mingled on one of the stunning patios facing the ocean. Huge potted flowers and graceful palm trees lined the property, and white lights, strewn overhead, echoed the starlight beyond them. Between the band's songs the air swelled with the sound of the surf. The ceremony had been beautiful—at least, Liam assumed it was. His mind was elsewhere for much of it. The meal had been delicious and now the dancing was well underway.

Liam excused himself from a conversation about the Actors Guild and went to stand by the low stone wall edging the patio. The party was hopping, guests crammed onto the makeshift dance floor, bopping to the beat of "Love Shack."

"You should be out there." Daisy appeared at his side, gorgeous in a sleeveless gown. "I happen to know you've got some moves."

He leaned in for a hug. "You make a beautiful bride. It's been an amazing evening. Where's your other half?"

"He stopped off for a much-needed drink, and I let him since he's getting me one too."

"Smart man. So . . . next stop, the Maldives?"

"I can't wait. It's been a busy few months, and I'm ready to chill out on a beautiful beach."

He couldn't help but think of their summer on Stillwater Bay . . . and Chloe. "Sounds perfect."

Daisy set her hand on his arm. "Sorry you're going through all the tabloid crap right now. Take it from me, it'll pass."

Daisy had had her own share of scandals. "I know that. This one just feels more personal than most."

"You might've had a PR relationship with Chloe—"

He started to speak.

She held up a hand. "I don't need the details. You're a great actor, Liam, but there was nothing fake about the way you looked at her."

Liam's heart gave a tight squeeze. No, there was definitely nothing fake about his feelings. But he didn't want to think about his loss on this happy occasion. He forced a smile. "So what's after the honeymoon? Is David moving to LA?"

"We'll split our time between here and New York as much as we can. And of course, I'll be gone on set sometimes."

Here was a couple who was attempting to manage a long-distance relationship. "How has that worked, living on opposite coasts?"

"It hasn't been easy. I miss him when we aren't together, but we FaceTime and text a lot. His work situation is seasonal and somewhat flexible, so he flies out to see me at least once a month when I'm home, and I stay in New York a lot when I'm not on set. He works for the Mets."

"I can see why he'd hate to give that up."

"So for now we just have to be flexible, play it by ear. Not everyone has a nine-to-five, picket-fence life. And that'll always be the case when you're an actor." She nudged him with an elbow. "No matter where the love of your life lives."

Chloe was certainly that. "I'm glad the two of you are making it work."

"A lot of couples do. Not just actors but people who serve in the military. Love can overcome a lot of obstacles—even geography."

He gave a wan smile.

Daisy glanced over his shoulder. "Uh-oh. David's been ambushed by my nosy great-aunt. I'd better go rescue him." She hugged him again. "Thank you for coming, Liam. I'm glad you were able to make it."

"My pleasure. Have a wonderful time in the Maldives."

And then she was off, skirt clutched in one hand, beating a path for her husband. They seemed like a good couple. Jealousy pricked hard.

His phone vibrated with a text. Welcoming the distraction, he pulled the phone from his pants pocket.

He froze at the name on the screen. The text was from Chloe.

*I know I was wrong. I'm sorry, Liam.*

# Chapter 43

*Thank you for that.*

Liam's response to her text had been rolling around Chloe's head for the past twenty-four hours. Her heart had beat out a tattoo and her fingers had trembled as they tapped out that apology on her phone. She paused with her thumb over the Send button for a full minute. And then after she sent it, she waited.

And waited.

Finally his response came—and it wasn't exactly a conversation starter. She told herself she hadn't held out hope her apology would develop into more. But her disappointment at his response told her everything she needed to know.

It was now the next day, almost one o'clock, and she was still down in the dumps. It had taken all her courage to unblock him. To write those words. She hoped he knew how much she meant them.

She shook the thoughts away as she loaded another plate in her mom's dishwasher, then went to work on a spatula. *Well, what did you expect?* How could she blame him for shutting down after what she'd done? Still, there was no comforting her bruised heart. It wobbled in her chest like a rickety chair.

Mom plunked a handful of silverware into the sink. "That's the last of it."

Chloe took hold of her arm. "Mom."

The woman's gaze sharpened on her daughter's expression, her eyes questioning. "What is it, honey?"

"I'm sorry I lied to you guys about Liam."

Mom squeezed her hand. "Honey, you already apologized and we already forgave you. Please, let it go. It pains me to see you so upset."

"I shouldn't have pretended to have feelings for him, especially not to you and Dad."

Mom gave her a knowing smile. "I'm not convinced there was all that much pretending going on."

Chloe's lips trembled. "You're right."

Mom cupped her cheek. "I'm sorry you're hurting. If that Liam Hamilton can't see what he had in my daughter, he's not the man I thought he was."

"It's not his fault, Mom. I'm the one who blew it."

"And you're gonna give up on him just like that?"

"I didn't give up on him, but I'm pretty sure he's given up on me." Chloe drew in a brave breath. "I'll be okay though. I'll get through this."

"You bet you will. And we'll be right with you every step of the way."

"Thanks, Mom."

Her mother gave her a side hug and went to wipe down the table.

Dad was still on the patio, cleaning the grill. And Sean and Meghan had retired to the living room, probably to make out if recent experience was anything to go by.

Shaking her gloomy mood, Chloe finished loading the silverware, sprayed down the sink, and started the dishwasher. Then she headed to the living room where the couple, it turned out, was not canoodling on the sofa.

"*Turn it.*" Sean reached for the remote.

But Meghan held it out of his reach. "No."

"She shouldn't have to—"

"We're leaving it," Meghan hissed.

Chloe arched a brow. "Arguing over the remote already?"

They both froze, comically posed with Meghan holding the remote in the air and Sean reaching for it.

Chloe's gaze swung to the TV to see what all the fuss was about. She caught an eyeful of Liam, apparently sitting for an interview. Before the program cut to a commercial.

Chloe's chest tightened in dread. She put a hand to her throat. "What is this? What's he doing?"

"He's getting ready to do an interview on *Celebrity Today*. I think you should watch this, Chloe."

"This is a bad idea," Sean said. "You've been hurt enough."

Her thoughts were scrambled. Why was Liam giving an interview? A last-ditch effort to prop up his career? But his fans were already forgiving him, according to the scuttlebutt Meghan passed on to her.

What else could it be though? Chloe didn't know—but she had to find out. And if nothing else, she was so desperate to *see* him. To *hear* him. She missed him so much. It humbled her to feel so needy, but not enough that she wouldn't give in to the longing. "Give me the remote."

Meghan handed it to her and Chloe perched on the sofa beside Meghan, waiting, her heart in her throat.

"You don't have to do this," Sean said. "We can just turn it off and go about our afternoon."

"I'll find out what he said one way or another. I'm sure it'll be all over town by tomorrow." All over the country, more like. She'd never known how exposed the spotlight of celebrity could make one feel.

Meghan glanced at Chloe. "They just played a little teaser. You haven't missed anything. I guess he decided to break his silence after all."

And on a live nationally televised show. "Go big or go home, I guess."

Mom appeared in the doorway, drying her hands on a dish towel. "What's going on in here?"

"Liam's giving an interview on *Celebrity Today*," Meghan said.

Mom's worried gaze darted to Chloe. "Right now?"

"I've already tried to dissuade her." Sean flopped back in his seat. "She's determined to torture herself."

Mom studied Chloe for a long moment. "Then we'll support her. I'll go get your dad."

Chloe clasped her hands to hide their trembling. She had no idea what was about to happen, but she could no sooner not watch than she could stop breathing. Would he talk about the scandal? The journalist would ask and she didn't see how he could avoid answering.

Oh, why were these commercials taking so long?

Meghan grabbed her hand. "It'll be okay. We've got you."

"I know you do." But they couldn't protect her heart. No one could—not even her.

Mom and Dad joined them and the program finally returned.

Meghan grabbed the remote and turned it up as the intro music swelled and the camera zoomed in on the host, Carmen Rodriguez. "Welcome to the weekend edition of *Celebrity Today*. We've got an exclusive interview with Liam Hamilton coming up. But first, let's go to Hollywood where Mina White is covering a new star on the block."

Chloe groaned. "They're gonna drag this out."

"It's bound to be their top story," Mom said. "But at least it's only a half-hour program."

Chloe stifled another groan. Thirty minutes seemed like an eternity. She had so much nervous energy, she couldn't sit still for the duration.

"Liam's up next," Dad called from the living room.

*Finally.* Chloe stopped pacing and joined the others. A commercial was on and there were only five minutes left in the program. Sure enough, they'd saved Liam's story for last.

The show returned and the camera zoomed in on Carmen and Liam in the small studio. Chloe drank in the sight of him. Those familiar broad shoulders. Those eyes that melted her into a puddle. Under the studio lights they appeared gray, but she'd been privy to the way the sunlight made them dance with specks of blue and silver. He was so handsome in his jeans and black button-down. He was trying for a smile but it traveled no farther than his lips.

Chloe was suddenly worried for him.

"He seems nervous," Sean said.

"Shh!" they all said as Carmen spoke. "Liam Hamilton joins us today in our LA studio. In the past he's been referred to as a 'cheater' and a 'player,' never having the same woman on his arm twice, and his reputation has suffered under such claims. This summer, though, a steady relationship with author Chloe Anderson made him one of Hollywood's most adored leading men.

"But recently there have been allegations that his very public relationship with Chloe was simply a ruse in a scandal known now as 'fake-dategate.' And his fans have questions. Both parties have been conspicuously silent on the subject since the story broke a week ago—until now. Welcome to the show, Liam."

He shifted. "Thank you for having me."

"Liam, can you tell us how you came to know Chloe Anderson?"

The camera zoomed in on his face. "Of course. The book she wrote, *Beneath the Summer Skies*, was being adapted into a movie, and when I read the script I fell in love with the story, the characters. I first spoke with her a few months before the movie began filming on a call with the movie's executive producer."

"What was your first impression of Chloe?"

"She was"—his lips twitched—"not what I expected."

"How so?"

"She didn't realize I was on the phone and she . . . expressed some concerns about my playing the lead in the movie."

Carmen's eyebrows rose. "Most authors would be thrilled to have an A-lister taking a role in their movie."

"The hero in *Summer Skies* is somewhat larger than life. And unlike any character I've played before. I understood her concerns." The corner of his mouth ticked up. "But I was also determined to prove her wrong."

"When did you first meet Chloe in person?"

"I arrived in North Carolina, the set location, a week early to get a feel for the area and ran into her while I was out and about."

"And how did that go?"

His eyes lit with mischief. "There were a lot of sparks."

Carmen raised an eyebrow. "The good kind?"

He chuckled, glanced down, adorably sheepish. "All the kinds."

"What happened from there?"

Liam drew a breath, his expression sobering. "As I said, she was concerned about the role of Ledger—due in large part to my reputation, which I'd been increasingly concerned about also. Just before the filming of the movie began, I offered Chloe a proposal. I'd take her direction on the role if she'd pretend to be my steady girlfriend."

"It was *your* idea."

"It was 100 percent my idea. In fact, she was reluctant. I had to convince her to go along with the idea."

Carmen tilted her head. "Forgive me if I sound skeptical, but it's hard to believe any single woman would turn down the opportunity to be Liam Hamilton's summer girlfriend, fake or otherwise."

His eyes took on a wistful look. "You'd have to know Chloe. She's different, special. She didn't like the idea of subterfuge. She doesn't care for the spotlight or the attention. She wasn't too impressed with *me* either." He chuckled. Lifted a shoulder. "I kinda dug that about her."

"The rumor mill has been pretty hard on Chloe this week. She's been called an opportunist, a gold digger, a parasite, and worse."

"That's why I'm here tonight. I want to be very clear. This wasn't Chloe's fault; it was mine. My idea, my fault. I offered her a deal that I hoped would salvage my reputation, and she took me up on it—only because the integrity of her story was so important to her."

"So all those swoonworthy pictures you posted on social media, all those articles about the blossoming relationship . . . it was all fake news?"

"It was . . ." He shifted in his seat. "Until it wasn't. Chloe and I spent a lot of time together this summer, running lines for the movie. We got to know each other, became good friends. I enjoyed her company and found myself seeking her out even when we weren't working." He flashed a shy grin. "And then there were those sparks."

"So you're saying the relationship shifted into something real?"

The camera zoomed in. Liam's eyes softened. "It became very real. More real than any relationship I've ever had."

"And now?"

He wet his lips. "Unfortunately, we're not together anymore. Something I'm not ready to talk about yet. But Chloe is a good person. She's one of a kind. And she doesn't deserve to be ridiculed because of her association with me."

"Sounds as if you're throwing yourself on the sword."

"Just setting the record straight." He stared into the camera. "I set out to deceive my fans and I'm truly sorry for that. It was wrong. I owe my supporters more than that. But Chloe was just a pawn in my game. So please, I'd be grateful if you'd show her a little mercy and let her have her privacy."

The camera zoomed in on Carmen, smiling widely. "And there you have it, folks. The answers to Hollywood's latest scandal, right here on *Celebrity Today*. Join us tomorrow as we talk to Katelyn Bauer in her first appearance since she dissolved her facial fillers."

Meghan turned off the TV.

Chloe's mind was spinning with everything Liam had said.

"He took all the blame," Meghan said.

"His career . . ." It was all Chloe could think of. "This won't be good for his career. If he'd just let this play out awhile longer, he probably would've been fine. Why did he do this?"

Mom gave a secret little smile. "I can think of only one reason."

Could it be true? He'd been unbelievably kind to her, especially after the way she'd treated him. Did he love her like she loved him? But why had his response to her text seemed so . . . distant?

Chloe's gaze swung to Sean, seeking answers from the one person in the room who wouldn't hold back.

He gave a wry grin. "Don't look at me. Even I can admit when I'm wrong."

And there she had it. Liam had won over the most jaded person she knew. Her heart felt as if it might pound right out of her chest. She had to talk to him. Not on the phone but face-to-face.

Meghan nudged her with an elbow. "Come on, girl. If you don't go after him, I will."

"Hey . . . ," Sean complained.

Meghan grabbed his hand. "I'll get him for *her*. I've already got my own man."

Chloe still couldn't believe he'd gone on national TV and taken the heat for her. His fans could very well turn on him now, and where would that leave him? She didn't even want to consider that.

Unable to sit still for another moment, Chloe popped to her feet. "I have to go see him."

Meghan grabbed her phone. "I'll book the flight."

"I just knew that young man had his head on straight." Mom grabbed her in a hug. "Go get him, honey."

# Chapter 44

Chloe fidgeted through both flights to LA, her mind turning with what she would say to Liam. How could she even describe the depth of her regret? He'd opened his heart to her, even to the point of sharing about his mother, and she'd abused his trust.

During her quick stop in Charlotte, she'd called Simone to get Liam's address. And now, as the Uber driver carried on a monologue about his electric Tesla, Chloe put her hand over her nervous stomach. The rambling hillside road climbed and curved, revealing hidden driveways and meticulously landscaped lawns and gardens.

From up here she had fleeting views of the Pacific sunset. Any other time she might appreciate the glorious golden glow swathing the horizon—the same view Liam must enjoy each night. But right now all she could think about was . . .

*What if he doesn't want to see me?*

She pressed her hand to her heart, which felt as if it might burst from her chest. It would be the ultimate rejection. She wasn't sure her heart would survive it. And yet . . .

The driver slowed on a downward slope, pulled into a paved driveway, and stopped in front of a formidable black iron gate.

Stupid her. She hadn't considered she might not even have access to his front door. If he wasn't home, she'd need a ride to a hotel.

"Can you wait here a minute?"

"Sure thing." The driver turned off the engine.

Chloe exited the car and approached the daunting gate—a stark reminder of just who Liam Hamilton was. She glanced down at the clothing she hadn't had a chance to change before rushing to catch her Wilmington flight—black leggings and a black tee with white lettering. *I am a writer. (Anything you say or do may be used in a story.)*

There was probably a camera somewhere. She glanced around even as she fluffed her plane-smooshed hair. Then she homed in on the keypad. The Call button.

He might not answer at all. Or he might refuse to see her. Her stomach twisted. This was the scariest thing she'd ever done. But she would never know if she didn't find the faith to put herself out there.

*All right, Chloe. You can do this.*

She sucked in a deep breath, blew it out, then pressed the Call button. She waited, pulse racing.

She peered up the drive. Only the roofline was visible over the hill. Was he home? Could he see her even now? She glanced back at the keypad. Had she hit the right button? Other than numbers, it was the only option. She pressed Call again and waited.

And waited.

He wasn't home. Or he wasn't answering. She wet her very dry lips. What now? She could simply camp out here and wait. But what if he'd flown somewhere after the interview? What if he wouldn't be home for days?

She could call him, but she didn't want to give him the chance to turn her down over the phone. It would be all too easy. It was why she hadn't called him to begin with. This was something she had to do face-to-face. When he saw her—when she saw his face—she'd know how he truly felt about her.

Wouldn't she?

How could she find out where he was? Spencer would know, but she didn't have his number. Maybe Simone did though.

"Miss, you gonna need another ride?"

"Another minute please. I'll pay you for the trouble." She tapped Simone's name, praying she'd answer the call.

"Did you make it to LA?" Simone asked by way of greeting.

"I did. I'm sorry to bother you again, but Liam's not home. Do you happen to have his manager's number?"

"Of course. Just a second."

There was a rustling sound as Simone messed with her phone. Would Spencer even give her the information she wanted? He was no doubt privy to what she'd done.

"Got it." Simone rattled off the number and wished Chloe good luck.

Without waiting another second Chloe tapped out the number and waited. The phone rang once. Twice. Three times.

She was giving up hope when the call was answered. "Hello?"

"Um, is this Spencer?"

"Yes . . ."

"This is Chloe Anderson. I'm sorry to bother you, but I was hoping you might be able to tell me where Liam is tonight. I know you have no reason to—"

"Why are you asking?" His tone was guarded, and no wonder.

"I have to see him. It's personal."

"Where are you?"

"Here, in Santa Monica." She glanced up the drive. "In his driveway actually. It's entirely possible he's home and just not letting me through the gate."

Spencer snorted. "He's not home. And I know exactly where he is."

"Please tell me. I really blew it with him and I need to see him. I need to tell him how I feel even if—even if he doesn't feel the same way."

The long pause on the other end of the line tightened the knot in her throat. "I realize you have no reason to trust me. But I care about him deeply. The last thing I want to do is hurt him." Another long pause had Chloe squeezing back tears.

"I'll give you the address. Do you have a ride?"

Chloe exhaled. "Yes, an Uber."

She returned to the vehicle, and as he rattled off the address she repeated it to the driver.

"Thank you, Spencer. You have no idea how much I appreciate this."

"Good luck, Chloe."

All the way back to LA Chloe repeated those last three words in her mind. Tried to decipher Spencer's tone. Was it "Good luck, Chloe" as in *You're gonna need it*? Or "Good luck" as in *I'm pulling for you*?

She still hadn't decided when the Tesla pulled up in front of a beautiful hotel. She thanked the driver and headed toward the entrance. He'd said the Pinnacle Room. She had no idea what or where that was. The doorkeeper swept open the door and she stepped inside the grand gilded lobby. A woman slinked past in a little black dress and skinny heels that defied gravity, making Chloe doubly aware of her street clothes and white tennis shoes.

She strode toward the front desk to ask for directions.

But before she reached it, someone called her name. A brown-haired, thirtysomething man in a tuxedo approached. He wasn't smiling. But he wasn't frowning either. He had piercing green eyes and a little cowlick at his forehead.

"Spencer?"

He gave a nod. "Right this way. It's a ticketed event but I can get you in."

Event? She glanced down at her outfit. "Oh. Uh, maybe I should just wait till it's over."

"Not at all." He took her arm and ushered her toward the elevator, which swept open at their approach. They stepped inside and he pressed the 20 button—the highest floor in the building. The elevator lurched and they started upward.

Her mouth felt like the Sahara. "Are you sure this is okay? I left in a hurry and didn't have time to change." *And also, he might take one look at me and turn the other way, and I'm not sure my heart can bear it.*

"You saw his interview?"

"I did." She was desperate to know how Liam felt about her. But it wouldn't be fair to put Spencer in that position. Besides, he'd hardly be helping her if he didn't think Liam would welcome her sudden appearance. Would he?

Unless . . .

He thought it would be the perfect revenge.

The elevator doors whooshed open. They were at the back of a huge ballroom. Spencer ushered her out, nodding at the two security guards standing sentinel. The dim room was filled with round tables, seated with guests who were eating . . . cheesecake, it appeared.

Where was Liam?

She scanned the seated crowd, finding tuxedo-clad men along with women draped in glittering gowns and dazzling diamonds. Chloe's apparel blended more with the staff than the guests. Scratch that. Even the servers wore dress shirts and pants.

The voice coming over the speaker captured Chloe's attention. She stopped in her tracks.

*Liam.*

Her eyes darted to the large screen at the front of the ballroom. If she'd thought he was handsome in a black tee and jeans . . . that tux elevated him to downright gorgeous. His gaze swept the crowd as he spoke, but his words faded into the background as the sight of him filled her senses.

Her heart squeezed tight. To her, he wasn't Liam Hamilton the celebrity. He was Liam Hamilton, keeper of her heart. She would do whatever it took to make him see that she loved him for who he was inside. He deserved to know he was loved that way. Even if he didn't return her affection.

His strident tone pulled her from her thoughts. "I'm more grateful than I can say that you chose to support at-risk youth by attending and giving at tonight's benefit. Your generosity will go a long way toward carrying my foundation through the year, and it's our hope that—"

Liam's gaze froze on her. He blinked. Blinked again. His mouth moved, but no words came out.

Chloe couldn't read his expression from this distance, not even on the jumbo screen. Her feet were rooted to the floor. Heat flooded through her as the moment lengthened. As people turned to see what had distracted him.

Then he glanced down at his notes. "It's, uh, it's our hope that today we can work together to change the lives of children for a better tomorrow. Thank you."

Applause rippled through the room. Liam exited the stage.

Chloe's breath hitched as he headed her way. Her eyes were glued to his advancing form. To his lovely face. She'd missed that face so much.

His attention was laser-focused on her. But even as he neared his expression was unreadable. Was he happy to see her? Angry she'd turned up so suddenly? Had Spencer set her up for the biggest, most public heartbreak of her life?

And then he was there, just a step away, and she couldn't think rationally anymore. All the words she'd rehearsed on the long flight fled at his nearness.

"You're here," he said.

She couldn't tell by his tone if he was pleased or annoyed, only that he was surprised.

Chloe searched those familiar features, remembering the boy who hadn't quite been loved by his mother. The man who was often used by others as a means to an end. Regret for the callous way she'd treated him pierced her heart, making her eyes swim with tears.

"Liam, I am so sorry about what I said to you. How I treated you. It was wrong and you didn't deserve that."

A bit of the guardedness dropped away. "I got your text."

"I know. I just want to explain that there was more behind my reaction than either of us probably realized. It's taken me a while to figure out that I was so afraid you'd come back to LA and forget about me . . . that I sabotaged our relationship. I ended things before you could." She gave her head a sharp shake. "I'm not offering an excuse. I was wrong, so wrong, to do what I did."

He stepped closer, his eyes softening. "I think I understand—because I was afraid too. I was worried about a long-distance relationship. You . . . made me feel things I hadn't felt before."

Her heart did a slow, cautious roll. "I did?"

"I shouldn't have let you go so easily."

His words were like salve on her wounds. She remembered to breathe. Remembered why else she'd come. "I saw you on TV today. Oh, Liam, why did you do that? Why did you put your career in jeopardy just when things were starting to get better?"

His eyebrows slammed together. "Better for *me*. I couldn't let people talk about you that way."

"It's no more than I deserve."

"That's not true."

When he stared at her like that, she could almost believe he felt the same way. Was it possible? She forced herself to maintain eye contact though her courage was faltering and her stomach was twisted in knots. "Liam . . . I came here not only to apologize again but to tell you"—she swallowed hard—"to tell you I love you. I know you can't possibly—"

Then his lips were on hers. His hands lifted to frame her face. His fingers plowed into her hair. The kiss was soft and commanding. Seeking, searching. Giving, receiving. A little desperate. A lot breathtaking.

Chloe wrapped her arms around him and sank into his embrace, the assurance of his affection warming her through. That he would welcome her after the way she'd treated him humbled her. She would never hurt him again. Would rather have every gossip site publicly humiliate her than cause him a single ounce of pain.

When he drew away, he gazed into her eyes, connected to her as if by an invisible thread. It took several seconds before Chloe heard the applause swelling around them.

His eyes smiled. "We seem to be in the spotlight again."

Her attention dropped to the circle of light on the carpet around their feet. "Um, literally."

He chuckled. She loved the way his eyes smiled too. The way he gazed at her as if she were the only woman in the room.

Then his expression turned serious. "I'm afraid in my world it goes with the territory."

"I understand that."

"Do you? Because there'll be a lot more of this. Plus a lot of gossip and misreported events and outright lies, printed for the whole world to see. We have to trust each other."

"I'll trust you to be truthful with me. And I promise to be the same with you."

"I like the sound of that." His eyes lowered to her lips. She'd missed that sleepy-eyed look. "Let's get out of here."

Who was she to argue?

He pressed a quick kiss to her mouth, then he took her hand and guided her to the elevator. Spencer stood off to the side in the shadows. *Thank you*, she mouthed. She caught a glimpse of his smile before the elevator swept open, allowing Liam and her to enter. The closing doors ushered in silence.

Liam swept her up in his arms and flashed her a grin. "Alone at last."

# Epilogue

### The following June

"You're staring," Chloe said.

"I can't help it."

The limo that swept Liam and her through LA sported plush leather seats, mood lighting, a flat-screen TV, and a full bar. She still wasn't quite used to the extravagance that came with Liam's life.

"That dress." Liam's low, throaty voice said it all. "Those shoes."

For a moment she forgot her pinched toes and the shaper that had her wedged into the red gown. The hungry look in his eyes was worth the momentary discomfort.

"You're quite a vision yourself." She laced her fingers through his. Over the past year she'd seen him in jeans and trunks and suits, but the man did know how to fill out a tux.

"Is my tie straight?"

"It's perfect. How's your mom doing? I forgot to ask." While Chloe had been preparing for tonight, Liam spent time with his mom. She was nine months sober and had recently purchased a condo in nearby Pasadena.

"She got a promotion at work. She's pretty happy about that."

Chloe smiled. "That's great. I think the move was good for her."

"Between that and the therapy, she's well on her way to reclaiming her life—and finally being over my dad."

"I'm glad the two of you have gotten closer these past few months. Family is important."

"Speaking of family . . . that picture Meghan took of us is making the rounds."

"I saw that." Meghan was family now. She and Sean had married in a simple ceremony on Christmas Eve. It was a whirlwind courtship but even Chloe had to admit—they were perfect together. It was an intimate ceremony at Dad's church followed by a larger reception at Docksiders.

Unfortunately, their sister, Tiffany, hadn't been able to make the event, but she promised to fly in this summer to finally meet them in person. They'd been communicating regularly. Their dad was still pretending his marriage to Chloe's mom had never happened. That Chloe and Sean had never happened. But now that Chloe was seeing Sean's therapist, she was coming to terms with all that. She couldn't control her father. And she'd decided she was finished letting the past dictate her future.

Liam squeezed her hand. "Are you ready for your big night?"

"I'm ready for the movie—the spotlight I could happily skip."

He gave her a rueful grin. "It's a red-carpet premiere, sweetheart, and you're the star. There's no skipping the spotlight tonight."

"I'm just the author—you're the real star."

He chuckled. "Keep telling yourself that. Did Katie prep you? Do you feel like you know what to do?"

Knowing and doing were two different things. "We'll do the red-carpet thing, media interviews, you'll do selfies with fans, then we'll head for the theater where I can hide in the dark."

The viewing was just a formality as they'd already previewed it. It had turned out beautifully. Liam had exceeded all Chloe's expectations as Ledger. The higher-ups were confident *Summer Skies* would be a box office hit. Liam and Daisy were doing the talk show circuit to promote it, and Rosewood Press also had Chloe doing national interviews the week of the movie's release.

"We'll be one of the last cars to arrive," Liam said. "Once we enter, the reporters will be behind stanchions with the movie graphics behind us. We'll stop every few feet, answer questions, pose. It's called the 'step-and-repeat' for a reason."

"Got it. And of course they're bound to ask about this." She held out her left hand, fingers splayed.

The emerald-cut diamond winked under the interior lights. Because yes, Liam had proposed two weeks ago in Stillwater Bay on the anniversary of their first meeting. After a quiet dinner at Main Street Grill, they took a stroll on the beach. That's where he dropped to one knee and popped the question. It was simple and special—the most magical moment of her life. She gave a wistful sigh.

As if he was also remembering the night, Liam gazed at her with affection in his eyes. He tipped her chin up and set a gentle kiss on her lips. "I must be the luckiest man alive."

"Two minutes out," the driver called back.

"Thanks, Paul."

She could hardly believe this movie was really happening. The past nine months had been so busy she'd barely had time to process it. She'd written that second book—an epic World War II saga—and turned it in last month. It would release next spring. She'd spent weeks at a time in Santa Monica, where she'd done most of her writing. But after the premiere she would return to Stillwater Bay and help out at Docksiders. Which worked out perfectly because Liam had scored a wonderful role in a TV series that was filming just up north. He would play a Coast Guard commander in a show that featured two other big-name actors and was expected to run for several seasons.

The limo slowed. A glance out the window revealed blocked-off streets, media vans, and black SUVs. When the limo stopped Chloe's pulse kicked up a notch.

Liam peered out the window. "Okay, we're here. I'll be right beside you every minute." Liam pressed a tender kiss to the back of her hand. "This is your big night, sweetheart. Try to enjoy it."

Chloe was seeing spots from all the flashes. Her smile felt like plastic after holding it in place through the step-and-repeat. A lot of the questions had been for Liam about the role in her movie, but they asked her questions about the story as well. And of course, they asked about the engagement.

They answered a couple of questions, then Liam directed the attention back to the movie—that's what they were here for, after all.

Chloe shifted on her heels and wiggled her toes. She tried to keep her grin in place as she waited for Liam to finish answering questions from the last outlet in the long line of media. He was doing a great job promoting the film. He was a natural at this.

She glanced around the red carpet, spotting people she knew: Simone chatting with the director, Spencer and Gwenn answering questions, Daisy and David posing for a shot. Cameras flashed. Reporters called out questions—it was quite the fray.

Chloe could hardly believe she was at her own movie premiere. And with her soulmate—who, as it turned out, didn't much resemble the larger-than-life character she'd written in her book.

But she'd learned a lot this past year—therapy had a way of illuminating things. After being abandoned by her father, followed by several romantic failures, she'd desperately needed to believe the perfect man existed. So she'd written him into a book. But in real life it wasn't about finding the perfect man—he didn't even exist.

It was about finding the perfect man for her.

And it hadn't taken long to figure out Liam was that man. He was kind and loyal. Generous and fiercely protective. He made her laugh and he made her feel. It seemed something unique and magical happened when two flawed people who were meant for each other came together. Liam and Chloe had that potent magic.

That didn't mean it was always easy. She was still figuring this out—and so was he. They both had issues to work on, but they were doing it together.

Liam finished answering the question, then they posed against the backdrop for the photographer. And then . . . they were done.

Liam ushered Chloe toward the area where fans gathered for selfies with the talent. He pulled her close and brushed her lips with a lingering kiss. She forgot about the people and cameras and little sound bites she'd memorized for tonight. His kisses still swept her away to someplace quiet even as her heart turned over in her chest.

When he drew away, his eyes were full of warmth and affection. "You did great, sweetheart. I am so proud of you."

"I didn't even trip."

He laughed. "And in those shoes, that's quite a feat." He gave her a squeeze.

"Hey, Chloe," a reporter called from behind the stanchions. "When's the big day?"

She smiled into Liam's eyes. "We haven't set a date yet."

"Where you gonna call home, Liam?" another reporter called.

The reporters, the cameras, and the flashes faded into the background as he gazed at her with forever in his eyes and answered, "Wherever Chloe is."

# Acknowledgments

Bringing a book to market takes a lot of effort from many different people. I'm so incredibly blessed to partner with the fabulous team at HarperCollins Christian Fiction, led by publisher Amanda Bostic: Patrick Aprea, Savannah Breedlove, Kimberly Carlton, Caitlin Halstead, Margaret Kercher, Becky Monds, Kerri Potts, Nekasha Pratt, Taylor Ward, and Laura Wheeler.

Not to mention all the wonderful sales reps and amazing people in the rights department—special shout-out to Robert Downs!

Thanks especially to my editor, Kimberly Carlton. Your incredible insight and inspiration help me take the story deeper, and for that I am so grateful! Thanks also to my line editor, Julee Schwarzburg, whose attention to detail makes me look like a better writer than I really am.

My experience with my own book-to-movie adaptations (*The Convenient Groom*, *A December Bride*, and *The Goodbye Bride*) was very helpful in the process of writing about Chloe's experience. But I would've been lost without the direction of movie producer extraordinaire Maura Dunbar. Her expertise of the film world helped me bring this story to life. Any mistakes that made it into print are my own.

Author Colleen Coble is my first reader and sister of my heart. Thank you, friend! This writing journey has been ever so much more fun because of you.

I'm grateful to my agent, Karen Solem, who's able to somehow make sense of the legal garble of contracts and, even more amazing, help me understand it.

To my husband, Kevin, who has supported my dreams in every way possible—I'm so grateful! To all our kiddos: Chad and Taylor, Trevor and Babette, and Justin and Hannah, who have favored us with three beautiful grandchildren. Every stage of parenthood has been a grand adventure, and I look forward to all the wonderful memories we have yet to make!

A hearty thank-you to all the booksellers who make room on their shelves for my books—I'm deeply indebted! And to all the book bloggers and reviewers, whose passion for fiction is contagious—thank you!

Lastly, thank you, friends, for letting me share this story with you! I wouldn't be doing this without you. Your notes, posts, and reviews keep me going on the days when writing doesn't flow so easily. I appreciate your support more than you know.

I enjoy connecting with friends on my Facebook page: www.facebook.com/authordenisehunter. Please pop over and say hello. Visit my website at www.DeniseHunterBooks.com or just drop me a note at Deniseahunter@comcast.net. I'd love to hear from you!

# Discussion Questions

1. Who is your favorite character in the novel and why?

2. Have you ever dreamed of being a famous celebrity like Liam? Discuss what you might like and dislike about living such a lifestyle.

3. Chloe wrote her ideal man into a novel, complete with all the traits she most desired. Discuss her motivations behind that act and how those motivations played into her decision to say yes to Liam's fake dating proposal.

4. Discuss Liam's reasons for being afraid of loving someone. Have you ever been afraid of falling in love? Why? Did you overcome that fear? If so, how?

5. Discuss how Chloe's abandonment issues prevented her from having a healthy relationship with a man.

6. Liam and Chloe fell apart over a misunderstanding—but their fears also played into the breakup. Discuss. Share a time when your fears held you back from something you really wanted.

7. If you were in Chloe's shoes, would you have welcomed your half sister into your life? Discuss how their pasts might make this relationship difficult.

8. Did you hope Chloe's father might reenter her life? Why or why not?

9. Meghan said, "People can't love you until they know you. And they can't know you until you open yourself to them

and show them who you are." Have you ever struggled to be vulnerable? Discuss how this has played out in your life.

10. Spencer told Liam, "You've gotta get good at forgiving. 'Cause believe me, brother, you'll be the one needing it next time." Have you found that to be true in your relationships? Discuss a time when forgiveness was not easy but was worth it in the end.

# About the Author

*Photo by Amber Zimmerman*

**Denise Hunter** is the internationally published, bestselling author of more than forty books, three of which have been adapted into original Hallmark Channel movies. She has won the Holt Medallion Award, the Reader's Choice Award, the Carol Award, the Foreword Book of the Year Award, and is a RITA finalist. When Denise isn't orchestrating love lives on the written page, she enjoys traveling with her family, drinking chai lattes, and playing drums. Denise makes her home in Indiana, where she and her husband raised three boys and are now enjoying an empty nest and three beautiful grandchildren.

DeniseHunterBooks.com
Facebook: @AuthorDeniseHunter
Twitter: @DeniseAHunter
Instagram: @deniseahunter